Praise for Donna Gra[nt]

"A captivating romance no[...] [mak]ing this perfect for anyone who loves a steamy romantic read." —*Fresh Fiction* on *My Favorite Cowboy*

"This first-class thrill ride will leave readers eager for more." —*Publishers Weekly* (starred review) on *The Hero*

"Dangerous, steamy, and full of intrigue." —*Booklist* on *The Hero*

"Grant's dizzying mix of danger and romance dazzles . . . off-the-charts chemistry and a breath-stealing plot." —*Publishers Weekly* (starred review) on *The Protector*

The Dark Kings series

"Grant's ability to quickly convey complicated backstory makes this jam-packed love story accessible even to new or periodic readers." —*Publishers Weekly* on *Fever*

"A sweet and steamy romance." —*Fresh Fiction* on *Fever*

The Dark Warrior series

"The world of the Immortal Warriors is a thoroughly engaging one, blending powerful ancient gods, fiery desire, and touchingly human love, which readers will surely want to revisit." —*RT Book Reviews*

"Sizzling love scenes and engaging characters."
—*Publishers Weekly*

The Dark Sword series

"Grant creates a vivid picture of Britain centuries after the Celts and Druids tried to expel the Romans, deftly merging magic and history. The result is a wonderfully dark, delightfully well-written [series]. Readers will eagerly await the next Dark Sword book."

—*RT Book Reviews*

"Another fantastic series that melds the paranormal with the historical life of the Scottish highlander in this arousing and exciting adventure." —*Bitten by Books*

"Will keep readers spellbound."
—*Romance Reviews Today*

ALSO BY DONNA GRANT

A **COWBOY**
KIND OF LOVE

DONNA GRANT

St. Martin's Paperbacks

This is a work of fiction. All of the characters, organizations, and events portrayed in this novel are either products of the author's imagination or are used fictitiously.

First published in the United States by St. Martin's Paperbacks, an imprint of St. Martin's Publishing Group

A COWBOY KIND OF LOVE

For information, address St. Martin's Publishing Group, 120 Broadway, New York, NY 10271.

www.stmartins.com

ISBN: 978-1-250-25009-4

Our books may be purchased in bulk for promotional, educational, or business use. Please contact your local bookseller or the Macmillan Corporate and Premium Sales Department at 1-800-221-7945, ext. 5442, or by email at MacmillanSpecialMarkets@macmillan.com.

Printed in the United States of America

St. Martin's Paperbacks edition 2021

10 9 8 7 6 5 4 3 2 1

Chapter 1

"Stay right here," Police Chief Ryan Wells commanded.

Jace chuckled at his friend.

"I'm not joking, Jace. Stay put. I'm not picking your ass up off the ground, and you can't walk for shit right now."

Jace couldn't keep the smile from his face. It had been quite a while since anyone had spoken to him like he was a five-year-old. He blinked and tilted back his head to look at the stars above him. For a heartbeat, the sky spun out of control, but it eventually righted itself.

He didn't know what Ryan was doing in the truck. Jace heard the stray cat he'd been feeding for a few months now meow and looked toward the sound. The black and white feline stood by the front door, staring at him. It wasn't a long walk from where Jace had propped himself against Ryan's truck. He could make it.

Jace pushed away from the vehicle and took a tentative step. He didn't fall or even wobble, which meant that Ryan didn't know what he was talking about. Jace took another few steps while remaining on his feet. With a smile on his face, he proudly walked along the curving path to his door as the cat turned in a circle, waiting for him. Only when Jace decided to bend down to pet the cat did he get dizzy.

"That wasn't a good idea," he mumbled to himself.

Jace used the doorframe to straighten and took a couple of deep breaths. He twisted the knob, and the door opened easily. Had Ryan already opened it? Jace decided that he didn't care. He wanted inside.

It had been a few months since he had gotten this drunk. Sometimes, the only way to dull the pain that the past continued to throw at him was to become so numb that he couldn't feel anything. Alcohol was just the fix he needed when things got to be too much.

And today had been one of those days.

"Dammit," Ryan grumbled. "Where are the keys?"

Jace didn't bother looking behind him. He entered his house, stumbling slightly over the front step. Thankfully, he still had a hand on the door. He released the panel and careened into the table his mother had insisted he needed against the wall. Jace then grabbed hold of the wall and watched the table—as well as the lamp—wobble before settling back in place, thankfully without falling. He was grateful because he didn't want to explain to anyone why the table was broken.

With that taken care of, Jace tried to swallow, only to find his mouth dry. He wanted water. He turned his head to look across the foyer to where it intersected with the kitchen. It seemed so far away, but he was thirsty. Jace decided to try and make it, but things spun again when he let go of the wall. That's when he realized that the water wasn't worth the hassle of falling—and proving Ryan right.

Instead, Jace turned to the living area that was much

closer. He frowned, wondering why the kitchen light was on and shining into the room. He must have forgotten to turn it off. Suddenly, his feet were too heavy to lift. And nothing sounded as good as sleep.

He blinked and tried to focus, but everything was blurry and getting worse by the second. Something moved in the shadows, drawing his attention. His dulled senses still warned him to be wary. Jace tried to make his brain sort through what was happening. As if conjured from his mind, Taryn materialized from the shadows. His heart skipped a beat. It always did when she visited him in his dreams. No matter how much she had hurt him, he couldn't stop loving her.

In an effort to bring her into focus, Jace blinked once more. And just like that, the vision disappeared. The pain that lanced through him made him rub his chest as his heart broke all over again. Would he ever stop pining for her? When would he be able to let go of his love for her and move on? Everyone kept telling him that he'd be over her someday, but it had been years, and he loved her still.

He swallowed past the lump in his throat. Despite the amount of alcohol he had consumed, the pain and emptiness he tried to bury rose to swallow him. He knew firsthand there were no guarantees in life, but he'd thought he had found the love of his life with Taryn.

"Jace?" Ryan said from behind him.

Jace reached out his hand, wishing and hoping he could touch Taryn. His eyes filled with tears as he realized that he couldn't will her image to return, just as he hadn't been able to make her love him. Jace felt himself pitching forward. Ryan called out his name seconds before Jace slammed into the floor.

He groaned, his head pounding from hitting the hard

wood. Ryan rushed to him. Jace closed his eyes, seeking the comfort of sleep, where he knew he would find her and the love they'd once shared.

Taryn.

Jace tried to hold back the bellow of agony as the guards beat him with their hands and wooden batons. He was strapped to a chair, unable to twist away or defend himself—or land a punch of his own.

Between the beatings and the lack of food and water, Jace knew he would likely die in this godforsaken hellhole. It was one thing to die where his family could learn what'd happened to him and possibly have his body returned. It was an entirely different matter with prisoners of war. His family might never know that he was no longer alive. His mom would hold out hope of his return until the day she died. He didn't want to hurt his mother like that. She deserved better.

"Jace."

He opened his eyes at the sound of the soft voice he knew all too well and looked past the guards with their gleeful smiles to Taryn's beautiful form. The prison was dirty and dank, infested with rodents and the stench of death so powerful it was difficult to remember a time when he had inhaled fresh air. Yet Taryn's skin and clothes were spotless, as if the grime knew better than to get near her.

She wore a cream-colored shirt that made her skin glisten. Her deep brown hair that bordered on black brushed her shoulders in soft waves. A full skirt in the same cream as her shirt swirled around her bare feet. He sighed when he realized that he could see through the thin fabric.

Her lips curled into a soft smile as she held out her hand. "Come with me. You don't have to stay here."

He desperately wanted to go, but he was bound. Still, he pulled at the ropes. To his shock, they loosened, and he was able to get to his feet. He waited for the guards to come at him and force him back down, but they let him pass without any struggle.

Jace swung his head back to Taryn to find her waiting for him. He hurried to her, reaching for her hand. Just as he was about to take it, he held back when he saw his fingers. He was filthy He didn't want to get any of the grime on her.

She laughed and grabbed his hand. "I've been waiting all day to go for a ride. Are you going to make me beg?"

He had never been able to refuse her anything she wanted. "No," he said, shaking his head.

Jace wrapped his fingers around her hand. The moment he did, the prison and the hell that he had endured as a POW faded away, replaced by the beautiful wide open spaces of his family's ranch. When he looked down, he saw he was in clean clothes, his many and various injuries now healed. The sound of Taryn's laughter brought his head up. She was already on the chestnut mare, looking back at him from beneath the cowboy hat atop her black hair, now in its natural state of curls. She wore jeans and a red plaid shirt that was his favorite.

"I'll race you!" she shouted before nudging the horse into a run.

There was a smile on his face as he mounted his gelding and raced after her. She stayed ahead of him for some time, but the gelding eventually caught up. They both pulled back on the reins and drew the horses into a canter as they rode side by side to the river. Jace raised his face to the sun, grateful to have clean air in his lungs once more.

The sound of a splash caught his attention. Taryn had shed her clothes and dived into the river. Her inviting smile had him quickly joining her. Once in the water, he pulled her against him and took her lips in a languid kiss. He couldn't get enough of her.

As the kiss deepened, he could feel Taryn pulling away. He leaned back to see what was wrong. Something had cut a slice in the sky above them, reaching out to wrap a hand around Taryn to yank her out of his arms.

"Jaaaaaaaace!!" she screamed, her face filled with terror.

He tried to hold onto her with everything he had, but she slipped from his fingers. He was instantly plunged into darkness, pulled back into the pit of Hell with his captors. Jace wasn't prepared for the fist to his ribs that knocked the breath from him.

Jace came awake suddenly from the nightmare. He took a few moments to make sure the dream had faded away enough that he wouldn't get dragged back into those memories. It had taken him a long time to pull himself from those. Thankfully, they only bothered him occasionally now, which was much better than when he had first been rescued, and the nightmares plagued him every time he closed his eyes.

With his head feeling as if an entire football team took turns kicking him, he saw the bright light from the window from behind his closed lids. His mouth felt like cotton. He tried to swallow and realized that he was lying face down on the sofa. That's when he heard a jingle on repeat.

He cracked open one eye to find his best friend, Cooper Owens, sitting in a chair opposite him, playing the stupid game on his phone that drove Jace bananas simply because Cooper always had to leave the music on. *Because* it annoyed Jace.

"Rise and shine, Sleeping Beauty," Cooper said without looking away from the screen.

Jace shut his eye and wished he could go back to sleep. But first, he needed to stop the pounding in his head. He used his arms to push himself up. The effort that took told him that he had imbibed a little too much the night before. The problem was that it took more and more each time he needed to numb himself from the pain.

"What are you doing here?" he asked as he rolled onto his side.

Cooper didn't immediately answer until he had won his level. Then, he lowered the phone and looked at Jace. "Ryan. He didn't think you should be left alone. He got called to an emergency, so he phoned me."

"Stop giving me that holier-than-thou look," Jace grumbled. "I seem to recall babysitting you when you got drunk."

Cooper scratched his neck. "Yep. You sure have. But this is your second time *this* week."

"No, it isn't," Jace said. But the minute the words were out of his mouth, he knew that his friend was right.

Cooper leaned forward and put his phone on the coffee table between them. "I'd just crawled into bed with Marlee when Ryan called."

It went unsaid that both Cooper and Marlee were irritated with Jace. Not that he blamed them. He would feel the same in their shoes. Jace managed to shift so he was sitting on the couch. That's when he looked down and found himself in nothing but his boxer briefs.

"You can thank Ryan for that," Cooper said, not bothering to hide his smile. "Apparently, you were adamant about getting naked. He somehow managed to make you keep your briefs on, though I'm not sure I want to know how." The smile died as he licked his lips. "You're spiraling out of control."

Jace ran a hand down his face and closed his eyes. The phrase *rode hard and put up wet* didn't even come close to describing how poorly he felt. That in itself should have been enough to make sure he didn't drink that much again for some time. But he knew it wouldn't.

"Jace?" Cooper said.

He looked at his best friend, noting the seriousness on Cooper's face. "I know."

"Do you? Because you're worrying the hell out of me. We've been down this road before."

Thankfully, Cooper didn't say her name. Jace never said it either—except in his dreams. He leaned forward and propped his elbows on his thighs as he dropped his face into his hands. "Fuck."

The chair creaked as Cooper rose. Jace heard him go into the kitchen. A moment later, Cooper returned and set something on the table. "Hair of the dog."

Jace immediately reached for the shot of tequila and drank it. He wiped his mouth with the back of his hand and set the glass back on the coffee table. The shot helped a little, but only time—as well as some water and food—would mend what the alcohol had done. "Thanks."

Cooper sat back down and released a sigh. "Do you want to talk about it?"

"Nope." The last thing Jace wanted to do was re-hash what had happened the day before that'd sent him straight to the bottle. After all these years, he should be over her. Why couldn't his heart let her go? Why couldn't he find someone new? His three friends had. Was he destined to spend his life alone?

Maybe that was it. Perhaps he'd had his shot with her and had done something to screw it up, which then caused her to leave. He'd never know since she hadn't said anything to him. He'd simply gone to her house one morning, and she was gone. No trace left behind. Not even his friends in law enforcement could find her.

"Maybe you need to go back to your therapist," Cooper offered. "He did wonders to help you get past everything that happened when you were a POW."

Jace shot him a smile and said, "You sound like my mom."

Cooper didn't respond to the jest. "Because we're worried."

"I know," he said and got to his feet. He moved too quickly, and the room spun. Jace fell back onto the sofa and dropped his head onto the cushion. "How many more times do I have to say that I'm all right before y'all start believing me?"

"I think you've reached the limit."

Jace twisted his lips as he stared at the ceiling. "Yeah. You're probably right."

"You aren't alone in this."

But he was. Jace didn't argue with Cooper because he knew what his friend meant. However, Cooper, Brice, and Caleb all had women of their own now. Brice was a father, as well. Their families came before anything else.

Jace lifted his head and met Cooper's forest green eyes. "Go home to Marlee and have breakfast with her."

"It's nearly one in the afternoon."

Jace shrugged. "Then have lunch."

"She's with her parents. You and I are going to grab some food. Take a shower. You need it."

Jace made a face but got up—slower this time—and headed to his room. Once in the shower, he stood beneath the spray for a long time before starting to wash. As he did, his mind drifted. He recalled coming home the night before and thinking he saw Taryn. She had looked so real, but he knew that wasn't the case. Jace tried to put it out of his mind as he finished bathing and dried off.

He raked his hands through his hair and opted not to shave since the last thing he needed was to put a razor in a hand that still shook from the effects of the alcohol. He found some clothes and dressed before walking from his room to find Cooper returning from feeding the cat on the back porch.

"You look better," Cooper said.

Jace shrugged. "Showers can do wonders."

"How's the head?"

"Still pounding."

"Your truck is at the bar. I'll drop you by after you've gotten some food. You always feel better after you eat," Cooper said.

Jace couldn't argue with him. After putting on his cowboy hat and grabbing some sunglasses, the two of them walked from the house and were immediately blasted by the Texas heat.

"It's going to be a scorcher of a summer," Cooper said when Jace made a sound. "Especially if it's this hot in June."

Jace put on his sunglasses as he hurried to the truck. Cooper's chuckle didn't help matters. The bright sun after a night of hard drinking was always difficult to bear. A comfortable silence fell between them as Cooper drove to one of their favorite places to eat. They didn't speak until they were inside the restaurant and greeted by the employees who knew them both by name.

In minutes, they were in their preferred booth at the back, their hats hanging on hooks on the wall. After they ordered, Cooper put his arms on the table. He looked Jace square in the eyes and said, "What happened yesterday?"

"Nothing."

He shot Jace a dry look. "I know it wasn't the date she left."

Jace sighed loudly. "If you must know, it was the anniversary of the first time I saw her."

"You keep up with that?" Cooper asked incredulously. "I can't remember when I first met Marlee."

"Bullshit. You can try that on anyone else. Not me."

Cooper's face broke into a grin. "All right. You've got me. I do know. But only because it wasn't that long ago."

"Trust me. If Marlee left, you'd remember all sorts of dates. The day you first saw her, the day you asked her out, the day you first kissed, the day you first told her you loved her."

"And the day she left," Cooper replied in a soft voice.

Without bothering to answer, Jace looked out the window to the parking lot. The pain had been unbearable yesterday, and it wasn't much better today. Especially not after the dream he'd had about her. That day with the ride out to the river had been a perfect one. The weather had been temperate, the sky the brightest blue he'd ever seen, and the river slow. They had made love in the water before basking beneath the sun on a blanket. Then they had ridden around the property, stopping to walk, talk, kiss and make love again.

Every day with Taryn had been special.

"It's been almost five years. We may not be blood, but you're my brother in any way I look at it. I know you loved her, but it's time to let her go. It's time to move on."

Jace jerked his head back to Cooper. "Don't you think I've tried?"

"I don't think you've tried hard enough," Cooper replied, though there was no heat in his words. "I think you're holding on because you believe she was your one and only chance."

"Maybe she was."

Cooper rolled his eyes and sat back. "Now I'm the one calling bullshit. If you really wanted to move on, you could."

"Some people don't."

"After everything you survived while in the military—"

Jace glared at him. "Don't finish that sentence."

"Fair enough," Cooper said as he raised his hands in defeat.

Jace shook his head, angry at himself for getting so riled up at his friend voicing the very things he told himself. "I'm sorry."

"No, you're right. I shouldn't have gone there," Cooper said.

"You're my friend, my brother. You've never hesitated to tell me the harsh reality, just as I never spared you. I shouldn't ask you to do it now."

Cooper put his hands in his lap. "You're one of the best men I know. You've been through hell and back. And despite it all, you smile. If anyone deserves to find happiness, it's you. I want you to know that. Just because she gave up on you doesn't mean there isn't someone out there who won't. Someone whose family accepts you and welcomes you into their lives. Someone who won't keep things from you or run off in the middle of the night."

"There are things we probably don't know."

"Maybe."

Jace narrowed his eyes at Cooper. Something in his friend's voice caused Jace to be wary. "What does that mean?"

"Nothing," Cooper said with a shrug. "I'm agreeing with you."

"No, you know something."

Cooper spread his arms. "I don't."

"You contacted Cash, didn't you?" Jace stated.

Cooper dropped his chin to his chest and blew out a breath. After a moment, he looked at Jace. "I did."

"When?"

Cooper briefly lowered his gaze to the table. "A couple of months ago."

"And?"

"Cash was having problems locating her. And when Marlee found out that I hired Cash, she chewed my ass real good for butting my nose into your business. She said that if you wanted to hire someone, you could have. I realized she was right, and I told Cash to stop looking for her."

"Good." But the more Jace thought about it, the more he considered hiring Cash himself. He needed answers about why Taryn had left. Cash could give that to him.

If he dared to look.

Chapter 2

What the hell was she doing?

Taryn had been asking herself that since she returned from Jace's house. She paced the small motel room while trying to think of a way out of her predicament. She was in so deep, she wasn't sure there was a way out for her.

She sat on the bed and put a hand to her forehead. Exhaustion weighed heavily on her, but no matter how tired she was, she couldn't sleep. That tended to happen when people's lives were on the line. She'd been backed into a corner, and for a brief moment, she had lost her mind. And went to Jace.

Seeing him had made her think everything could be all right again. Especially when he smiled at her. His face had lit up with such excitement that she had been overcome with emotion. But it hadn't taken her long to realize that he was drunk—and not alone. The instant that dawned on her, Taryn knew she needed to leave.

She had needed someone to lean on, and she hadn't even stopped to think that Jace might not be alone. She had left the house through the side door and hurried to her car she had parked at the curb. With every step, she chastised herself for going to Jace. It was wrong to bring him into her problems, but she hadn't been able to help herself. Thankfully, she had come to her senses with enough time to get away. And given how drunk he'd been, Jace likely wouldn't remember the encounter.

At least, she hoped he wouldn't. The very last thing she wanted was to have Jace confront her. He would demand answers that she simply couldn't give.

Taryn fell back onto the bed and stared at the ceiling. From the moment she met Jace at that party, she'd known he was something wonderful. They could've had something special if given a chance, but too many obstacles had been in their way. Her father had been the biggest one. If she had had the guts to stand up to him and the rest of her family, she likely wouldn't be in the situation she was in now. But she couldn't change the past, and it wouldn't do to dwell on such things.

She drew in a deep breath and sat up. Her options had run out long ago, leaving her one last resort. Why had she thought she could do this? But she knew the answer. She was desperate, and desperate people did desperate things. Taryn didn't want to make the phone call, but she didn't have any other choice. Her time was running out. She had already wasted too much of it going to Jace's house.

"Only because I don't want to make the damn call," she told herself and released a long sigh.

Still, there was no alternative, no other place she could turn.

That wasn't entirely true. She could get in her car

and drive south until she reached Mexico. She could start a new life there with a clean slate. As appealing as that sounded, she couldn't do it. Her younger sister was counting on her, and Taryn wouldn't put anyone else's life in jeopardy.

She reached for her phone and pulled out the folded piece of paper her father had given her several years ago when their nightmare first began. On it was a name and a number. She had thrown the note aside at the time, causing her father to yell at her.

"You might need him one day."

Taryn had sneered at the thought. "Never."

"Don't ever say never. It'll come back to bite you in the ass."

Her father's words had never been truer than in that moment. Back then, she had sworn she'd never be in a place where she needed the people her father had called friends. And yet, here she was. She would have to do some major groveling—if Big Pete even spoke to her.

She could sit here for several more hours, trying to find another way, only to end up right back where she was. There was no use putting it off any longer. Taryn dialed the number but couldn't make herself hit SEND. The very thought of it made her stomach roil so violently that she tossed aside the cell phone and ran to the toilet. She sat on the vinyl floor and leaned back against the tub as she drew her knees up to her chest and gave in to the tears that had been threatening since she drove into Clearview. She was so tired of being the responsible one. The one always sorting things out.

The one everyone leaned on.

She'd had so many dreams, so many things she wanted to do. She never imagined herself little more than an indentured servant to one of the most feared drug kingpins in Texas. Her mother was probably rolling over in her grave.

Taryn couldn't think about her mother. If she did, she would never be able to do what had to be done. Like it or not, this was her fate. She had accepted things as they were.

If she could carry out this plan, she would finally free herself and Payton. If Boyd kept to his promise, once Taryn returned with the money, her family's debt would be repaid, and she could take Payton and get as far away as possible.

Taryn picked herself off the floor and splashed water on her face. Then she got her phone and purse and left the motel room. She walked down the stairs to her car and threw her bag onto the passenger seat next to her. Once more, she held her phone in her hands and stared down at the numbers already displayed. Just as she was about to hit SEND, something hit her car. She jumped and turned in her seat to find a group of kids.

"Sorry!" one of them yelled as they held up a baseball.

No doubt it'd left a dent in the side, but why should that concern her when there were much bigger problems at hand? Taryn dropped the phone into the cupholder and started the car. She was famished, and while the thought of food made her slightly ill, she knew if she didn't get something in her stomach, she really would be sick.

Besides, she had a couple of days. It would be better to get things over with as soon as possible, but this was the first time she had been free in . . . years. She planned to take advantage of it while she could.

She backed up and pulled out of the parking lot and

onto the street. It felt weird to be back in her hometown. While many of her friends had hungered to get out and live somewhere else, she had always found Clearview charming. And it was close enough to the big cities to get in some culture whenever she could.

Her family had taken advantage of that often when her mother was alive. Everything had gone downhill after that.

Taryn decided to drive around for a bit to relax. She passed her high school, which made her smile at the memories. She'd had a good life back then, even if her mother's untimely death had disrupted it. After graduation, she had gotten an associate degree in dental hygiene. Teeth had always fascinated her, and if she had to work, she always figured she would do something she enjoyed.

After the two-year degree, she had found a job quickly enough and began bringing in decent money. Her future had been open, with so many opportunities. Not once had she ever counted on someone like Jace.

She drove past the rodeo grounds where she had first met him at a party. Taryn pulled into the parking lot and put her car in park as she thought about that night. It felt like a lifetime ago. And in many ways it was, because she was a completely different person now.

It had been a hot summer night, and her friends had talked her into going to the rodeo. She hadn't found out until after they arrived that one of her friends was interested in one of the bull riders. Being from Texas and living in a huge ranching community, Taryn had been aware of rodeos and everything involved with them from an early age. She remembered wanting to leave and begging her friends to go instead of staying for the afterparty. Then came the steer wrestling. The moment she saw Jace shoot from the gate atop his horse, she had been utterly enthralled. He captivated her, mainly because of his bright smile.

He'd gotten the steer easily with a great time, winning the event. Taryn thought that would be the last time she saw him, but she found herself being introduced to him at the afterparty.

And the rest of the world had faded away to nothing.

They'd spent hours talking that night. It had been magical and ended with the most amazing kiss at dawn. She had been floating on air when she returned home. She didn't think anything could put her in a bad mood. But her father had been waiting for her.

He had a particular hatred for the rodeo—and ranchers especially. It all stemmed from when he was a teenager and had been fired from a ranch job. Her father had never let it go. Her mother had been able to temper him, though. She had been his anchor, for lack of a better word. And when she died, her father hadn't known what to do. Taryn had hated him for a while, but after some time, she began to pity him. Which, in his eyes, was even worse. Whatever relationship they had died with her mother.

Taryn had tried to keep her involvement with Jace from her father, but her brother had ratted her out. That's when their budding relationship nearly got derailed. It would have, but Jace hadn't given up on her. And how had she repaid him? By leaving in the middle of the night with only a hastily written text right before her phone was destroyed.

A tear rolled down her cheek that she hastily swiped away. The time for crying was long gone. She was no longer the girl from before. She was someone who'd learned the world was a harsh place where only the strong survived.

If her father had taught her anything, it was how to survive—no matter what she had to do.

A sheriff's car drove past. A part of her wished they would pull in and ask what she was doing. She could tell them everything. It would solve her current dilemma, and it would be so easy. But she wouldn't do it for the very same reason she hadn't spoken to Jace.

Her phone vibrated. She looked down to see a new text message. The number wasn't one she recognized, but that didn't matter. She knew it was from Boyd or one of his thugs.

Tick tock.

Taryn put the car into gear and drove away. She had given her word. What she had to do was a small price to pay for her and Payton's freedom.

Chapter 3

Jace rubbed his temples, trying to ease the headache. The food had helped, but then again, he and Cooper had been in this condition more times than either wanted to admit. The majority of them had been when they were much younger. Jace didn't want to become an alcoholic, which meant he had to face some hard facts.

Probably sooner than he wanted.

"You all right?"

Jace swiveled his head to Cooper as they drove from the restaurant to the bar where Jace had left his truck. "Much of last night is nothing but a blur."

"You really should've called me if things were that bad."

At one time, Jace wouldn't have hesitated. But now that his friends had all settled down, he didn't want to bother them.

"And if you tell me you didn't because you didn't want to disturb Marlee and me, I'm going to punch you," Cooper stated with a hard look as they came to a red light.

Jace shot him an attempt at a smile. "You and Marlee are busy hiring people to help in her private investigation business, finalizing the plans for her new headquarters here in town, as well as getting her parents settled. Not to mention the house the two of you are building. As for Brice and Naomi, they have little Nate, who takes up all their spare time. Caleb and Audrey split their time between the ranch and the animal sanctuary. So, yeah, I'm aware that everyone has other obligations."

"If I weren't driving, I would absolutely punch you," Cooper said and shook his head. "After everything that Brice, Caleb, you, and I have been through, you should know each one of us would drop whatever we were doing for you and each other."

"I know." And Jace did know, but that didn't make it any easier to call them.

Cooper blew out a breath. "Going to a bar makes me think you were looking for trouble."

"I wasn't. Well, maybe subconsciously, I was. I don't know."

"You were surrounded by three women. All of which wanted you to go home with them."

Jace laughed. "I suppose Ryan told you that?"

"That he did. It's a good thing he happened to stop by when he spotted your truck. He thought he'd have a beer or two with you. But he said you were already pretty drunk when he arrived."

Jace twisted his lips. "I started drinking around four."

"So, you were lit." Cooper made a sound in the back of his throat. "Ryan also said that you kept saying her name after he got you home."

There were some kindnesses in life. Cooper not

saying Taryn's name was one of them. "I don't remember that."

"Is there anything you *do* remember?"

"I recall Ryan being at the bar and getting in his truck. While I don't remember getting home, I could almost swear I saw her."

Cooper's head jerked to him. "Her? As in . . . *her*?"

Jace pointed to the road and waited for Cooper to return his focus on driving. "Yeah."

"Why do you think she was there?"

"I don't know. It was probably just my mind playing tricks on me. But even drunk, I swear I saw a person move out of the shadows."

Cooper was silent for a moment. With one hand on the steering wheel, he propped his left elbow on the door and scrubbed his hand over his mouth and jaw. "She was the reason you were drinking in the first place. Memories and all that. Maybe it was just thinking about her that made you believe she was there."

"If it wasn't her, then someone else was in my house. I saw a person. I can swear to that."

Cooper briefly met his gaze. "I don't have an answer for that. But, think about this . . . If she had been there, wouldn't she have spoken to you? And how did she get in?"

"The light in the kitchen was on," Jace said as he tried to push past the fog of the night before. "I don't remember unlocking the front door either."

"You still keep the spare key in the same place," Cooper said.

Jace nodded slowly. "Probably not a good idea."

"Maybe you should move it."

Instead of answering him, Jace pulled out his phone and called Ryan, who picked up immediately. He put it on speaker so Cooper could listen in, as well. "Thanks for last night."

"Anytime," Ryan said with a chuckle. "I don't think I've ever seen you so bad before."

"Yeah, about that. Did you unlock my front door?"

"Your door?" Ryan was quiet for a heartbeat. "No. I told you to stay by the truck while I searched for the keys to your house that you lost between the seats right as we drove up. When I looked up, you were already inside the house."

Jace exchanged a look with Cooper. "I'm very good about keeping my doors locked, and the front door opened for me. I do keep a spare key that some people know about, though. Did you see anyone?"

"I didn't, but I was more intent on getting to you. When I finally made it into the house, you had fallen on the floor, face down."

Jace rubbed his head. "So that explains some of my pain. Did you hear anything that sounded odd?"

"Nothing out of the ordinary. Then again, I was only there a little while before Cooper showed up."

Cooper quickly added, "And I didn't see anyone."

"Why?" Ryan asked. "What's going on?"

"Jace thinks someone was there when y'all arrived," Cooper said.

There was a frown in Ryan's words when he asked, "Who?"

"My ex," Jace replied.

"Ah," Ryan said, drawing out the word. "I'm sorry I can't help."

Jace's lips twisted. It had been a long shot. "No worries. I owe you for last night."

"You owe me nothing," Ryan said.

Cooper shot Jace a knowing look as the call disconnected. Jace pocketed his phone. He had now heard from the two people who had been in his house when he arrived home, and neither of them had seen anyone. Had he imagined Taryn? Was it like Cooper said? Had his memories manifested her? Jace wished he knew because he couldn't shake the feeling that she had been there. If only he hadn't been so drunk, he might be able to remember.

By the time Cooper dropped him off at his truck, his headache was worse, and all because he was trying to think too hard. He gave his friend a wave and climbed into his vehicle before starting it. After he fastened his seatbelt and put the truck in reverse, he paused. It was probably his memories that had pulled Taryn from his head.

This wasn't the first time some type of anniversary with her had brought him low, but it was the first that he had imagined her. Could've sworn she had been there. He knew the difference between seeing her in his dreams and in real life. And last night seemed so real.

Jace turned the wheel, heading in the opposite direction of his therapist and pulled out of the parking lot. He took roads he hadn't been on since she'd left. Jace found himself driving past her house. It was a two-story and had once been nice, but time and uncaring owners had let it deteriorate badly.

He remembered the first time he had visited her there. Her father had met him on the front porch with a rifle cradled in his arms. Phil Hillman had had nothing but hate in his eyes for Jace that day, but that hadn't deterred Jace. Her father had told him in no uncertain terms that he didn't want his daughter around cowboys.

Jace pulled over to the side of the road and looked at the house, recalling that occurrence and several after where Phil had continued to do his best to stop Jace from seeing Taryn. All he knew was that Taryn took his breath away, and he wanted to be with her.

Phil never stopped trying to break them up, though. And it seemed Phil finally got his wish when the family left. Based on the brief text Taryn had sent, they were starting over in a new town with no ties to anything in Clearview. Since Jace had thought he and Taryn had something real, the kind of love that lasted lifetimes, he was blindsided.

Jace called, he texted, but Taryn never answered. He even went so far as to contact her sister, brother, and father, but none of them answered him either. That's when Jace turned to Danny Oldman. As the local sheriff, he had been able to dig deeper than Jace could. All Danny had found was that someone had cut off the Hillman family's cell phones. Danny had done his bit, as had Ryan, but since Jace was the only one making a fuss, and there was nothing else to go on, they'd had to set aside the case.

All these years later, Jace still carried that hurt around as if it had just happened. He blew out a breath and pulled back onto the road to turn his truck around to head home. He knew that what he and Taryn had was real love. There was no doubt in his mind. But no matter how certain he was, he couldn't explain how the family had disappeared in one night. Even more disturbing was the fact that they had left a lot behind. For a family wanting to start over, they hadn't taken much with them.

His thoughts remained in turmoil as he continued driving. He decided not to visit his therapist because he was still sorting through everything. Jace wasn't in the mood to talk to anyone but driving with a distracted mind wasn't smart either. He headed to his parents' house and parked at the stables.

Thankfully, he didn't see anyone when he walked inside. He let out a whistle, and his horse stuck her head over the gate and nickered in response. Jace smiled when he reached the blue roan mare and rubbed the animal's head. He had been at the ranch for Cinder's birth, and he, along with Caleb, had trained the mare. She was by far the best horse he'd ever owned.

Jace took her out of the stall and tied her to a post so he could begin saddling her. He didn't breathe easy until he was riding Cinder into the pasture. He loved everything about his parents' home. It had been a great place for him and Cooper to get into trouble. His father, however, had quickly taken the two of them and put them to work. His father had taught Cooper how to ride.

Jace's family was from a long line of professional steer wrestlers, and his father had given up on the rodeo circuit when he met Jace's mom. The two of them had started the ranch, which had been a good decision since people from all over the state came to learn steer wrestling from a family known for the trade.

Over a year ago, Jace had taken over the training duties from his father. Jace loved nothing more than being on a horse. The fact that he got paid to teach the very thing he loved to do still boggled his mind.

"Come on, girl," he whispered to the mare.

Cinder easily moved from a walk to a lope. But that wasn't enough for either of them. The mare wanted to run, and Jace wasn't about to hold her back. He gave Cinder her head and leaned low as she increased her speed until the ground was a blur beneath her hooves. For the next hour, Jace rode the mare around the property before returning to brush her down and put the tack back. Riding had been exactly what he needed.

He glanced at his parents' house as he stood by his truck, but he still wasn't ready to talk to anyone. After climbing into his vehicle, he started the engine and drove away. On the way back to his house, he pulled up to an intersection to await the light.

Jace happened to look over when a car pulled up next to him. He was gut-punched when he saw none other than Taryn. There was no time for him to comprehend what he saw before she drove away when the light turned green.

He jumped when someone honked behind him. Jace realized that he had been sitting through the green light. He knew he had to follow Taryn, so he punched the accelerator and managed to get through right as the light turned yellow. As he sped down the road, he searched for the newer model silver Camry that he'd seen, but he couldn't find it anywhere. There were several places it could've turned off, and with all the traffic, she could've gone anywhere.

Finally, he gave up and started for home again. On the way, he convinced himself that it hadn't been Taryn in the car. Just as she hadn't been in his house the night before. It was only his memories, making him see her everywhere.

Though he wasn't sure if that was any better.

Chapter 4

Her hands were clammy. Taryn was nearly hyperventilating by the time she pulled up in Big Pete's drive. It didn't matter how much money he brought in, or how much he remodeled the old home he lived in, there was no getting around the fact that he was white trash. She had detested him from the moment she saw him. And she had made no bones about letting him know it, either.

Taryn couldn't stop the shudder that ran down her back. She didn't want to be here, nor did she want to talk to Pete. But she had already decided that she wouldn't involve anyone else. This was the path she had chosen. On the way there, she had decided not to call. Showing up was better because there was less chance that he would turn her away.

She drew in a deep breath and opened the door before she changed her mind. The minute she stepped out of her car, two men appeared seemingly out of nowhere to stand at the red front door. While they didn't brandish any weapons, she knew they had them on their person. This wasn't the first time she had been to Pete's or encountered his muscle. If only it were.

She raised her hands by her head to show she was unarmed. "I need to see Big Pete."

"You have an appointment?" the man on the left asked.

His and his partner's penchant for steroids to help build their insanely large muscles made them brutes for sure—and not anyone she wanted to mess with. Taryn was certain that most people felt the same.

"I don't. Please tell him Taryn Hillman wants to see him," she called out, not wanting to get closer until she had to.

The guy on the right turned and opened the front door to step inside. It closed behind him, leaving her with the other one. Taryn wasn't much for small talk, much less with someone she didn't like. She lowered her arms when they began to hurt and looked anywhere but at the muscle staring at her. She took in the overgrown flower beds running along the house's perimeter, the tree branches hanging too near the house that caused green mildew to grow on the white siding, and the immaculate, bright blue Corvette sitting in the driveway.

It took forever before the second man finally returned. He didn't say anything, only nodded at his partner.

Lefty said, "Mr. Pete will see you now."

Taryn nearly laughed out loud. Pete had really come a long way in the few years she'd been gone if they called him "mister" now. She kept that to herself as she made her way to the house. With every step, she wanted to turn and run the other way, pretend she was anywhere but here. And yet, here she was, walking up to a house that gave her the willies, to talk to a man who made her want to puke, to ask for something that would likely take whatever freedom she got from Boyd.

Her knees knocked, and it took everything she had to keep her breathing relatively calm. She was walking into a nest of vipers, and she needed to have her wits about her. Before her current situation, she hadn't known how to handle people like Big Pete. But thanks to her time with Boyd, she had learned quite a lot.

The moment she walked into the house, she wanted to cringe. Just like the outside, someone had refurnished the inside, but the big dog chewing on the arm of the sofa, as well as the filth, cigarette trays, and beer cans everywhere, reaffirmed that money couldn't fix everything. Pete might have the cash to have nice things, but he and his . . . friends . . . couldn't take care of it.

They led her to the kitchen, where it took everything she had not to gag at the horrible smell that assaulted her. A young woman in a white negligee cheerfully cooked something that the dog probably wouldn't even eat. Taryn swung her gaze from the woman to find Pete sitting at the table with all kinds of drugs and money laid out before him.

He was only ten years older than Taryn, but he had a baby face that belied his age. That face now wore a sneer as he looked her over. She had known this was coming. It didn't make it any better, though.

"Well, well, well. Look what the cat dragged in," Pete stated.

You need him. You need him. Remember that and stay calm. "Thank you for seeing me."

Big Pete, who was actually barely above five feet tall and skinny as a reed, sat forward in his stained, white wife beater and cut-off jeans. His blue eyes narrowed on her. "You drive up after being gone for all these years, you bet I'm going to get your sweet ass inside."

Remain calm. You need his help. Don't let him rile you. They're just words. Words can't hurt you—not when freedom is so close at hand.

She held his gaze, waiting for him to say more. Pete ran a hand over his close-cut blond hair as he sat back and laughed. He crossed his bare feet on the chair near him, his soles black. Behind her, Taryn could feel the eyes of the two men who'd brought her inside. No doubt other armed men were in the house, as well. A nest of vipers, for sure.

"Your father was a good client," Pete said with a smile. He lifted his hands and looked around the house. "Thanks to his constant need for drugs, I was able to get all of this."

Taryn had expected this comment. The first time she'd met Pete was when she came to get her father, passed out from drugs. Pete had told her that she could pay her father's debt with sex, and she had slapped him. It was an instinctive reaction that she immediately regretted since Pete and his goons could've easily killed her. But if she'd thought that would anger Pete, she had been wrong. He liked that she had spirit.

And that had frightened her more than anything.

Because she knew people like Pete could do very, *very* bad things to her. That's when she really started hating her father. If he had only dealt with his grief in another way, she never would have been exposed to such lowlifes.

Pete raised a barely visible brow on his pale face. There were only a few whiskers about, proving that he couldn't grow a proper beard. His pale blue eyes unnerved her, but then everything about him made her want to bathe in hand sanitizer.

"Not interested in small talk, eh?" he asked, disdain filling his voice.

Taryn glanced at the floor and inwardly kicked herself. "My apologies. I've been traveling."

"You got into town last night."

Her heart clutched as she held his gaze. The fact that he had known she was in town didn't sit well with her at all. "It was late. And I slept in this morning."

"Where have you been, my beautiful flower?"

How she hated when he called her that.

Pete lowered his feet and stood. He looked behind her to the two men. "She's stunning, isn't she?"

"Yes, sir," the one who'd spoken to her outside answered.

Pete walked to her and ran the backs of his fingers down her arm. "Your skin is so soft and pale, but during the summers in the sun, it turns a lovely bronze. And those eyes of yours. I've never seen a green like it."

Taryn noted that the girl had stopped cooking and now stared at Taryn as if she were the devil herself.

Pete looked up at her, lust filling his visage. "You get more beautiful with age, Taryn."

She took a half-step back to put some distance between them without being obstinate. Pete had always told her that he wanted her, and she knew she had to appeal to his ego. It was the way with men like him. "I came because you're the only one who can help me."

"Is that right?" he asked skeptically.

"It is."

He studied her for a long minute as he leaned back against the table. "All right. I'll bite. What is it you want?"

"I need half a million dollars."

His eyes bugged out as he gaped at her, then he laughed and walked back to his seat. "You think I'm just going to give you that kind of money?"

"I'll work for it," she said, fisting her hands as she tried not to think of how he'd make her *work* for it.

"That's assuming I give it to you."

She raised her chin and took a long shot. "You will."

He quirked a brow. "You've got some balls, woman. Why would I give you anything? Look at the way you've treated me. Hell, even now."

"I always squared my father's debts with you. Always."

Pete seemed to think about that and then nodded slowly. "That's true. And you were timely, too."

"We just need to negotiate how I pay you back."

"Whoa," he said, lifting his hands. "Hold up a moment. You've skipped some steps. Like finding out if I even have that kind of cash."

And here's where she went for it all. She had no choice. Because five years under Boyd's thumb was enough. And it was time she did something and got herself and Payton out. "You do."

"Is that right? What makes you say that?"

"Because if you didn't, we wouldn't be having this conversation."

Pete's smile was slow as it spread across his face. "You're fierce, woman. If you had a mind to do it, you could have your own business. Anyone you work for will make loads of money."

"I've got another job at present that isn't negotiable. That changes when I bring the money."

He reached for a toothpick near him and speared one

of the olives sitting on a plate. He popped it into his mouth and swallowed before he said, "So you say."

"It's the truth." God, she really hoped it was. She didn't want to think about being indebted to both Boyd *and* Pete.

"Sounds like you're in a bit of a pickle."

"Can you help me or not? I don't have time for this."

"If I don't help, where else are you going to go? Perhaps to your old boyfriend? His family is well-off, but nothing like the Easts. Then again, you know that."

Just the fact that Pete had brought up Jace made Taryn want to kick him in the balls. She fisted her hands in a bid to keep a lid on her temper, proving once more that she had learned a lot while working for Boyd. "I'm here with you."

"So you are." Pete laughed. "So you are."

"Are you willing to negotiate with me?"

Pete stuck the toothpick into his mouth and crossed his arms over his chest. "The thing is, darlin', I'll want you to pay off the debt in my bed—or anywhere else I want your fine body. You can't do that if you're . . . otherwise employed."

"As I said, that will be taken care of."

Pete pulled a face. "And I'm just supposed to take your word for it?"

"I'll pay it back with ten percent interest." When Pete hesitated, she tried one more thing. "I'll do anything. I'm desperate."

"The last thing you should tell anyone you're negotiating with is that you're desperate," he told her, though he had the look of a wolf about to go in for the kill.

"I don't have a choice. I have to get this money, and my deadline is closing in. You're the only one I know who can help. With our . . . past . . . you know I wouldn't be here—begging—if it wasn't serious."

He nodded again. "That I do. Did your father put you in this position?"

"It doesn't matter whose fault it is."

"Actually, it does. That man doesn't deserve you or your siblings. I told him a long time ago that he was dead weight, that he would pull all of you down. It wasn't but a few months later that your entire family vanished."

Taryn shifted uncomfortably, praying that Pete didn't prod more. "Bad things happen to people all the time."

"Why did you leave?"

"There was an . . . unavoidable situation."

Pete pulled the toothpick from his mouth and tossed it onto the table. "Apparently, pretty bad if it caused all of you to leave. And yet, here you are once more. So, I'll ask again. Why did you leave?"

"Men came for us," she said through clenched teeth.

"Now, that wasn't so hard, was it? Sit. Brandi over there is cooking dinner. You're going to join us. I have a feeling it's going to take hours for us to hash out this . . . negotiation. But you can start by telling me everything I want to know." Pete kicked out the chair next to him so she could take a seat.

Taryn knew this was her very last chance to leave. She sank into the chair.

Chapter 5

No matter what Jace did, he couldn't stop thinking about Taryn. He paced the living room as his mind went over everything again and again, trying to sift through his foggy memories. Was it just coincidence that he swore she had been in his home the night before? Was it mere happenstance that he believed he'd pulled up beside her earlier?

The answer was no.

He hadn't seen her in years. Hadn't heard from her via text, email, or phone. Just hours after she'd sent him that final text, her cell number had been disconnected. Now, all of a sudden, he'd seen her twice in two days.

"*Thought* I saw her," he corrected himself.

He'd been too drunk the night before to know for sure. And today . . . well, he couldn't be positive there either. The driver had been at an angle where he couldn't get a good look at her profile. But he'd *known* it was her. A gut feeling.

Jace halted. The car. The Camry might be one of the most popular vehicles on the roads, and the color made it easy to blend in. But he wasn't going to give up. He could've made things easier on himself if he had caught the license plate number, but that wouldn't stop him. Just before he turned and headed to where he'd left his keys, he paused.

"She left you," he said aloud. "She didn't bother to tell you to your face or allow you to talk to her to get more of an explanation. For months, you did everything you could to find her. Why would you chase her again?"

The simple reason was that he loved her. No amount of anger over her leaving or her absence had changed that.

"She obviously didn't love you as much as you thought she did. Only someone so self-centered would leave so callously."

Jace frowned. While that was true, she hadn't left on her own. Her father, brother, and younger sister had all gone with her. It reminded Jace of his time in the military when they were closing in on targets and entire families would steal away in the middle of the night, carrying only what they could hold in their hands.

He ran a hand down his face. Was that what happened? Jace shook his head. No, that couldn't be. Because if Taryn and her family had been in danger, she would've come to him for help.

"Unless she couldn't."

He was searching for explanations that weren't there, just as he had when Taryn first left. The need to punch something was great. Before he put his hand through a wall, Jace spun around and stalked to his keys. He swiped them from the table and strode from the house, anger in every step. He didn't realize he wasn't sure what to do until he was in his truck with the engine running. He could always go to his friends for help. They would do everything they could for him, but they had already done so much.

He could call Cash, Cooper's Air Force buddy who had turned into a highly sought-after private investigator. Then there was Marlee, who was also a PI. But for some reason, Jace was hesitant to do any of that. He wasn't sure why. Following his gut had never led him wrong before. However, he was quickly reaching the end of his rope. Soon, he would contact Cash or Marlee and see if they could find Taryn.

After the two most recent incidents, Jace couldn't help thinking that Taryn was in Clearview. And if she were, then he would be able to find her. No one knew the roads like he did.

Jace put his truck in reverse and backed out of the drive. He returned to the intersection where he thought he'd seen Taryn in the car. After he pulled into a nearby parking lot, he surveyed the businesses and buildings. His gaze then went to the street he was sure she had pulled onto. It had some hotels as well as a few businesses

He waited until it was clear and pulled onto Main Street before moving into the left lane and turning onto Oak. Jace drove slowly, his gaze scanning the right side of the road, looking for any vehicle that even resembled a silver Camry. Oak was long and straight with a few side streets branching off, but he remained on it. When he reached the end, he turned around and made his way back, keeping his gaze focused to the right as he scanned for the car he'd seen.

Just as he was about to circle back to the intersection with Main, he spotted a back drive leading to a hotel. Jace quickly turned in and circled the lot. The moment he found the silver Camry parked at the end under a tall pine tree, he breathed a sigh of relief. He hadn't been seeing things.

Jace stopped the truck and looked around for an empty parking spot close by. Luckily, he found one behind him. He backed into it to look straight ahead at the hotel and still keep sight of the car. With his vehicle in park, he pulled out his phone and typed the license plate number in, just in case.

He left the truck idling because of the heat. But his tinted windows kept him partially hidden from anyone who might be looking. After about thirty minutes with no movement, Jace lowered his windows a few inches and turned off the engine. This wasn't the first time he'd been on a stakeout. He'd helped Danny and Ryan a few times when they needed extra eyes.

The sweltering Texas heat didn't make things comfortable. Sweat ran down his back and his face. When he could stand it no more, he started the truck again. A loud sigh escaped him when a blast of cold air hit him in the face. He closed his eyes in enjoyment. When he opened them once more, he just made out the back of a woman with long, dark hair as she climbed into the Camry.

His heart rate quickened because he knew right then that it was Taryn. Just seeing her from the back confirmed it. It was the way she moved, how she held herself. In those brief seconds he'd seen her getting into the car, he knew without a doubt that it was her.

He didn't take his eyes off her as she backed out of her spot and drove away. Jace saw her pull onto Oak and head toward the intersection with Main. He waited a few moments and then followed her. He was two cars behind when he pulled to a stop at the light. When it turned green, she made a right and drove for a quarter of a mile before she pulled into a restaurant parking lot.

By the time Jace drove in behind her, she was already inside. He parked several spaces from her and contemplated his next move. He could wait and see where she went after she ate. Or he could go in and confront her.

There was so much he wanted to say to her. How many times had he had imaginary conversations with her where he told her how hurt he was, how much he missed her, how furious he was that she hadn't told him goodbye to his face? That he loved her still?

Jace fisted his hands, arguing with himself over what to do. There were pros and cons to both options. The more he sat and thought about Taryn being back in Clearview without talking to him, the angrier he became. And yet he was thinking of staying in his truck instead of talking to her?

"Fuck that."

He shut off the engine and climbed out. Taryn owed him an explanation. And if by some chance it wasn't her . . . well, then Jace would go straight to his therapist.

As he walked toward the entrance, he wasn't sure if he wanted the woman inside to be her or not. If it was, then he might finally get some answers to the many questions that had formed over the years.

If it wasn't her, then he would hire Cash and find her once and for all. He needed closure. Both mentally and emotionally. His therapist had told him exactly that, when Taryn had first left. But he hadn't been ready to consider it. Now, he was. He wanted to move on with his life, and he couldn't do that until he had the closure she hadn't given him.

He pulled open the door to the restaurant and walked

inside. Jace removed his sunglasses and paused beside the hostess as she greeted him, letting his eyes adjust to the dimness of the interior. He hung his sunglasses on the neck of his shirt and ignored the hostess as he scanned the occupants until his gaze landed on Taryn. She sat facing the door, her head lowered as she looked at the menu.

"Sir?"

He blinked and looked at the petite brunette staring at him expectedly. "I'm meeting someone," he answered the hostess. Then he pointed to Taryn. "She's right over there."

Jace walked toward Taryn, his heart beating rapidly as all sorts of things ran through his head. Her thick hair was much longer now, the dark strands falling over to one side as she leaned her head into her hand and slid her fingers through the curls.

This was the first time he'd gotten a look at her face in years. The sight was like being kicked by a horse. He halted, unable to move. He had seen her so many times in his dreams, but looking at her now was like seeing her for the first time all over again. She had taken his breath away back then, and she was doing it again now.

Her oval face had delicate features, but her eyes were large and slanted slightly upward at the corners. Dark brows arched over her beautiful green orbs, the color the most unusual thing he had ever seen. There were no words to describe it. Her eyes had been the first thing he'd noticed about her all those years ago. The second was her lips. Wide, full, and utterly sensual. With just a smile, she could have him on his knees.

Even today.

But those were only a few of her assets. High cheek-bones, an hourglass figure that made his mouth water, and a laugh that could make anyone smile completed the package. She was stunning. The kind of striking that caused people to stop and stare because they weren't sure she was real.

The kind of beauty that generally went to someone's head.

Not Taryn. She could've had any man she wanted. For a brief time, she had chosen him. Those two years had been the best of Jace's life. They had made a great team. Or at least he'd thought they had. And the sex . . . it had been mind-blowing. He'd fallen head over heels for her in just a few days. Hell, he'd loved her at first sight. Jace had known almost immediately that he wanted her in his life forever.

Suddenly, Taryn looked up from the menu. The instant their eyes met, she stilled, surprise registering as if she hadn't been prepared for this moment. She straightened slowly, her arm falling to the table as her lips parted in shock.

Jace watched disbelief and astonishment cross her features, one emotion at a time. She slowly lowered the menu, and her hair fell back into place as she licked her lips—a nervous gesture he'd picked up on early in their relationship. She glanced away and took a drink of the water that had been placed on the table. Then, she slid her gaze back to him.

"Jace."

A shudder went through him at the sound of his name on her lips once again. He wasn't sure approaching her was a good idea. He realized he wasn't prepared for any of it, no matter what he had told himself. Not the sight of her, not her reaction to seeing him, and not the smooth sound of her voice.

Not the fierce, undeniable desire she still stirred within him.

He'd been raised to be a gentleman, but all of that went out the window as the hurt and pain of the last few years welled up within him. He wanted to shout at her, to release all the fury he'd held inside for so long. He wanted to shake her, to kiss her. To hold her against him and feel her soft curves as he tasted her sweet lips.

It surprised him how he could hold onto so much anger and passion for the same person. The two emotions swirled around each other, twining together until he couldn't tell one from the other. But the one thing he knew for certain was that she still had the ability to make him crave her as no one else could.

He walked the rest of the way to her table and slid into the booth without asking if it was okay. He didn't take his hat off or even offer a smile. The pain pushed past the desire then. "Where have you been?" he demanded.

Her eyes lowered to the table, showing him long lashes that used to tickle his cheek as she rested her head on his shoulder. "I know you're angry—"

"You don't know a damn thing," he said over her. "You left. In the middle of the night. And you thought a quick text was enough?"

"I know." She took a deep breath and looked up at him. "I'm sorry."

He shook his head. "You don't get to say that without an explanation."

"I—" she began as she glanced toward the door of the restaurant. She paused, her face going pale. She shifted uncomfortably. "Can we do this another time?"

"I've been waiting years for answers. I'm not going anywhere." He wanted to look over his shoulder to see what had caused her discomfort. But he wasn't going to take his eyes from her. The fact that she was so obviously upset caused him to want to protect her, which only pissed him off even more. But he wasn't entirely sure that she wasn't playing him.

She cut her eyes to the door again, then lowered her voice. "*Please.*"

He sat back and put one arm along the back of the booth. "No."

"Jace. Go," she urged.

Out of the corner of his eye, he saw someone approaching. He looked over to find a man in a suit. Jace gave him a once-over, noting the man's impeccable features. He was good-looking, and the stranger knew it. That didn't upset Jace, though. He was pissed because the man was there to see Taryn.

"Hello," the stranger said to Taryn, shooting her a smile. "I didn't know we were having company."

"We aren't," she said and looked pointedly at Jace.

Jace was about to tell them that he was staying, but a man could only take so much abuse before he reached his limit. And he was far past his. Without a word, he rose from the table. He looked the man in the eye and gave him a nod, then walked out of the building to his truck.

Once inside, he turned up the music and pointed the vehicle toward his house, the need for alcohol too strong to resist.

Chapter 6

Taryn was still in shock at seeing Jace at the restaurant. She wanted to call him back, to ask him to wait so she could tell him everything he wanted to know. But she didn't. She couldn't believe he had found her. Actually, that wasn't true. She hadn't exactly hidden when she came to town. A part of her had *wanted* him to find her.

It had been a beautiful daydream. One she had nearly every day. The chance to return to Clearview and find Jace, have him offer to rescue her without wanting to know all the details of what had happened. Him stating his love.

But the reality was much, much different. And it had hit her like a freight train when she found Jace standing before her. She had nearly wept at the sight of him. Somehow, he was more handsome than ever. How was that even possible?

She'd let her eyes run over his strong jaw, wide lips, and the hard body she knew firsthand was all lean muscle. But then he had demanded answers, and she hated him for it. Hated him because she couldn't give him what he wanted. Seeing him had her hurting all over again, and there was no denying the anger and pain in his hazel eyes.

When he sat down, she'd fought the urge to reach out and tuck his golden blond hair behind his ears where it poked out of his Stetson. He needed a haircut. He'd always put it off, and seeing it now reminded her of the many times she had trimmed it for him. He'd loved having her cut his hair.

And she had loved doing it.

"Is there a problem?"

Taryn started at the deep voice beside her. She had forgotten all about her meeting. She looked into the man's deep brown eyes and shook her head. "Not at all."

"I'm Jerome," he said as he motioned to the booth.

Taryn nodded for him to sit. "This is a very public place."

"Exactly. Transactions like ours are usually done here, which makes it perfect."

She sat back, instantly not liking Jerome. Maybe it was the way he spoke and acted, as if he were above the law. Or perhaps it was the way he stared at her. Taryn had gotten used to the looks from men at an early age, but some made her skin crawl. And Jerome was such a man.

"I don't like this."

He smiled, though it didn't reach his eyes. "Who was that man?"

"No one."

"I want to know his name."

She narrowed her eyes on him. "It's none of your business."

"I determine what's my business or not. And he's certainly my business after the way he looked at you."

Taryn wasn't going to listen to this anymore. She might be doing a trial run for Big Pete, but she could convince him to give her another try. Hopefully. Maybe.

Shit.

She was in so deep that she could no longer determine which way was up. That's how her brother had gotten killed. If she weren't careful, she'd soon follow in his footsteps. And that simply couldn't happen.

Taryn met Jerome's dark eyes and let her anger surface enough for him to see. "I don't give a rat's ass who you think you are. I won't conduct any business here, and if you think you're going to come in here and tell me what to do, you've got another thing coming."

Instead of lashing out, he laughed and sat back, mimicking Jace's pose with his arm along the back of the booth. "Pete told me you had spirit. Now I understand what he was referring to. I'm intrigued. How much?"

"Excuse me?" she asked, taken aback.

"How much do you want to be mine?"

Taryn shook her head in astonishment—and more than a little indignation. "Who the hell do you think you are? I'm not property to be bought."

"I'm willing to pay whatever you want to be mine," he said as his gaze intensified. "I can give you anything, take you anywhere you desire. Do anything you wish. Just give me a figure."

She was ready to tell him to kiss off when she

realized that his proposition was better than the one she had given Big Pete. It would get her out of the hole she currently found herself in. But it wasn't just money. Boyd would kill her sister if she didn't return on time. If, even for an instant, she'd thought Jerome might be able to help her with Boyd, she'd take him up on his offer.

The fact that she was putting herself in a position to be in Pete's debt, to do whatever he wanted—sexual or otherwise—for an unspecified period of time, was more than enough. All she was doing was trading one asshole for another, and Jerome wasn't any better than Pete or Boyd.

"I'm not interested," she replied.

A smile broke over Jerome's face. "But you considered it. I know you did."

"So what?" she asked with a shrug.

He leaned forward and put his arms on the table. "Why are you working for Pete? Whatever you went to him for, I can get you."

"I need half a million dollars."

"Done," Jerome said without blinking.

Taryn laughed and rubbed her forehead. "I have a debt to repay."

"I assumed. People don't ask for that kind of money unless it's important. I can write you a check right now. Come with me. I'll wipe away anything from your past that's hounding you."

"You'll never be able to do that. The money is only a portion of my debt."

"What's the rest?"

Taryn stared at him, refusing to speak.

Finally, Jerome lifted his hands. "All right. If you don't want to tell me, that's fine. I've got connections,

Taryn. I can untangle you from whatever mess you're in."

The more he spoke, the more she thought he might be able to do it. And while Jerome still wasn't her best option, he was someone other than Pete—who made her gag. She had only gone to Pete because there hadn't been anyone else. Now, she had options.

While she didn't know much of anything regarding Jerome, at least he seemed a better choice. The confidence with which he spoke told her that he was used to negotiating. He just might be able to go up against Boyd and ensure that she and Payton were able to get away. If Taryn played her cards right, she might be able to make sure Payton didn't get involved in whatever agreement she made with Jerome. Taryn hadn't been sure how Pete would respond, so she had left out any mention of Payton or Boyd in her discussion with him.

"Tell me who it is," Jerome urged. "There isn't anything you can say that will make me retract my offer. I promise."

"Boyd Walters."

Jerome's face paled. He slid from the booth and stood to button his suit jacket as beads of sweat dotted his forehead. He glanced around as if looking for someone. "Forget you know my name. I don't want anything to do with you. Our conversation never happened, and I never made any sort of offer to you."

"But you just said—"

"That was before you mentioned that name."

And just like that, her other option was gone.

Not to mention, she hadn't made the sale for Pete.

"Dammit," Taryn mumbled to herself.

She blew out a breath as a waitress walked up. She

needed to eat, and Brandi's food was inedible. Plus, she wasn't at all sure Jace wasn't waiting in the parking lot for her. She couldn't face him again. Not now, at least.

After she placed her order, Taryn dropped her head into her hands, elbows on the table. She had known that coming back to Clearview was a mistake, but she had been grasping at straws. That's what desperation did to a person. How had she ever imagined that things would work out as she wanted? And how the hell had she thought she could come back to town and not run into Jace?

"Please," she whispered to whatever higher power might be listening. "I'm tired and scared, and I don't know what to do now."

Her last few years had been hell, and it didn't look as if things were going to get any better. She raised her head and blinked rapidly to quell the tears that threatened. Thankfully, they retreated. She feared if she gave in and let them come again, they wouldn't stop. She was tipping into an abyss that threatened to eat her whole, and she had nothing and no one to hold onto.

Not true. There's someone you can turn to.

Taryn refused to think of Jace. He was furious with her, and for good reason. He was the type of man who was a natural hero, the kind who always did the right thing, who set aside their own wants and needs to help those they loved. He had come into her life at a time when she needed him. He'd swept her off her feet and loved her unconditionally. Gave her the kind of love that everyone dreamed of. She'd had that. For two blissful years, she had been in the arms of a man who had sheltered her, loved her, and adored her.

And in one horrible night, it had all gone away.

She left the restaurant forty minutes later. Her gaze swept the parking lot, but she didn't notice anyone sitting inside a vehicle. Taryn got into her car and headed back to Pete's, hoping to try and explain what had gone so terribly wrong with Jerome. All Pete had asked of her was to do one job. Then he'd give her the money she needed. It had been a simple exchange. In all honesty, it was Jerome's fault. If he had kept to their transaction, Boyd's name wouldn't have come up at all. Taryn would've made the sale and returned to Pete's to claim her funds. She would then be on her way back to Fort Worth to hand over Boyd's money in exchange for her and Payton's freedom.

Why had it all gone sideways? Taryn didn't want to dwell on that. What'd happened with Jerome was done. She needed to start thinking about how she would handle Pete, specifically what she planned to say to him.

When she pulled up to Pete's, several more cars filled the drive. She was instantly on edge. More people meant more witnesses to her exchange with Pete, and that couldn't be a good thing. She got out of her vehicle and started toward the front door. Before she reached it, one of the guards opened it for her. She nodded at him, recognizing him as the one who hadn't spoken the first time she came.

"There she is!"

She looked up at the sound of Pete's voice as he came down the curving staircase of his home. He wore a smile, but his eyes burned with fury. She knew that look well because she had seen it on Boyd's face right before he killed her father in front of her. No doubt

Jerome had told Pete what'd happened. So much for her getting to Pete first. She opened her lips to speak when she caught sight of something in her periphery. She turned her head and saw five new people who hadn't been there before.

Two men dressed casually in jeans and solid-colored tee shirts three sizes too big, and women next to them in short, tight-fitting dresses that dipped low and barely covered their asses, along with heels so high they should've been called stilts.

Pete reached the bottom of the stairs and put his arm around her. He squeezed her a tad too tightly, but Taryn hid her grimace. "I've been singing your praises all afternoon since you left. I had my best client come to you. My. Best. Client," he stated, spittle flying from his mouth.

Taryn tilted her head away. "Don't you want my side of what happened?"

"I don't give a flying fuck about your side. Customers are always right."

"He wanted to buy me away from you."

Pete looked at her for a moment, then threw back his head and laughed. "I would've attempted the same thing in his shoes. It's business."

"I'll make things right with him."

Pete shoved her away as if she were a hot coal in his hands. His lips twisted cruelly. "You didn't tell me who you were indebted to."

Dread filled her. Shit. *Shitshitshitshitshit.* "You didn't ask. Besides, it doesn't matter."

"The hell it doesn't. I'm not interfering in any business involving Boyd Walters. Do you know what kind of man he is?"

She knew *exactly* what kind of man Boyd was. She

was also aware that not too many people had seen the things she had and were still alive to talk about them. "This is for me, not Boyd. It's my debt."

Pete laughed, but there was no mirth in the sound. "You're beholden to him. That means any transactions I do with you, tie me to him. I don't want anything to do with him. He's a fucking maniac."

Taryn knew that for a fact. "Pete, I'm in a bad way. If I don't bring Boyd the money, he's going to— "

"Get out," Pete cut her off before she could finish. "Get out and never come back."

She hesitated, trying to think of something that might change Pete's mind. Just as she was about to offer herself to him for the remaining days she had in Clearview, Pete snapped his fingers, and the two hulking men who had barred her entrance earlier moved in on either side of her.

She knew then that if she didn't leave on her own, the two muscled men would make sure she did. She swallowed, feeling as if she were drowning and no one would help her, Taryn pulled the bag of pot from the front pocket of her jeans and tossed it at Pete, who caught it easily. Then she turned on her heel and walked away. She made it inside her Camry before the tears came.

Taryn gave in to them for a few moments, then wiped her eyes and drove away, both relieved not to be involved with Pete any longer and also angry that she still didn't have any money. And time was running out.

She drove for a few miles before she pulled over and allowed herself another good cry. The tears didn't fix her problems, but she was overwhelmed and fast losing hope. Eventually, the tears dried. She leaned her head

back against the seat and blinked, her eyes now sting-
ing from all the crying.

Taryn drew in a deep breath and did what she had
always done—she tried to find a solution. No matter
how many things she tried to concentrate on, all she
could think about was Jace.

You can go to him.

She knew that, but she also knew it wasn't wise.

*Why not? If anyone in the entire world wouldn't hes-
itate to help you, it's Jace.*

That was true. It was just part of what made Jace . . .
Jace. But did she really want to involve him in things
with someone like Boyd? Look how Pete and Jerome
had reacted.

They aren't Jace.

She shook her head at her subconscious. She had already hurt him enough. What kind of person did that
to someone and then went to them, asking for such a
hefty sum of money? The worst kind.

*Who else can you turn to? This isn't about you or
Jace. It's about Payton.*

Taryn slammed her hand against the steering wheel,
mainly because she knew the voice in her head was
right.

You're wasting time. Drive to Jace's now.

No. It was the worst idea ever.

But no matter how many times she tried to come
up with another plan, she got nothing. Taryn knew she
had nowhere else to turn, and Payton was counting on
her. She put the car in drive before she lost her nerve
and headed toward Jace's. She wasn't sure if she could
go in, but she would at least give it a try.

She only hoped that he would let her talk. Then
again, it wasn't as if she wanted to tell him everything.

The night he came for them, Boyd had made it impossible for her to send Jace anything but the curt text she had sent, breaking things off.

But Jace needed some answers.

And she had to give them.

Chapter 7

Fort Worth, Texas

"Well?" Boyd asked as he concentrated on hitting the golf ball on his private putting green situated on the penthouse's rooftop.

Brick, a tall, muscular man with black hair and dark eyes, stood behind Boyd. Brick was methodical, relentless. And he always got the job done the first time. Boyd tapped the golf ball and watched it roll into the hole. Only then did he turn to face Brick and lean on the putter.

"She's attempting to get the money," Brick replied.

Boyd glanced out over downtown Fort Worth, highlighted by the beautiful setting sun. "You trust what our people in Clearview are telling you?"

"I do."

"You still don't agree that I allowed her to go."

"I don't."

Boyd didn't bother to hide his grin. He'd known Brick for nearly ten years. In that time, the man had shown his true colors, as well as his loyalty to Boyd, time and again. The one thing that drew Boyd to him was the fact that Brick never pulled any punches. If he told you something, it was the truth. That was the main reason Brick had climbed the ranks in Boyd's organization to become someone Boyd trusted.

And he never gave trust easily. People had to earn it.

Brick clasped his hands in front of him and held Boyd's gaze. "By allowing her to leave, you've given Taryn a means of escape."

"I hold her sister as collateral. That's all the incentive Taryn will need to return."

Brick briefly lowered his gaze. "It's a lot of money you want Taryn to bring you—in a short amount of time. Even I'd have trouble doing that."

"She's intelligent. She'll figure something out." Boyd turned his attention back to the green and moved another ball into place with his club. "What else is on your mind?"

A sigh escaped Brick. "Let me go down to Clearview. I'd rather be there to watch Taryn and make sure she gets back as promised."

"I can't figure out if you're more worried about Taryn or her sister, Payton." Boyd slid his eyes to Brick. "Which is it?"

Brick's gaze was steady. "My concern is for you. It always has been."

"But?" Boyd pressed.

Brick only hesitated for a moment. "Those two women could be your downfall."

Boyd chuckled and made another perfect putt. "I think you give them too much credit."

"You killed the father and then the brother. Both in front of Taryn."

Boyd halted as he swung back his arms. He slowly straightened and faced Brick once more. "I did that because they left me no choice. Phil's death was retribution for thinking he could steal from me. Again. As for the brother." Boyd shrugged. "He tried to outsmart me and escape. I couldn't allow that to go unpunished."

"But you've given Taryn incentive not to try something . . . foolish."

Without a doubt, Boyd knew that Brick was worried about one of the women. If only Boyd could figure out which one. "You've always given me the truth, even when I didn't want to hear it."

"It's what I'm trying to do now."

"Or you're attempting to save one of the sisters."

Though Brick didn't move a muscle, his entire demeanor changed to one of outrage. "I would never pick a woman over you. I gave you my word when you allowed me to work for you that you would always come first."

"Then why all the concern?"

Brick let his arms fall to his sides as his brows drew together. "Because I've seen that kind of desperation in Taryn before. When someone is backed into a corner, they can do reckless, impulsive things to save themselves or their last remaining family member."

"You did tell me to leave the sisters in Clearview," Boyd said, recalling that long-ago night. "I thought it would be beneficial for Phil and his son to know that the girls' lives were in my hands."

"It didn't stop the·father or the brother from being idiotic."

Boyd twisted his lips ruefully. "No, it didn't. The fact is, Taryn will return because of her sister."

"If you say so."

What did he do now? Boyd didn't like complications. Brick was there because he sorted out such issues in whatever way was necessary. Sometimes, it was with negotiations. Other times, it was with force. But it was always done.

Boyd put away his putter and walked to the bar to fix himself another gin and tonic. He could leave things the way they were and hope that Taryn returned with all of the money she had promised, in exchange for her sister's life. Though Taryn also believed that she and Payton would be set free. That wasn't going to happen. And Boyd couldn't wait to see Taryn's face when she realized that.

However, there was still a chance that Taryn couldn't get all the money—or any of it. While Boyd took no pleasure in killing, it was sometimes necessary. Taryn had ensured they kept Payton out of their negotiations, which was fine with Boyd. As repayment, the older sister had taken up the work her father and brother had done for Boyd. Surprisingly, she had been more efficient and twice as good at selling his product. He hated to lose her—which was why he never intended to let her go.

If she tried to double-cross him, he'd send Brick to find her. After some weeks of torture, she'd come around to his way of thinking once more. Then, she'd be back to working. But he knew that Taryn wouldn't do anything stupid. She cared for her sister entirely too much for that.

Boyd still couldn't believe that Taryn had come to him with the offer. Five hundred thousand dollars. It was double what her father and brother owed him. No doubt that's why she had come up with the sum. She'd thought it would be enough to pay off the debt and free both herself and Payton.

The fact that Taryn actually believed he would hold

up his end of the bargain was laughable. Brick worried for nothing. Taryn would get the money, and she *would* return. Boyd would have more money and another worker, who had tasted her one chance at freedom that would never come her way again. Death was the only thing that would free her from him.

He paused as he recalled that Taryn had been involved with someone in Clearview. It was some years ago, so he couldn't remember properly, but he knew there had been some concern over the man finding out what had really happened to Taryn and her family. Boyd had to admit that Brick had a point. If he wanted Taryn to remain in his employ, then he needed to send Brick to ensure the outcome.

Boyd took a drink and lowered the glass as he made his way back to where Brick waited. "Taryn knows how much is at stake."

"She is also backed into a corner. If she can't get the money, then she knows there isn't any reason to return, because nothing she can say or do will stop you from killing Payton."

Boyd scratched his chin. "True. But Payton is all Taryn has left. She might plead for her sister's life."

"There comes a time when a person has to think of themselves. That time comes when they realize nothing can save them but themselves."

"And you think that's what Taryn is doing?"

Brick shrugged. "I'm saying it's certainly something I would consider."

That in itself said a lot since Brick's mother had risked death for Brick and herself when she fled an abusive husband to start a new life. Maybe that's why Brick was so troubled about the sisters. Their predicament wasn't far removed from Brick and his mother's.

"All right," Boyd relented. "Go to Clearview, but don't show yourself to Taryn unless you have to."

Brick's brows drew together. "Why do you believe she'll come through?"

"The girl is resourceful. How many times did she get more money from selling to cover what her father and brother couldn't?"

"Every time they were short," Brick responded, his features smoothing back into place.

Boyd grinned. "That's why I know she'll come through. But you gave a compelling argument. I've invested time in Taryn, and I don't intend to let her go."

A beat of silence passed before Brick said, "You gave your word that you would let her and Payton go if she got the money in time."

"So? After I instituted some of the procedures I noticed Taryn doing, our profits have increased companywide. She keeps the regulars returning but buying a little more each time. Not only that, she has also brought in a significant number of new clients. All while having the wherewithal to avoid notice. Just think what we could do if Taryn trained all of our dealers. I'd make five times . . . no, ten times what I bring in now."

Brick bowed his head. "You have ironclad control over all of Texas, Oklahoma, and the south. You rule all of it."

"I want more," Boyd said. "I can get that with Taryn."

"You put too much on one girl."

Boyd chuckled. "She's a woman, Brick. Even you have to notice that."

"She's carried a heavy load because of her family, but you keep pushing. She's either going to break or push back."

"By that time, it won't matter. I'll have everything I

need from her. Besides, I've got the best leverage over her there is—her sister. Now, I've made my decision. Go." Boyd lifted his drink to Brick and made his way back inside the penthouse and to the woman waiting for him.

It was going to be a decadent night.

Brick took the back exit from the penthouse and then rode the elevator down to the parking garage. He got into the black Jaguar XJS and drove home. After he pulled the Jag into the garage, he walked into the condo. It didn't take him long to pack a bag and water his plants before locking everything behind him, climbing into a dark green Jeep Wrangler, and backing out of the garage.

Then he pointed the Jeep toward Clearview and began driving.

Chapter 8

The last thing Jace wanted was company. So when a knock sounded on the door, he thought about ignoring it. Then he heard Brice call his name. If Jace didn't answer, Brice would use his key and enter anyway.

"We know you're in there," Caleb shouted.

Cooper then said, "We brought beer."

Jace loved his friends more than anything, but he wasn't in the mood for them tonight. They would know that something was wrong and keep prodding him until he told them what it was. And, frankly, he didn't want to hear anything they had to say—good or bad—about Taryn. But he didn't have a choice.

He pushed himself out of his chair and made his way from the living room to the back door, where the faces of his closest friends stared at him. He shook his head, a smile forming as he motioned them inside.

"Told you he'd want us," Caleb said as he entered first.

He was the youngest of the Harper siblings. Brice was the middle child, and Abby, the eldest, was married to

Clayton East, who happened to own the largest cattle ranch in the area. Jace watched as Caleb and Brice went to the fridge to put away the beer. He turned his head back to the door to find Cooper and Ryan watching him.

"What?" he asked them.

Ryan lifted a shoulder. "You look a sight better than you did last night."

"You should've seen him when he woke earlier," Cooper said with a grin.

Jace rolled his eyes and turned away. He took the beer Brice offered and sipped it. The one thing about being friends with such a group was that everyone knew everyone else's secrets. He didn't have to ask why they were there, and they didn't need to say it. They knew he was in need. It was as simple as that.

"Y'all didn't have to come," he said as he made his way back to the living area.

Caleb was right behind him and took a seat on the sofa. "I'm just sad I didn't get to see you fall on your face last night. From what I hear, it was pretty epic."

"It couldn't have been too bad," Brice said from the kitchen. "There aren't any bruises."

Ryan chuckled as he sat on the other end of the sofa. "I'm just curious to know if you could've handled the two women fawning over you last night."

"Women are always trying to get Jace." Cooper shot him a grin as he leaned a shoulder against the archway to the kitchen. "It's been that way for most of his life. He's never had to work as hard as the rest of us."

At that, Jace rolled his eyes. "For fuck's sake. Shall I remind each of you how easily you got your women?"

"Hey, don't put me in that bunch," Ryan said. "I'm still happily single. And I intend to stay that way."

Brice snorted then coughed since he had been taking a drink of beer at the time. "Happily single? You avoid women like the plague."

"You would too if you had gone through my divorce." Ryan gave him a nod, then took a long drink of his beer.

Jace found himself smiling. He and Cooper had been friends since the first day of kindergarten when they walked into the same class. They had been inseparable from that day on. They met the Harper brothers in their early teens, and the four of them had formed a bond that kept them together even when they went off to college and the military. It also allowed them to step right back into their roles when they returned home to Clearview.

Ryan had become a recent addition to their group. It had begun with his working relationship to another close friend of theirs—the sheriff, Danny Oldman. Soon, Ryan became part of poker night, and then he was just part of the group. Jace wasn't sure when it had happened, but he was glad to have someone else he could call a friend.

"I know it isn't poker night, but how about a couple of games?" Brice asked. "I've got a few hours before I need to get back home."

Jace was about to answer when another knock sounded on the door. He realized it was probably food one of them had ordered. Cooper, who was standing nearest to the front door, answered it.

A beat of silence passed, and Jace expected to hear someone mention whatever food they had ordered. Instead, he heard a soft, feminine voice but couldn't make out the words. It wasn't until Cooper looked his way that Jace knew something was wrong.

"Fuck me," Brice said when he looked at who was at the door.

Jace rose and walked to Cooper, who hadn't budged. When Jace's gaze landed on Taryn, the world stilled. All the anger and frustration he'd felt earlier came back, slamming into him like a tidal wave. He stared at her, uncertain if he wanted her in his house or not. But he knew that was bullshit. Of course, he wanted her. As much as he wanted to throttle her, he wanted to kiss her more.

"Hi," Taryn said hesitantly as she nervously swallowed. She had her fingers in the front pockets of her jeans. her green eyes watching him.

Cooper cleared his throat. "That's our cue, gentlemen."

There was a chorus of agreement as his friends filed out the door with a nod to Taryn as she turned to the side. They didn't welcome her, but they didn't snub her either. It was their way of letting Jace know that they would be courteous until he decided where he and Taryn stood.

Once the guys were gone, Jace wasn't sure what to do. "I didn't expect to see you again."

"If I'm honest, I didn't expect to be here."

"Then why are you?"

She bit her lip and glanced at the ground. "May I come in? You asked some questions earlier that I didn't answer."

"And you want to answer them now?" he asked, his tone full of suspicion.

"I deserved that," she said.

Jace gave her the opportunity to walk away again, but she didn't leave. He stepped aside, granting her access. After he'd shut the door behind her, he followed her to the living room. His gaze locked on her as she looked around.

"You've made some changes," she said with a grin. "I noticed that last night when I was waiting. I can't believe you actually chose the gray color for the paint in here. You were so against it when we talked about it."

Jace didn't reply. He stopped at the entrance and simply stared. So, she *had* been here. He hadn't imagined it, after all.

Taryn couldn't meet his gaze. "The place looks nice."

He realized that she needed the small talk, but he wasn't interested in it. "Based on how you spoke to me earlier, you don't want anything to do with me. You claim that you came to give me answers. Give them."

She shifted uncomfortably. "All right."

"Ah," he said as he walked to his chair and sat. "Is this where you give me *all* the answers I want?"

"As many as I can."

And there it was. Jace should've known there would be a catch. He raised a brow and motioned with his chin for her to sit. To his surprise, she chose the spot on the couch closest to him.

"It wasn't my choice to leave the way I did," she began after she set aside her purse.

He stopped short of rolling his eyes. "You could've called instead of sending that text. Could have given me *something*."

"That wasn't my choice either."

"You're a grown woman. You are now, and you were back then. There is no reason for you to do everything your father says."

There was a slight tremble to her lips as she said, "It wasn't him."

Jace narrowed his gaze on her. "Who, then?"

"It doesn't matter."

"It does," he insisted.

She held up her hand before he could say more. "I can't tell you. Suffice it to say I shouldn't be telling you any of this, but you deserve answers. What I can say is that Dad got himself into more trouble than I could pull him out of."

"Ben could've done something for once," Jace said, not hiding his loathing for her brother.

Taryn shrugged halfheartedly. "None of us were given a choice."

The two years that Jace and Taryn had been together, he had witnessed her coming up with money that her father owed to drug dealers, bookies, and anyone else he could borrow or buy from. Time and again, she rescued her father from having to take care of his problems. Jace had never agreed with any of it, but he had supported her.

The Hillmans were a family held together by only Taryn after her mother died. Only because of Taryn did Payton stay on the straight and narrow and not follow her father and brother down the road of drugs. Taryn had kept Payton away from as much of the ugliness as she could, which had given Payton at least a somewhat normal life.

And when Payton graduated from high school, Taryn had convinced her sister to move out with her. Unfortunately, Phil persuaded Payton that it would be wise to live with them as she attended college. Unknowingly, Payton shackled Taryn to more of the same by agreeing to stay. And Jace had been unable to convince Taryn to move out. She saw Payton as her responsibility, even though Payton was an adult and could take care of herself.

That went on for months, but it never changed the way Jace felt about Taryn. He knew he wanted her as his wife. He had been getting ready to propose and have her and Payton move in with him when the family vanished.

"*If* you were taken as you claim," he stated.

She shot him a hard glare. "I'm not lying."

"Years have passed since your text. You said you and your family wanted a fresh start. Now, you suddenly come back to town, and I'm just supposed to believe everything you say?"

"Yes."

"If they forced you out as you alluded to, then you wouldn't be here now, driving around as if you don't have a care in the world."

She rubbed her palms down her thighs and drew in a deep breath. "I know it's hard for you to understand, but I've told you the truth."

"Then why are you here now? Alone? Why did they let you leave? And why come back here at all? Better yet, why not go to the authorities for help? Hell, most people would've just run."

"Payton. The answer to everything you just asked is Payton."

That drew Jace up short. He should've realized that was the answer. "That explains why you didn't run or go to the authorities. But tell me why you're in Clearview."

"Ben thought he was smarter than the people who took us. He ignored my warnings, and it cost him his life."

"Jesus," Jace said as he got to his feet and ran a hand down his face. He walked a few paces before turning to look at her. "And your father?"

"Killed within months of us being taken because he stole—again. Though it was money that time."

Jace closed his eyes and put his hands on his hips as he shook his head. Fuck. Had the two people who should've been protecting Taryn and Payton really been killed? Sadly, he could believe it. Phil and Ben had only ever thought of themselves. After a moment, Jace looked at Taryn. "Are you telling me it's just you and Payton now?"

"Yes."

He returned to his seat but leaned forward and put his forearms on his thighs. "Why didn't these people kill your father immediately? You said he stole 'again,' so I assume that's what he did to get into trouble in the first place."

"It's a little more complicated than that. Dad began trying to deal. He thought he could earn more money that way. Which he did. At first. The problem was there was too much product around, and he started using it himself."

Jace was getting angrier on Taryn's behalf by the second. "Why didn't you tell me?"

"Dad and Ben kept it from me. They thought they could fix the problem because they knew if they kept doing the same things, I would leave."

Jace was taken aback. Not once had she said anything like that to him.

Taryn's lips twisted. "Yeah. I really did tell them that. Because I knew you were right. I couldn't continue to bail them out. I needed to start my life, which I intended to do with you."

"What happened?" Jace asked.

"The night we were taken, both Dad and Ben were

high from the last of the cocaine. I came home to find Payton trying to wake them up."

Jace fisted his hands. "You're telling me it was just you and Payton when they came for y'all?"

"Yes. I was getting ready to call 911—and then you—when they were suddenly in the house with guns trained on us. There was nothing I could do."

"Had you fought them, they probably would've killed you."

She lowered her gaze to the floor. "The only reason they didn't kill us is because I offered to work for them to make up the money that was owed."

"You did what!?" Jace shouted.

Taryn threw out her hands as she looked at him. "What else was I supposed to do? We were all about to die!"

Jace tried to get himself under control. "And when Phil and Ben came to?"

"I'd never seen Dad so scared. He sobered up real quick. Same for Ben. We had people with us at all times as they sent us out onto the streets to sell." She shuddered. "We had thirty thousand dollars of what Dad and Ben snorted to repay."

Jace frowned. "Even Payton worked for these people?"

"I kept her out of it. I promised I'd make twice as much if they didn't send her out with us."

Of course, she did. Taryn always came through for her family. It was part of why he loved her. "And when you paid off the money?"

"I don't know. Things were going smoothly, and I was actually proud of Dad and Ben. I thought we might survive."

Jace shook his head. "You were in their organization. You knew faces, names. They weren't going to let you leave."

"I came to that conclusion pretty quickly. I didn't say anything to Dad or Ben, but we never got to find out. Dad hid a little money when his handler wasn't looking. It was just one time. He told me it was his way of making sure that we had funds when we got out."

"He never was a bright man," Jace said.

Taryn's lips twisted. "He was different when Mom was alive." She was silent for a moment, and then she sighed slowly. "Of course, they discovered the missing money. They knew it was Dad. They brought us all into a room, hands tied behind our backs as they shoved us to our knees. I was between Ben and Dad. When the head guy showed up, Dad apologized and said he'd pay back what he had stolen. They put a bullet in his head before the last word left his mouth."

"I'm sorry." Jace wanted to reach out to her, to cover her hand with his, but he didn't.

Her gaze went distant. "I thought we were all going to die. Payton was crying. Ben was in shock. Then they took Payton away, and we were put back to work. That was the last time I saw my sister face-to-face."

"You've not seen her?"

"Only through a window if they're feeling generous. I've not spoken to her."

"So, you don't know if they're mistreating her."

Taryn shook her head, weariness crossing her features.

Jace rubbed a hand across his jaw again. The full picture was coming into view, and he didn't like what he saw. "How did your brother die?"

"He got sober, but instead of it making him smarter,

it made him more stupid. He thought he could actually free us. He devised an elaborate plan to escape and get to the authorities so Payton and I could be rescued. With the way they always watched us, I told him it was stupid. But he was always coming up with crazy ideas after Dad was killed. I thought this one would be forgotten like all the others."

"It wasn't."

She shook her head. "They caught him trying to break out. They shot him right there. I didn't know then that he had broken into one of the offices where they stored the money and took some. That's part of what I have to repay now."

"But they got their money back. They caught Ben before he left."

Taryn's lips flattened as she nodded. "I know."

"How much are we talking about?"

"I have to bring half a million dollars."

Jace jerked back. "There's no way Ben took that much."

"He had about twenty grand on him. I'm the one who came up with the figure. It encompasses everything my father and Ben stole and did, with more added in for my and Payton's freedom."

Something about this didn't sit right with Jace. What kind of criminals allowed someone like Taryn to leave? "And they just let you leave to get this money on your own?"

"If I don't return in two days, they're going to kill Payton."

"How do you know they haven't already?"

"I don't. I only have their word."

Jace slowly sat back. "Why didn't you come to me before? You knew I would help."

"I didn't want you involved. I told them that you and I fought that night. That I was breaking up with you. That's why they let me send that last text."

"You were protecting me." All this time, he'd thought she had abandoned him. He should've known better. All Taryn ever did was protect others.

It was time someone protected her.

Chapter 9

Getting it all out in the open was such a relief that Taryn wanted to cry at the weight that had been lifted from her. But it wasn't all gone. She still had Boyd to deal with, as well as getting her sister free.

"I can get you the money," Jace said.

Taryn had known he would say that. It was one of the reasons she had come to him. But that didn't mean she wanted to take the cash. "If there was anyone else—"

"You should've come to me first," he said before she could finish.

She licked her lips, hating her situation. "After what I did, I knew you'd be upset."

"Damn right, I was. And worried. Everyone looked for you and your family."

"I know. I'm sorry."

Jace released a long breath. "You don't have anything to apologize for. It's not like you left because you wanted to. You were forced."

"So, you believe me?"

He nodded. "I do."

Tears pricked her eyes again. "I'm glad because I'm not sure how I could prove it."

"I've got about sixty grand put away. The rest is locked in investments, which means I can't get to it for a day or so. I'd rather not cut it that close."

She blinked, completely taken aback by how easily he offered the money. But that was Jace. The hero. *Her* hero. "I'll pay back every cent. With interest."

"I don't give a shit about the money. I want you and Payton free of these people," he told her.

"That's the plan, but they are . . . well, they don't play by the rules. I expect them to try and go back on the promise."

Jace's hazel eyes turned hard. "Oh, they will. Without a doubt. Which is why I'm going to make sure they don't."

Fear locked itself around Taryn's chest like a band of steel. She had lived in dread for years, watching first her father and then her brother be killed. She couldn't stand to have Jace pulled into her mess. There had to be a way she could convince him to let her handle things.

The thought almost made her snort out loud. Jace was the epitome of a gentleman. Nothing she could say or do would make him let her go back to Boyd alone. But Taryn needed to try. She knew Boyd. The minute Jace showed up, Boyd would have a gun to his head and smile as he pulled the trigger. Taryn wouldn't survive that.

"No. Please," she said, "I don't want you involved. These people are ruthless. They shoot first and ask questions later. I've dealt with them for nearly five years. I'll make sure Payton and I are freed."

"You need the money to make sure Payton lives. I've

got that, but in order for me to let you hand it over, I'm coming with you. You might think you know them, but trust me, you don't. As you said, they're ruthless. They're not going to let you go so you can make a bee-line for the authorities and give information."

Taryn shook her head, but the words wouldn't fall past her lips. She knew there was no other place for her to go. She slid her gaze away, hating that Boyd had put her in such a predicament. Hating her father and brother for not being strong enough to stay off the drugs. Hating that she hadn't seen all of this coming so she could save herself and her family.

Her throat clogged with emotion again. She felt more tears prick her eyes. She never let anyone see her cry at Boyd's. Now, it seemed all those years of holding back had broken down the dam's walls.

Or maybe it was just being with Jace. Knowing he would help her.

"You know they don't expect you to get the money," Jace said.

She sniffed and nodded, refusing to look at him until she got herself under control. "I know."

"Payton could be dead already."

The stress of the last few days—hell, the past years—and seeing Jace again had her emotions running high. His words caused the tears she fought so hard to hide to fall down her cheeks. Mostly because she also feared that Payton was dead. That would mean that everything she had done, all of her plans, were for naught.

Taryn jumped when Jace touched her hand. She swung around to look at his long fingers, then raised her gaze to his face. He used his other hand to wipe away her tears. It felt so good to be back with him. But at the same time, Taryn knew that it was a terrible mistake.

The worst she could've made. Jace might be able to help her with the money, but she could very well lead him to his death if he insisted on returning to Boyd's with her.

"If Payton were . . . gone . . . what would you do?" Jace asked.

"There would be no reason for me to return. They know that."

"Exactly," he said. "You need to make sure you talk to her or see her—alive—before you go back. If they can't or won't accommodate that, then you have to assume it's because they've already killed your sister. Or . . ."

She frowned when he trailed off. "Or what? Say it."

"They've done something else with her."

Taryn's gut clenched when she thought of the women she had seen being loaded into a truck several months ago. She hadn't dared to question anyone about it, but there was no denying that the women had been frightened. It wouldn't surprise her to know that Boyd was into human trafficking, too.

Jace caught her attention. "What else are these people doing?"

"I don't know for sure. People are always coming and going. I can't be certain, but there's a chance they might be involved in human trafficking—among other things."

He blew out a breath, his lips flattening. "That doesn't surprise me. Do you have any names you can give me?"

"They killed my father without hesitation. Same with Ben. And for all I know, Payton, too. If I tell you anything about them, you're going to do something rash and possibly get yourself killed."

"Damn straight, I am. Sitting here twiddling my thumbs and hoping you get out on your own isn't the kind of man I am. You know that."

She did, but that didn't make her like that he wanted to put himself in danger. "Jace, please. I may have had my issues with my dad and brother, but they were family. Now they're gone. Payton is all I have left. And you. I might have already lost my sister. I can't lose you, too."

"You're not going to lose me."

"You don't know these people," she cried as she jumped to her feet and moved back. "Did you hear nothing I said? They're evil, vicious."

Jace remained calm, his expression filled with understanding as he waited for her to finish speaking. Then he said, "You're aware of what I did in the military. I was a Marine Raider. The elite. Trust me when I say this won't be the first time I've encountered such individuals."

"You had a team to back you up then."

"I won't be alone this time."

Taryn took another step back. She didn't have to ask to know that Jace referred to his friends who had been at the house when she arrived. It was bad enough that he was thinking of putting his life in danger. She couldn't handle knowing that more could potentially do the same.

What had she been thinking coming to Jace? But she knew. She was tired of being alone, tired of making all the decisions, and never knowing if they were right. She wanted someone to lean on, even if just for a moment. But in doing so, she might have made the worst mistake of her life.

All because she was scared, lonely, and needed Jace.

She should leave. Tonight. No returning to the hotel to gather the few meager items she had there. She would head back to Fort Worth and deal with the consequences of not having the money. She'd rather die than have Jace and his friends killed because of her. This was her family's problem. No one else's.

"If you leave, I'll track you," Jace said as he got to his feet and walked toward her. "I know that look on your face. You regret telling me anything. But know this, I lost you once, I'm not going to do it a second time."

Taryn wanted to scream, to hit something. There was no good choice here. If she were smarter, stronger, she might have done things differently with Jerome and even Big Pete. But she had screwed that up royally.

Looking up and seeing Jace standing there had given her such hope that she had nearly flung herself at him. Jace was the only one who had never let her down. He'd been as steady and true as the giant live oak she had played on as a child in front of her house. She had instinctively known that Jace was the answer.

Even now, knowing he could die, she understood that he was her best chance for freedom. Yet she couldn't allow him to do it. The time he had spent as a prisoner of war had left scars on his body and soul that would never heal. When they first met, he had told her that he was broken, but all she found was a gentle, kind, adoring man who showed her exactly what it was to be loved unconditionally.

He deserved better than her, and this fate she was leading him to.

"Did you hear me?" Jace asked. He closed the distance between them. "I'll follow you. I know the license plate of your car. Between Ryan as Chief of Police and

Danny as sheriff, there's nowhere you can go that I won't find you."

Her heart raced, having him near. She stared into his hazel eyes and felt more tears threaten at the love she saw reflected there. She didn't deserve Jace. The last thing he needed was more upheaval in his life. He had already lost so much of himself in the military. The fact that he was alive and hale spoke to the fighting spirit within him.

His hand brushed hers before his fingers trailed up her arm slowly. She forgot to breathe when his other hand came around to her lower back and pulled her close. How many nights had she dreamed of him? Holding her pillow and wishing it was him? Imagining his arms around her, cradling her so the world couldn't touch her?

From the moment she had first seen Jace, she had been inexplicably drawn to him. He was like an unstoppable force that pulled people in. She hadn't even tried to get away. The need to know him, to touch him had seized her, and the instant their eyes had met that long-ago night, she knew that she had known him—and loved him—in another life.

His nearness made her blood quicken through her veins as her body heated with need. The minute he looked down at her mouth and lowered his head to hers, she stopped breathing. No air flowed into her lungs until their lips met.

The chaos that had surrounded her these past years halted as if Jace's very presence commanded the cosmos. His mouth moved over hers, teasing and tasting and nipping. She sighed and wrapped her arms around his neck. A moan rumbled through his chest as he held her firmly and slid his tongue between her lips.

An inferno of need and a longing so intense, so potent that the rest of the world ceased to exist, engulfed her. Jace kissed her as he did everything else—with everything that he had and was. He knew just how to hold her, how to move his hands over her back. When to deepen the kiss in a way that sent her already hungry body into overdrive.

His kiss was like a drug, and she was experiencing her first taste after what felt like an eternity. The future was uncertain, but she had tonight. In the arms of the man she loved so much that it hurt.

Tears fell down her cheeks as he ended the kiss. They were both breathless, their passions running high. Jace gently brushed away her tears with his fingertips. She smiled to let him know that they weren't tears of sadness.

"I never thought I'd have you in my arms again," he said.

The tears fell faster. "I didn't either."

"I don't think I can let you go. Not tonight. Not ever."

"You won't have to if I'm holding onto you."

This time when his mouth descended on hers, the kiss was fueled with desire that she couldn't ignore. They tore at each other's clothes until they were finally skin to skin. She didn't have to tell him about her need because it was his, as well.

Jace pressed her against the wall, helped her wrap her legs around his waist, and was inside her in one thrust. Both of them stilled for a heartbeat, taking in the feeling of their bodies joined once more. When he began to move, all Taryn could think about was how right it felt to have his cock sliding in and out of her.

She threaded her fingers into his hair as their bodies moved as one. Their gazes locked as they got lost in each other's eyes. Her breath hitched when she felt her orgasm building. A pleased smile graced Jace's lips as he recognized that she was tumbling toward her climax. He shifted just slightly, and that's all it took for her body to tighten as bliss filled her. Taryn clung to Jace as he shouted and climaxed, as well.

They clung to each other for several minutes, and then Jace pushed away from the wall and carried her to the sofa, lowering both of them down. With their bodies still joined, they lay entwined, his fingers brushing at her hair.

"I like it longer," he said.

She smiled, so happy she thought her heart might burst.

"I meant what I said earlier. If you leave, I'll follow you."

She looked into his hazel eyes and nodded. "I know."

"How long do you have before you need to return to them?"

"Two and a half days."

"I've got the money, but I can't get to it that quick. I'll need to talk to a few people to see if I can get a short-term loan until I can pull the rest of the cash from my investments. I'll start everything first thing in the morning. Hopefully, I'll have all five hundred thousand for you by lunch. I take it you need to bring cash?"

Taryn nodded, her throat tight with emotion.

Jace paused and twirled a lock of her hair around his finger. "Stay here tonight. Please."

"Are you worried I'll leave?"

"You want help, but you don't want me involved. And since you know I won't give you the money otherwise, you're telling me what I want to hear but are considering returning to these people alone. Tell me I'm wrong."

Taryn drew in a shaky breath and looked at Jace. It was because she loved him so deeply that she was trying to do everything possible to keep him out of the shitstorm she was in. "I believe Payton is still alive. You're right in saying that I need confirmation, which I'm going to get. Since I think she's waiting for me, and I need the money, it means I also need you. Even if I would do anything possible to keep you out of all of this."

He stared at her for a long, silent minute. Taryn prayed that she looked convincing because she was crying rivers of regret and guilt inside. The first time she'd left Clearview in the middle of the night, she had done so against her will. The second time would be her decision.

She detested herself for giving in to her need to see Jace again and explain. She could tell herself it was so he didn't hate her, but she had known exactly how he would react. Now, Taryn told herself it was all right since it was all for Payton, that Jace was a grown man with combat experience. And if anyone could help, it was him.

But looking into his beautiful hazel eyes, hearing that deep, silky voice of his, and having him make love to her once more had brought back all the memories of their years together. Reminded her how much she had loved him. Jace and the love he had given her had kept her going in those dark days.

Unfortunately, she had been too weak to realize that until she stood before him once more. Had she accepted that earlier, she never would've come to see him. Weakness and love had brought her to him again. But the strength of her love for him would help her walk away.

"What's going through that mind of yours?" Jace asked in a soft voice.

"Thinking of when we were still together. My biggest problem was Dad."

Jace's lips twisted ruefully. "We'll get this sorted. I give you my word."

"You're the best man I know, Jace. I'm sorry I brought this to you."

"I'm only sorry you didn't come sooner. We could've had a few days to come up with a plan. But it'll be fine. You don't need to worry about anything."

She wished with all her heart that she could believe him. This was her family's mess, and it was her responsibility to deal with it—no one else's. Jace had seen her as no one else ever had. He loved all of her, accepted everything about her, and had given her a glimpse of a future she had been looking forward to.

If only she could return to that time and do things differently. She would've moved out and left her father and brother to their own devices. Her life would certainly be different now. So would Payton's. But her sister was counting on her. Taryn wished she could come through for her, but maybe this was the better alternative.

"I've got to get my things," she told him.

He frowned but nodded. "I'll come with you."

She put a hand on his bare chest and raised a brow. "Don't you trust me?"

"I'd feel better if I went with you."

"I'll be right back. Promise."

Jace bowed his head. "All right."

They rose and began to dress. As she hooked her bra, she caught sight of the many scars that crisscrossed Jace's back, shoulders, and sides. There were more on his chest, arms, and legs. They were more faded now. She used to kiss them when they lay together. She'd told him that her love would heal his soul as medicine had healed his body. Things had been so much simpler back then. She was happy to see that he was doing well.

When she finished dressing, she faced him as he looked at her. Unable to resist, Taryn wrapped her arms around him and held him tight as she squeezed her eyes closed. This would be the last time she got to touch Jace. "Thank you," she whispered.

His arms came around her, and they simply stood there for several moments, holding each other. Taryn released him and backed away. She flashed him a smile and waved as she walked out the door. The tears fell before she even reached her car in the driveway. Right before she drove away, she looked at the house to find Jace still standing with the front door open, watching her.

Chapter 10

The moment the taillights of Taryn's car were out of sight, Jace pulled out his cell phone and called Cooper.

"Hey," Cooper answered, a smile in his voice. "I didn't expect to hear from you for a few days. Figured you and Taryn needed to catch up."

"I need your help."

Cooper's attitude instantly shifted to one of business. "What is it?"

"Are you still with the other three?"

"Yeah. They're right here."

"Put me on speaker."

A heartbeat later, Caleb said, "We're listening, Jace."

"I need someone to head out to the Hilton Hotel off Oak and see if Taryn's silver Camry is there. If it is, great. Just make sure she heads back to my place. Everyone else, pick the main roads out of town and look for the Camry. I'll text the license plate number. I'm not sure if she's headed north or south."

Brice asked, "What's going on?"

"All those years ago, Taryn left because drug dealers forced her family to leave in order to pay off her father's debt. Her father and brother are now dead, killed by the drug dealer. But the people who took them still have Taryn's younger sister. Taryn's in town to get half a million to pay off her family's debt and try to free Payton and herself," Jace explained.

"Fuck me," Cooper murmured.

Ryan then said, "Tell me her license plate. I'll get it to my deputies immediately."

Jace quickly rattled off the numbers and letters, his gut twisting because he knew Taryn wasn't coming back. She had said and done all the right things, but he knew her too well. Once she realized that he planned to put himself in the middle of the situation, her body language immediately told him that she wanted to do what she always did with those she loved—she wanted to protect.

"We're heading out now," Cooper said and disconnected.

Jace wanted to be out there with them, but he still held onto a thin shred of hope that he was wrong, and Taryn would come back to him. He debated calling his folks. They had adored Taryn and had been upset by her disappearance. He was close with his parents, and he knew how they would react to the news, especially his father. Which was why Jace decided not to fill them in on any of what was going on. Not yet, at least.

Each second that passed as he paced his house felt like an eternity. He wished something could occupy him as his mind raced in twenty million different directions, including the path of how wonderful it had felt to hold her once more. Still, his mind kept returning to the story she had told him.

He'd believed every word. The truth had been in each syllable, in her voice and face. He knew there were likely other horrors there she hadn't described, but he had an idea of what they were. He'd served in the military and been held prisoner. He knew all about those kinds of hell because he'd lived them. And it made him insane with fury that she had been subjected to any of it.

The fact that Jace had seen the same vacant look in Taryn's eyes that he'd seen in his when he looked in the mirror infuriated him. Phil and Ben had put her in that situation. Jace couldn't take his anger out on them because they were already gone from this world. But he sure as shit could turn his rage on the assholes who dared to keep Taryn in their grasp.

His phone rang. He glanced at the screen to see Brice's name and quickly answered it. "Did you find her?"

"I'm at the hotel."

Jace closed his eyes. "I'm not sure what number she's in, but she parked on the far right-hand side of the lot earlier."

"There's no way she could've beaten me here. I'll stay for a while to see if she shows."

"Thanks."

"And, Jace," Brice said. "If you decide to help her, it goes without saying that we'll be right there with you. Especially after everything you've done for me, Caleb, and Cooper."

Jace rubbed his eyes with his thumb and forefinger. "Thanks."

"I'm talking about more than just the money."

"I was counting on that." Jace dropped his hand to his side. "I'm terrified for her. It's a kind of fear I've never experienced before. I don't know what all they did to her, but she's endured a lot. Probably more than I want to know."

Brice made a sound in the back of his throat. "I'll give Clayton and Danny a call to fill them in on what you've told us."

"I gave you the condensed version. I'd prefer if Taryn told you herself. If we find her."

"We'll find her," Brice assured him.

They ended the call. Jace wished he could believe Brice, but he knew Taryn too well. She always put others ahead of herself. He wished he would've insisted on going with her, or even driven her, but he hadn't wanted to push. Instead, he had to rely on his friends to do what he wished he was doing.

Jace found himself in the kitchen. He turned and slammed both fists down on the granite countertop as he let out a bellow of frustration. When he was more composed, he laid his hands on the granite and hung his head, his chin to his chest. The last time he'd felt this frustrated was when he'd been held prisoner.

This time, his life wasn't in danger. It was that of the woman he loved.

Jace might not be out there searching for Taryn, but he could at least begin formulating a plan. Taryn had told him nothing of the people who had taken her or even where she had been held. And he hadn't pushed her on purpose. He'd known she'd attempted to keep that from him, but he intended to uncover the information one way or another.

His military training had prepared him for any type of mission—large or small. But no matter how hard he tried to devise any sort of plan, he came up empty—mostly because he couldn't stop thinking about Taryn.

There were too many variables he didn't know. Location and the number of guards were two of the main ones.

He went back to pacing the house, his mind drifting between recalling every second of his time holding her as they found pleasure, and her story. Thankfully, his phone rang, distracting him. He wasn't surprised to see Danny Oldman's name on the screen. "Sheriff," Jace answered.

"Skylar and I were with Clayton and Abby for dinner when Brice called. Tell me what you know about these drug dealers," Danny urged.

Jace blew out a breath. "Not much, unfortunately. Taryn kept a lot to herself, but given the way she talked, it's a big organization. Nothing local."

"We've got some heavy hitters around here. My narcotics division has been busy, especially since we're between Dallas/Fort Worth, Austin, and Houston."

"When you say heavy hitters, what are we talking about?"

Danny paused for a moment before he said, "The kind of people who do exactly what was done to Taryn. If we can get her to tell us who, and possibly testify, I'm sure the federal district attorney will offer her witness protection."

"First, I need to make sure Taryn is still in town."

"Surely Taryn wouldn't leave after coming to see you. You're going to help her."

Jace ran a hand down his face. "I think she did. Because I told her that if I give her the money, I was going with her to deliver it."

"Shit," Danny said.

"I know. I just wanted to protect her. I should've held off saying that part. As soon as I did, she freaked out. Then I made things worse by stating it again."

Danny blew out a breath. "Love makes us do crazy things. She might have run. Brice gave me the plate number. I've already sent it to the station so everyone on duty could keep their eyes peeled for her. Look, I know you want to do this on your own, and I know firsthand that you, Brice, Caleb, and Cooper could do it yourselves, but if you're smart, you'll let me or Ryan call the FBI and pull them in on this to help out."

"Let me find Taryn first. Then we can all sit down and talk."

"Sounds good. I'll keep you posted," Danny said before hanging up.

Jace dropped his phone into his front pocket, strode to the living room, and plopped down in his chair. Leaning forward, he put his face in his hands, Danny's words about the drug dealers still ringing in his head. It might be wise to enlist the FBI, but Jace knew better than most how efficient a small tactical team could be.

Not to mention, there was less chance of someone leaking the information. Jace wanted these men brought down, but he trusted his circle of friends implicitly. He couldn't say the same for the Feds.

The longer he sat there, the more irritated he became. He was a doer, a fixer. The worst thing for Jace was to be sitting still, and yet that was exactly what he was doing. Forty minutes later, Brice sent a text stating there was still no sign of Taryn or her car at the hotel.

Then Cooper called.

"Tell me you found her," Jace said.

"I found her."

Jace let out a relieved sigh. Then he frowned as he heard the wariness in his friend's voice. "What is it?"

"I'm not the only one following her."

"Who else is?"

"Not sure. He must have spotted me because he turned off. I've not seen him since. She's headed toward the Dallas/Fort Worth area."

Jace tried not to be angry that she was gone. He might understand what motivated her, but that didn't mean it didn't hurt like hell. "Let Ryan and Danny know. They can get others involved to keep track of her when she crosses county lines."

"She pulled off to get gas. I'm turning in behind her at the Exxon station. I'm going to confront her and hopefully change her mind about leaving."

"And the other vehicle that was following her?" Jace asked.

"Don't worry. I'll keep my eyes open. He kept his distance from her, just as I did. But there was no doubt that he was following her."

Jace filed that information away. "When did you find her?"

"I was at the rest stop, hoping I'd see her if she went north. I did, as well as the Jeep following her. I took my time catching up with them, but even still, he spotted me."

"A professional," Jace said.

Cooper grunted. "Or someone with the same military experience as us. Either way, someone who knows what they're doing."

"Danny called. He told me about some big dealers in the area. There's a real chance that whoever has Payton didn't allow Taryn to come on her own."

"I thought that, as well. Trust me, I'm not stupid. I want to return home to Marlee. Who, by the way, is itching to put her private investigator skills to work on this."

Jace rubbed his forehead as he shook his head. "It's

bad enough I asked you and the guys for help. I don't want to involve the women."

"Too late," Cooper said with a chuckle that quickly died. "All right. I'm parked. Taryn is stopped and filling up."

"Leave me on the line. I want to listen," Jace said.

Cooper blew out a breath. "You sure that's wise? You might not like what you hear."

"I want to hear, Coop."

"Suit yourself."

Jace braced himself as the sounds of a busy highway soon filled his ears. Then he heard Cooper say, "Hey, Taryn."

Chapter 11

Taryn whirled around at the sound of the voice behind her. She gasped at the sight of Cooper. There was no anger in his forest green eyes, only disappointment. Taryn looked away and put the nozzle in her gas tank to begin filling up. Something had told her to try and get farther out of town, but she had already been running on fumes. She was surprised she'd made it as far as she had with the menger fuel in her tank.

"I don't think running is a good idea," Cooper said as he came to stand beside her.

Flashing lights caught her attention. She turned her head to find two sheriff's deputy cars, and one Clearview police department cruiser headed toward the gas station. Their sirens weren't on, but that didn't matter. She knew they were after her. And the only one who could've pulled a stunt like that was Jace.

Because he'd known she would run. It was how Cooper had found her. Taryn inwardly shook her head. So much for thinking she had gotten one up on Jace.

"It's all right," Cooper said, though there was alarm in his voice.

Taryn stopped the pump. There was no way she could get the nozzle put away, her gas cap on, and inside her car before the authorities were upon her. There was no reason for them to come after her. She had done nothing illegal. Well, nothing in Clearview, anyway. But she wasn't entirely sure what might happen to Payton if Boyd discovered that she had been detained. For all she knew, Boyd would think she'd told the cops everything and kill her sister. The thought of that had Taryn looking around for an escape.

A sheriff's deputy unfolded his big frame from the car, his gaze locked on her. When he started toward her and Cooper, the other two cruisers blocked the entrances so no one could get in or out. Taryn was trapped.

Suddenly, the deputy halted. He spoke into the radio on his shoulder, his gaze laser-focused on her. Taryn swallowed nervously, her palms sweating as she thought about all her plans going up in flames. Suddenly, the deputy did an about-face and returned to his car. He shut off the red and blue lights and pulled away. The other two patrol cars followed.

Taryn slumped against the Camry in relief as she dragged in huge mouthfuls of air to reinflate her starved lungs. She tried to continue filling up the gas tank, but her hands shook too badly to manage it. Cooper reached over and took the nozzle from her. He said nothing more until it had been replaced along with her gas cap. He had set his phone on the trunk of her car as he helped, and that's when she realized he was on a call with Jace. Her gaze moved to him.

Cooper raised a brow. "You disappeared once. Did you really think he'd let you go again without a fight?"

"This isn't his problem."

"You brought it to him and asked for his help."

She fisted her hands. "I asked for money. I didn't want him or anyone else involved."

"You know him. What did you expect? Besides, that's what we do," Cooper said with a shrug. "We get involved in the lives of those we love."

"Like I told Jace, I already lost two family members. I don't want to lose anyone else."

Cooper braced a hand on her car and blew out a breath. "One way or another, Jace will find out who these people are. We'll come up with a plan and go after them. Or, you can come back with me, tell us their names and locations, and we can come up with a better plan. Together. One that will ensure we're more prepared and it's less likely anyone will get hurt."

"They have my sister," she stated. "I know Jace thinks she might already be dead—and she very well could be. But I can't make any decisions based on a *might*. I've got to continue believing she's alive until I know otherwise."

Cooper nodded as he listened. "I would do the same thing in your place. The difference is, I'd trust the people I turned to for help."

Taryn brushed her hair out of her face when the wind lifted it. "I trust Jace. I trust all of you. But I know these people. I've seen firsthand how brutal and cruel they can be."

"They allowed you to come by yourself."

She snorted at that and crossed her arms over her chest. "If you believe that, you're an idiot. And I know you're not stupid."

"No, ma'am, I'm not," Cooper said with a crooked smile. "So, you know someone's been watching you?"

She shrugged and glanced around. "I always assume they're watching me. They always have been."

"And yet you went to Jace's."

"They didn't know who I planned to see while here, and I didn't tell him. If I'm asked about where I went, I'll come up with a story."

"Him."

She frowned, not understanding. "What?"

"You've said '*they*' and '*them*' numerous times. Just now, you said '*I didn't tell him.*' Who is he?"

Her stomach clenched painfully. Taryn shook her head and walked around the hood of her car to get to the driver's side door. She had been so careful not to reveal anything about Boyd. How could she have been so stupid as to let something like that slip?

"Taryn," Cooper called.

She paused as she got into the car and looked at him. He hadn't moved from his spot. He beseeched her with his gaze. Then he lifted the phone and held it up so she could see the screen and a picture of Jace and Cooper smiling, reminding her of why Cooper was here—as if she needed the reminder.

Taryn sank onto the seat but left the door open as her mind raced. She had come to Clearview for help. Maybe she had known all along the answer was Jace. If anyone could get her out of this, Jace had the brains, guts, and heart to do it. That was until she determined exactly what he planned and realized that he could be killed.

Knowing that Jace had been in the military and hearing his stories was quite different from knowing that he intended to actively engage one of the States' biggest drug kingpins. She loved Jace all the more for wanting to do it. But she couldn't let him.

The sound of footsteps coming around the car had

her looking up at Cooper. She shook her head and looked out her windshield at the people going about their lives. "So far, the only people who have been affected by all of this is my family. If Jace or any of you help me, more lives will be ruined."

"That's not on you," Cooper told her. "It'll be our decision."

"None of you would be making such choices had I not gone to Jace."

Cooper shot her a small smile. "Why *did* you go to Jace? Was it simply because you knew he'd somehow get you the money?"

"No." Her gaze dropped to the phone in Cooper's hand. "I went because I needed to see him, to talk to him. But more than anything, I wanted him to know why I left."

"You could've called him."

She lifted one shoulder in a shrug. "He was the only man in my life who never let me down."

"We can get you the money. Come back with me to Jace's so we can continue talking. Listen to what we have to say. If you still refuse to give us any information, then I'll hand you the money and make sure Jace can't follow you."

"Coop! What the fuck?" Jace yelled through the phone.

They both ignored him. Taryn held Cooper's gaze, looking for any signs of deception. It didn't take her long to conclude that he wasn't lying. "All right."

"I'll follow you," Cooper said.

Taryn was still shaking from the arrival of the authorities. A person could only handle so much stress, and she was at her wits' end with everything. She wanted nothing more than to turn it all over to someone else so she could have a few hours to herself. But that wasn't possible. Too much rested on her shoulders.

She closed her door, buckled her seat belt, and started her car. After a glance to see that Cooper was behind her, she started back to Jace's. On the way, she weighed the options of telling Jace every detail or keeping it all to herself. Boyd needed to be taken down. Taryn wouldn't argue that fact, but it wasn't only her life on the line. It was also Payton's.

Taryn would never forgive herself if she gave in to Jace's plan, and Boyd killed Payton. The guilt of her father's and brother's murders wasn't something she carried. If she lost her sister because she wanted to be free, Taryn wouldn't be able to have a future. She'd shoulder that responsibility for the rest of her life.

When Taryn pulled up to Jace's, she still hadn't decided what to do. No sooner had she put the car in park than Jace opened her door. He tugged her out of the car and pulled her into his arms.

"I'm glad you came back," he said against her neck.

She looked up at the stars as she held him. "I'm not sure it was the smartest thing to do."

"Trust me." He pulled back and met her gaze.

"I've always trusted you."

He shut her door after she grabbed her purse, then they walked to the house. Cooper was already inside, waiting for them.

"Prepare yourself," Cooper warned.

When he didn't elaborate, Taryn swung her gaze to Jace, who shrugged. "When I suspected you might leave, I called the others."

"And now they want to hear everything from you," Cooper said as he opened a beer and took a drink.

"Are there more of those?" she asked, nodding at the beer.

Cooper grinned and pulled another bottle out of the fridge, removed the cap, and handed it to her. "Plenty more where that came from."

"Thanks," Taryn said and took a long drink. Then she turned to Jace.

He held up a hand before she could speak. "I'm sure if I were in your shoes, I would've tried to leave, too. You're scared and confused. But you're safe here."

"Until I'm not. Then, all of you will be in danger. He won't hesitate to kill every one of you. Men. Women. Children." She shrugged. "He doesn't care."

"Who doesn't care?" Clayton East asked as he strode in through the side door.

Taryn hadn't been sure she would ever see these people again. She watched as Sheriff Danny Oldman walked in behind Clayton. Bringing up the rear was a man she had seen earlier.

"This is the chief of police, Ryan Wells," Jace told her.

The sheriff and the chief. Why was she not surprised that Jace had them as friends? She looked at Jace, wondering what all she had missed during the years she had been gone. She imagined quite a bit. It made her hate Boyd even more.

"The others pulled up behind me," Ryan said.

Cooper finished off his beer and tossed the bottle into the trash. Then a bright smile spread over his face as a woman with auburn curls walked in and went straight to Cooper. They embraced and shared a quick kiss. Then bourbon-colored eyes landed on Taryn.

"You're gorgeous," the woman said.

Cooper chuckled. "Sweetheart, this is Taryn Hillman.

Taryn, this is my fiancée, Marlee Frampton. She's a private investigator."

"So nice to meet you," Marlee said as she walked to Taryn and held out her hand.

Taryn smiled and shook it. "Nice to meet you, as well. Congrats to you both."

"And then there's the rest," Jace replied with a grin.

Without missing a beat, Caleb and Brice entered the house with two women. Bringing up the rear was Abby, Clayton's wife, who held a baby in her arms as she chatted with a blond-haired woman.

Jace let out a whistle that quieted everyone. "We're going to do this quickly because there's a lot to discuss, and frankly, time isn't on our side. Everyone, this is Taryn."

"So glad you're back," Abby said with a welcoming grin.

Taryn returned the smile and waved, genuinely happy to see Abby again.

Jace cleared his throat and wrapped an arm around Taryn as he pointed to Clayton. "You remember Clayton and Abby?"

"I do," Taryn replied and nodded in their direction. Clayton had aged handsomely as only men could. And Abby was still quite a beauty, her eyes sparkling every time she and Clayton looked at each other.

Jace then motioned to Brice and the pretty woman beside him, her wheat-colored hair gleaming. "Somehow, Brice convinced Naomi to marry him. She's a photographer—and a damn good one. She's quite in demand. They adopted the little darling Abby is holding. His name is Nathanial, but we call him Nate."

Taryn barely registered all of that before Jace moved on. She did manage to flash Naomi a smile in greeting.

"Caleb somehow roped in the best equine vet in all of Texas. Audrey. However, none of us can quite figure out how he convinced her to marry him."

There were chuckles all around.

Taryn waved at the gorgeous Audrey with her thick, black hair and dark eyes, denoting her Hispanic heritage.

"Then we have Skylar, who not so long ago became Skylar Oldman," Jace said, a smile in his voice.

Taryn nodded but couldn't look away from Skylar's stunning azure eyes as she smiled at Taryn.

"And that's everyone." Jace looked at her expectantly. "Ready?"

Taryn took another drink of beer, feeling twelve pairs of eyes on her. "I suppose."

"Let's get comfortable," Marlee said.

Jace took Taryn's hand and led her to the living room where he put her in his chair. Abby, Naomi, Audrey, and Skylar squeezed onto the sofa with little Nate, while Marlee took the other chair, a pen and paper at the ready. The men brought in dining room chairs, leaving Jace to stand against the wall near her.

Taryn drew in a long breath then started the tale from the very beginning, which for her was when Boyd and his men came into her life in the middle of the night five years prior and changed everything.

Chapter 12

Hearing Taryn's story again didn't make it any easier to bear the second time. But Jace hung on every word, catching things he was sure he'd missed the first time when he had too many other things going on in his head.

Taryn still held off giving any names or locations, but he understood why. Hopefully, the others would be able to help persuade her to give up that last little bit of information. He remained silent while Ryan, Danny, and even Marlee asked pointed questions like what drugs she sold, how much, and for how long.

"Did they ask you to do anything else?"

Jace's head snapped to Danny. There was no apology in the sheriff's eyes when he glanced at Jace. It didn't matter that Danny was doing his job. This was Taryn. There might be things she didn't want others to know, stuff too painful to speak about—like rape. The mere thought of someone putting their hands on her had him seeing red.

Somehow, Jace pulled himself from the brink in time to hear Taryn say, "I was good at selling. I don't think he wanted to disrupt that. At least, that's what I assume because no one ever bothered me after the first few months."

"And during those first few months?" Ryan prodded.

Jace told himself to remain calm, that regardless of what had happened to Taryn, she was here now. Which meant she had survived.

Taryn shrugged half-heartedly. "The guards made lewd comments and tried to touch both me and Payton. They kept us separated from Dad and Ben. One night, the men entered the room where we were and went after Payton. I kicked one in the balls and elbowed another in the nose."

"That's my girl," Jace said with a smile, recognizing some of the moves he'd taught her.

She glanced at him and grinned briefly. "The commotion caught the others' notice. The muscle then came in and broke it up. Once it was learned what had happened, the men were ordered not to touch us."

"That's interesting," Danny said.

Jace frowned. "Why?"

"Why would they protect Taryn and Payton?" Ryan asked. "Based on what Taryn has told us so far, they were nothing more than slaves. It's been my experience that whoever took Taryn and her family wouldn't care about what happened to them, as long as they did their jobs."

Clayton's face was filled with concern. "Did Payton sell, as well?"

"I told them to keep her out of it," Taryn explained. "It was my dad's and Ben's problem."

Marlee tapped her pencil on the pad of paper. "But you felt obligated to work."

"I've always looked after Payton. I wanted to keep

as much of this from her as I could, so I offered to work twice as hard to make up her share," Taryn said.

Brice made a sound with his lips. "And this drug lord agreed? That sounds a bit suspicious."

"When did they take Payton away?" Danny asked.

Jace watched Taryn's face as her mind drifted through her memories. He hated that she had to relive all of this again and hoped it would end soon.

Taryn shifted in her chair. "They took Payton away when they killed my father. Our captor told us it was to make sure Ben and I didn't do anything stupid."

"The perfect leverage," Marlee commented.

Taryn nodded slowly. "Yes."

"How long after y'all were taken did all of this happen?" Cooper asked.

Taryn's dark brows drew together as she thought about that for a moment. "Within the first three months. Those were the worst. Dad and Ben were detoxing from all the drugs, but as soon as they were able, they were out on the streets with me." She paused and looked at the floor. "When I was out there alone, I had to work three times as hard to make up for Dad and Ben being unable to work. I was told that if I didn't sell a certain amount, one of them would die."

"Fucking assholes," Caleb murmured.

Brice, Clayton, and Cooper nodded in agreement. All Jace could think about was finding whoever these people were and ripping their heads off. It took a special kind of bastard to put people in those kinds of situations and make money off them.

They deserved the worst kind of hell for it.

"And that's the last time you saw your sister?" Marlee asked.

Taryn shook her head. "No. Well, yes. Face-to-face

anyway. My requests to talk to her were always denied, but after a while, they caved and allowed me to see her through an upstairs window."

"How did she look?" Jace asked.

Taryn turned her head to him. "She looked well. I couldn't tell if she'd been harmed, but rape doesn't always leave marks."

"No, it doesn't," Ryan said in a soft voice.

Danny leaned forward and clasped his hands together as he rested his forearms on his thighs. "I know you're scared, Taryn, but these people need to be stopped. Tell me names. But more than that, we need you to testify once we have them in custody. I've no doubt that the federal district attorney in Texas will ensure that you're put in the witness protection program for your safety."

There was a moment of silence before Taryn issued a bark of laughter. "That's not going to happen."

"These men have to be stopped," Clayton said.

Taryn twisted her lips and shrugged. "I learned a lot while I was a slave for these people. There is nowhere I could go where they wouldn't find me. Nowhere. They're very powerful, and they have their fingers in everything, everywhere. Do you think only junkies need drugs? It's businesspeople, housewives, congressmen, the elite you don't suspect because they don't *look* like junkies. None of them want to get caught with drugs, so they do whatever is necessary to ensure that what they're doing—and who they've gotten their goods from—remains quiet. I've seen it firsthand."

"That's just it," Ryan said. "You've been on the inside. You can give us information we've never had."

"At what cost?" Taryn asked, anger coloring her words. "My sister's life? Mine? Yours? Everyone's here? Because that's what's going to happen. I can guarantee it. No amount of witness protection will stop them from getting to me. That, I can promise you."

Cooper cleared his throat. "She was followed when I found her."

Taryn started at that revelation. She blinked at Cooper, then frowned.

"A Jeep. About ten years old, is my guess," Cooper said. "I didn't see inside the vehicle, but he was definitely following Taryn."

Marlee tapped her pen on her pad of paper again. "These people want to make sure that she does what she said she would do. They gave her the appearance of freedom, but the moment it looks as if she's going to the authorities or leaving, they'll come for her. I saw it happen when I was still a cop in California."

"Were any of you followed here?" Jace asked. If one person was following Taryn, there were most likely more.

Ryan shook his head. "No."

"How can you be sure?" Jace pressed. Danny and Ryan exchanged a look that had Jace pushing away from the wall. "What aren't you two telling me?"

Cooper stretched out his legs in front of him and crossed his ankles as he linked his fingers behind his head. "I'm guessing it has something to do with the fact that three patrol cars pulled into the gas station with lights on when I was there with Taryn. One deputy got out and started to approach Taryn as if he were coming for her, but he was called back. Then, all three left."

"I think it's time you two share with the rest of us," Clayton told Danny and Ryan.

Danny blew out a breath and dropped his chin to his chest for a moment. Then he straightened in his chair.

"I got a call from the FBI, stating there was an under-cover agent in the area."

"And you took that to mean it had something to do with Taryn?" Skylar asked her husband.

Danny raised his brows and nodded. "That's what I was told."

"Who is it?" Marlee asked. "If we can talk to who-ever it is, they might be able to shed even more light."

Jace watched Taryn during all of this. He went to her and kneeled beside her chair when he saw her face turn pale. "You all right?"

"If someone in the organization is undercover, Boyd will find them. He always does. He doesn't do anything stupid, so the Feds won't know he's the one who killed their agent, but he will end their life. Whoever this person is needs to be careful. If they're smart, they'll stay away from anyone who looks even remotely like a cop."

Ryan caught her attention. "We sent the patrols out looking for you because Jace was worried. We weren't going to have you arrested. The officers were simply going to ask that you remain until we could get Jace there to talk to you."

"Not to mention, both you and Danny wanted infor-mation," Taryn said, a hard edge to her voice.

Ryan threw up his hands. "I'm not denying it. The thought of getting a criminal such as this off the streets is too much to resist. However, I've got a feeling this is out of both my and Danny's jurisdictions."

"I can't imagine the Feds were too happy about your interference," Abby pointed out.

Jace put his hand atop Taryn's. He wanted to say so much to her, but he saw her exhaustion. She was weary, and she needed some time.

"Thank you all for helping us tonight," Jace said. "I know y'all probably have a lot more questions, but they'll have to wait. It's been a long day, and Taryn needs to rest."

Audrey got to her feet. "You're absolutely right. Taryn, I hope we girls can catch up soon. Until then, please don't hesitate to reach out to any of us if you need anything."

Caleb brought his chair back to the dining room and waved at Jace and Taryn as he walked Audrey out of the house. The others followed one by one until only Ryan remained.

He stood and rocked back on his heels. "Thank you for sharing your story. You've given us a lot without giving us what we really need. I know you want out, and if you don't want to trust me or Danny, then trust Jace. He'd do anything for you."

"I know," Taryn said.

Once they were alone, Jace moved to the sofa. "You hungry? Thirsty?"

"No, thank you."

"Do you regret coming back?" He hadn't wanted to ask the question, but he had to know the answer.

Her head swiveled to him as she smiled. "The one thing about my life I don't regret in any fashion is you. To answer your question, no, I don't regret coming back to you tonight. I'm just scared of what might happen because I did."

"We're a pretty resourceful group. We've been through quite a lot together." Jace grinned as he thought back. "Naomi's best friend used to be a rodeo queen who was blackmailed and used for sex by some business owners in town. Naomi found out, and then she was threatened. Brice immediately stepped up to help her, and the rest of us joined in. In the end, we stopped the individuals, and they were arrested."

"Really?" Taryn asked, genuine interest in her green eyes.

Jace nodded. "Then there were the dying horses at an auction house. Audrey was blamed. As it turned out, a woman jealous of Audrey did all of it, but we helped Caleb and Audrey sort through it all. It actually involved a couple of shoot-outs and some scary situations."

"Y'all have been busy," Taryn replied with wide eyes.

Jace scratched his head as he frowned. "I think you're right. Skylar came back to town while running from an abusive, controlling ex-boyfriend who came from a wealthy and well-connected family. The ex-boyfriend kidnapped Danny and nearly had him beaten to death. We helped to track him down and then helped him find Skylar and free her from her ex."

"Shit," Taryn whispered. "That sounds intense."

"It was."

"Is that all?"

Jace shook his head. "About seven months ago, Marlee came to town. She specializes in locating kidnapped babies and children. When her twin, Macey, was eight months pregnant, she was murdered, and the baby was stolen."

"Dear God."

"Marlee thought Brice and Naomi had adopted the child but it turned out there was a kidnapping ring right here in Clearview. We helped her locate it and bring it down. Marlee was nearly killed, Cooper was kidnapped and locked in a building rigged with a bomb, and I was hit over the head and left for dead."

Taryn rose from the chair and came to sit beside him.

She took his hand in hers and held his gaze. "I'm so happy that all of those stories ended happily for everyone. I don't think this one will."

"We'll have to see about that."

"You're amazing, but you can't do everything," she said.

Jace linked his fingers with hers. "What I do know is that I'll do whatever it takes to free you and your sister."

He felt her pull, the same one that had brought them together so long ago. Blood surged to his cock as he thought about earlier when they had given in to the urge to have each other. Jace slid his hand under the fall of her hair to her neck and then leaned toward her. She met him halfway, their lips meeting for a slow, languid kiss that had them both breathing heavily within moments.

Taryn broke the kiss as she rose to her feet. She shot him a seductive smile and motioned with her finger for him to follow her. As she walked away, she began undressing. Jace pulled off his boots before he stood and yanked off his shirt, tossing it aside. He had his jeans unfastened and pushed down his hips by the time he reached his room.

When he looked at the bed, Taryn was already stretched out on it, waiting for him. His hard cock jumped at the thought of being inside her again. He strode to the bed and moved over her, yet she pushed against his shoulder until he was on his back. Then, with her eyes locked on his, she kissed down his chest, stopping at every scar to run her tongue over it like she used to. She traveled down his abdomen until she reached his arousal.

Her long fingers wrapped around him as she slowly

slid her hand up and down his length once. Twice. She flipped her hair to one side and licked the tip of his rod. Jace groaned in anticipation of her amazing mouth.

He kept his gaze on her. His heart raced when she parted her lips and wrapped them around his cock. She moved her hand and mouth up and down, stroking him as she gradually increased her speed. Jace dropped his head back onto the bed and closed his eyes as he was overcome with desire, the type that only Taryn could bring out in him.

Though they hadn't had sex that long ago, her amazing hands and mouth had him on the edge quicker than he would've liked. As if sensing that he was close, she lifted her head and straddled him, then guided his aching cock into her body.

Jace clamped his hands on her hips as she began rocking back and forth. He reached up to fondle her ample breasts, teasing the nipples as he knew she liked. When her breath hitched, he knew she was closing in on another orgasm, as well. Earlier, things had been quick because they both needed it. He wanted to extend this time for as long as he could. Which meant he needed to get her off him if he didn't want to come. Because nothing could make him climax quicker than having Taryn on top.

He flipped them, then pulled out of her to rise up onto his knees. She readily got on all fours facing away from him and looked at him over her shoulder. He entered her from behind and moaned. He kept her hips still with his hands as he drove into her again and again. Faster, harder. Deeper.

But even this couldn't keep the orgasm at bay. He wasn't going without her, though. Jace reached around and found her swollen clit. The moment he made contact with the nub, Taryn groaned in response. He swirled his finger around it as he continued thrusting, exciting her, tantalizing her, and urging her into another climax.

Suddenly, she stiffened and cried out. The moment he felt her clenching around him, he tumbled headfirst into his orgasm, as well.

Chapter 13

The last thing Taryn expected was to actually sleep. She couldn't remember the last time she had rested fully. She had always been a light sleeper, but from the moment Boyd took her and her family, every little sound woke her. So, for her to sleep so heavily the moment her head hit the pillow after she and Jace curled up against each other meant only one thing—she felt safe.

The smell of coffee and Jace's amazing cinnamon pancakes pulled her from a dreamless sleep. She smiled as she looked at the sun coming through the blinds on the window.

Taryn rolled onto her back and stretched her arms over her head as she yawned. She threw back the covers, swung her legs over the side of the bed, and sat up, a smile on her face as she thought about the night before and how she and Jace had loved each other's bodies.

While she understood that she and Jace couldn't just pick up where they had left off, it almost felt as if that had happened. But she wouldn't take anything for granted. She had done that once and had lost five years. Jace had welcomed her back into his life—partly because she was in trouble, but she also knew that he still loved her. His actions the night before had proven that.

Which made her love him all the more.

She rose from the bed and put on some clothes, then made her way from the master to the kitchen. Jace had his back to her as he whistled softly to the sound of the radio. Taryn grinned as she recalled many such mornings that she had risen to find him in the kitchen.

Her gaze darted to the hallway that branched off from the entryway and led to the two other rooms of the house. She walked across the living area to the hall, wondering what he had done to the other rooms since he had changed other parts of the house. She wasn't at all surprised to find that one space was full of weights and workout equipment, including a punching bag in the corner.

She moved to the next door, the shared bath. Then she came to the last room. She thought she might find a spare bed or perhaps boxes. Instead, the room was almost completely empty except for two boxes that held the things she had left.

"I always hoped you'd come back."

Her head jerked around at the sound of his voice. He stood behind her with a cup of coffee in hand. He held it out to her with a grin.

Taryn took it and offered him a smile of gratitude. "The smell of food pulled me from sleep."

"I thought it might. You were sleeping pretty good, but I was hungry." He shot her one of his sexy grins that always made her knees weak.

She lowered her face to inhale the heady scent of

coffee and honey before she took a drink. She closed her eyes and savored the taste. "I missed your coffee."

"You're the only one who likes it," Jace said with a chuckle as he turned and started back to the kitchen.

She followed him, her bare feet not making any sound on the hardwood floor. "I've not slept that hard in years."

"I'm glad you got some much-needed rest." Jace returned to the stove and flipped a pancake. "I wanted to have some food ready for when you did get up."

She climbed up onto the stool and smiled. "Are you kidding? It's the best way to get woken up. All of this. I can't tell you how much I've missed it. Thank you."

His hazel eyes met hers briefly as they shared a smile. "Does that mean you aren't too upset that I pulled out all the stops to get you back last night?"

"Not at all. I wanted this. All of it." Her smile faded. "What I don't want is any of you being pulled into the hell I've lived with."

Jace put the last pancake atop the others and set the dish before her. "That isn't going to happen."

"You can't promise me that."

"Nope. I can't. What I can promise is that I'll make or buy all your favorites while you're here. So, eat up and enjoy."

"You do know how to spoil me."

Taryn didn't hesitate to take three of the pancakes when Jace handed her a plate and fork. She put some butter on each pancake, then poured some syrup on a separate plate.

Jace shook his head and chuckled. "Still not wanting your syrup and pancakes to touch?"

"Never," she said around a mouthful of food. She grinned at him and stuffed another bite into her mouth.

Not one to sit idly by when there was food, Jace got a plate, sat beside her, and proceeded to drown his pancakes in syrup. They ate in silence. Taryn enjoyed the food too much to think of anything to say. Besides, there would be a lot more questions later.

By the time she'd swallowed the last bite, her stomach hurt from eating so much, but she didn't regret a moment of it. Jace laughed as he rinsed their plates and put them into the dishwasher. Then he straightened to look at her.

Taryn shifted uncomfortably with his stare. "What?"

"I had your belongings gathered from the hotel. Thought you might want to know."

As always, Jace had thought of everything. Taryn slid off the stool and walked to stand before him. She gazed up at him before she rose on tiptoe and placed a kiss on his mouth. "Thank you. I think I'll jump in the shower. Want to join me?"

"Tempting. Very tempting," he murmured as he kissed down her neck. "But the others will be here before we know it, and if I start licking your body now, I won't stop."

She laughed and pushed him back so she could look in his eyes. "If you change your mind, you know where to find me."

She turned and started toward the master as she thought about how this was exactly how she'd expected her life to be with Jace. Maybe she shouldn't have returned to Clearview and put those she cared about in danger. Perhaps she should've told Boyd that her brother's mistake was his own, and that she would no longer pay for her family's crimes. Things could be vastly different right now if she had.

"Taryn."

She halted and looked over her shoulder at Jace, hope blossoming that he would join her in the shower. He stood holding her bag. She went to retrieve it, but he held it back until she gave him a scorching kiss. Only then did he hand it to her.

"Damn, woman," he said as he adjusted his thickening cock.

She laughed and winked at him, but she didn't tempt him more. As much as she would love to have a day with just the two of them, it wasn't meant to be right now. If things worked to her advantage, she might very well have it later, though. It was a big if, however. One that scared her as much as the thought of losing Payton.

Taryn gave herself the time in the shower to shake off the melancholy and put herself in a better frame of mind. Unfortunately, it didn't quite work as she had planned. Instead of letting go of what her mind had conjured, all she could think about now was whether she was being selfish by turning to the one person in the entire world she knew would help her no matter what.

She wanted to think that she was a better person than that. One strong enough to fight her battles, smart enough to figure a way out of the toughest situations. That had gotten her as far as today, but she could no longer claim to be strong or smart. She felt . . . beaten down. Like she had been treading water for hours and something continued to yank on her feet, threatening to pull her beneath the waves once and for all.

If only Payton hadn't been caught up in this with her. Without her sister in the picture, Taryn would've handled things differently. Every move she'd made, every decision, every action had been about doing whatever was necessary to ensure that Payton wasn't harmed or made to do anything illegal.

"She's all I have left," Taryn whispered.

She isn't all you have left. There's Jace.

Taryn blinked back the unbidden tears. She didn't like the fearful woman who currently stared back at her in the mirror. The woman who second-guessed everything. She had survived all kinds of horrors while in slavery to Boyd. Though she had never been raped. In the grand scheme of things, that was a huge win.

She finished drying off and put on a clean pair of jeans and an olive-green V-neck tee. Taryn cleaned up her mess in the bathroom and gathered her dirty clothes in her arms. She carried them out of the room in search of Jace. When she didn't find him, she put a load of her clothes into the washer.

When she finished, she found him outside on the back porch, sitting in a chair with the fan on above him. A cat, who opened her eyes long enough to get a glimpse of Taryn, sat on his lap. Once it realized Taryn was no threat, the feline settled more comfortably on Jace's lap and purred louder with each stroke of his hand.

Taryn knew just how good his touch was. She envied the cat. That was something she'd never thought to tell herself. She bit back a chuckle and smiled when Jace turned his head to her.

"I put some clothes in to wash. Hope you don't mind," she told him as she took a chair beside him.

He shook his head. "Not at all."

"When did you get a cat?"

His hazel eyes lowered to the feline, who looked up at him adoringly. "She showed up one day. Next thing I knew, I had a cat."

"Have you named her?"

"Cat," he said with a shrug of his shoulders.

Taryn laughed and leaned over to offer her hand to the animal to sniff. When the cat was satisfied, it bumped its head against her hand. Taryn smiled as she scratched the feline beneath its chin. The animal purred loudly. Taryn then stopped and sat back, hoping the cat would curl up in her lap. But it didn't budge from Jace's. Not that she blamed her.

"She's very pretty."

"I've become quite fond of her." Jace glanced at the cat then said, "Clayton is on his way over with the cash for you."

And just like that, she was reminded of her past and why she was at Jace's to begin with. She forced a smile. "All right."

"Danny and Ryan are with him. They're going to want more information."

"I know."

"Will you give it to them?"

Images of everyone she had seen Boyd or his men kill flashed in her head. There was a real possibility that Jace could be another fatality.

Or he might be the one to free you and Payton.

Taryn opened her mouth to reply when the doorbell rang.

Chapter 14

Jace might have been expecting his friends, but that didn't mean he liked their interruption. He should've held off texting to let them know that Taryn was awake. That would've at least given them a little more time together.

For what? He wasn't sure. Jace had missed Taryn so much that he wanted any and all time he could have with her. That was selfish, considering the shit her father and brother had pulled her into. After Jace got all of that sorted out, they could finally sit down and talk about their future.

The doorbell rang a second time, but Jace still didn't move.

"Want me to get it?" Taryn asked.

He shook his head and gently lifted the cat from his lap. Then he stood and held out a hand for her. Taryn slid her fingers into his, and Jace pulled her up to stare into her beautiful green eyes.

"What is it?" she pressed.

Taryn always knew when something was on his

mind. Maybe it was because she read him so well. He thought it was because she saw him better than anyone else ever had. "I'm happy you're back."

"I wish I never left."

"That wasn't your fault. It was your father's and brother's faults."

She shrugged, her lips turning up in a grin. "I should've listened to you and moved out. I should've taken Payton with me, like you said. We never would've gotten mixed up in any of this if I had."

"Don't," he told her. "Wondering what might have been is pointless. The deeds are done. Now is when you look ahead and plan for the outcome you want."

Taryn put her hand on his chest. "What I'm trying to say is that every day I was away from you, I blamed myself. You tried for so long to get me to walk away from my family and let them fix their own messes. I don't know why I didn't listen."

"Because your mother told you to look after them. You took that to heart and did way more than anyone should have."

"I know that now," she said and opened the sliding glass door, pulling him into the house after her. "Had I made my father and brother settle their debts, things would be different. I've learned my lesson. I paid for their crimes, and I'm all right with that. I'm not okay with Payton doing it, as well."

Jace tightened his hand on hers as they made their way to the side door. "Agreed."

He unlocked the door and let Clayton, Ryan, and Danny inside. Clayton had a black duffle filled with cash in his hand. Jace took it into his closet and put it in his large gun safe. When he returned, the four of them were seated in the living room.

"I was just telling Taryn that she looks rested," Clayton said.

Taryn gave Jace a huge smile. "And I told him it was because I slept for the first time in years."

"I'm glad you feel as if you're safe here," Ryan said.

Danny pushed his cowboy hat back on his head. "You are safe here. The sheriff's department, as well as the Clearview PD, have undercover officers in the area."

"That's not a good idea," Taryn said as her smile vanished, and trepidation filled her visage.

Jace lowered himself to the arm of the sofa and took Taryn's hand. "I agree with her."

"You don't honestly think we wouldn't have officers patrolling the area," Ryan said in disbelief.

Clayton cleared his throat. "I think what both Taryn and Jace are trying to tell you is that they're worried that whoever she's been working for will be told what's going on. If police are in the area, it'll look like she's working with you."

Ryan ran a hand down his face. "I put my best men on the case. Those I would lay down my life for."

"I know you think that," Taryn said in a soft voice. "The reality is much different when the people I've been forced to work for are involved."

Danny blew out a frustrated breath. "Does that mean you won't tell us who it is?"

Jace looked down at Taryn at the same time she slid her gaze to him. He saw the hesitation there, the bone-deep fear. Her fingers gripped his hand tightly as if begging him to see what she knew as truth.

"Danny. Ryan. Thank you," Jace said as he turned his head to them. "You've both been amazing friends that I've turned to countless times. You've both selflessly helped when you didn't have to. I owe you both a huge debt."

Danny snorted and shook his head. "I'm the one in *your* debt, Jace. No doubt about it."

"I take friendship seriously," Ryan said. "There's no need to thank me."

Jace got to his feet as he released Taryn's hand. "There is when I'm asking both of you to step away from this. For now," he added when both men began to argue.

Clayton watched it all without saying a word.

Ryan got to his feet first. He shook his head in annoyance before he looked at Jace and then Taryn. "You might think you're doing the right thing by excluding us, but I hope you'll see that isn't the case. Give me a call. I'll always be here."

"Thank you," Taryn told him.

Once Ryan left, seconds ticked by before Danny spoke. "This is a bad decision."

"But it's my decision," Jace said.

The look in Danny's eyes was hard when he said, "It's actually Taryn's. That you're making on her behalf."

"He's doing exactly what I want," Taryn replied. "I've been with these people for years, up close and personal. No amount of reports or pictures can explain what they're like. No movies or books or TV shows. I broke the law every day. Did whatever was needed to stay alive."

"I understand that," Danny said.

Taryn shook her head. "You can't possibly. Neither does Jace or anyone else. But what Jace *does* understand is that these people have connections everywhere. If there's even the slightest chance that I can walk away with my sister, I'm going to take it. But for that to happen, the authorities can't be involved in any way."

Disapproval showed on Danny's face as he stood. "You're talking about taking justice into your own hands. Jace, I've told you, there is only so much you can do before it comes back to bite you in the ass. This might be the occasion."

"It might be," Jace said.

Danny looked at Clayton. "Say something?"

"He's a grown man, and Taryn is a grown woman. They can decide for themselves."

Danny mumbled something under his breath as he stalked from the house without another word.

After the door slammed shut, Clayton said, "Do not think what I just said means I condone what the two of you are planning."

"I don't know what I'm planning," Jace said as he moved to sit beside Taryn.

Taryn shifted and licked her lips. "I used Danny and Ryan as excuses not to speak any names."

"And now that they're gone?" Clayton said as he watched Taryn with his pale green eyes. "Will you tell us?"

Jace didn't want to push her, but time was swiftly ticking away. If he was to go after these people, he needed names and locations. He silently urged Taryn to trust him, to tell him what he needed so he could free her from her prison.

A single tear slipped from her eye to fall onto her cheek as she looked at him. "Boyd. Boyd Walters."

"Son of a bitch," Clayton swore as he jumped to his feet and started to pace.

Jace frowned as he watched Clayton. "What is it? Do you know the man?"

Several moments passed before Clayton stopped and rested his hands on the back of the chair, letting his gaze rest on Jace. "I read over some reports on the known crime bosses in Texas. The worst, the one at the top of the most wanted list, is Boyd Walters."

"So?" Jace said.

Clayton looked at the ceiling briefly. "They've tried to pin tons of crimes on him, but he's slippery as an eel. He's gotten to people in witness protection. No section of any branch of our justice system has been able to hold anyone who can testify against Boyd."

"His men are that good," Taryn said in a soft voice.

Jace inhaled deeply. "That's the kind of information I need."

"That doesn't sway you at all?" Taryn asked in disbelief.

Jace twisted his lips. "Not in the least." Not when it came to helping the woman he loved.

"If you're going to do this, then you'll need a lot of help." Clayton sighed loudly. "I'll start making some calls."

Taryn shook her head. "You've got a family."

"You don't need to get involved more than you already are," Jace told him.

Clayton gave him a hard look. "I was a SEAL. And I can still hold my own. Not to mention, I can call in some favors. I'll be back." Clayton started to turn away, then pointed a finger at Jace. "You know who you need to call now."

Taryn looked from Jace to Clayton's retreating back before she asked, "Who do you need to call?"

"Cooper, Brice, and Caleb," Jace said as he sent a text.

Taryn turned to face him. "There's still time for you

to back out. You don't have to do anything. I'll take the money and pay Boyd."

"Then what?" Jace pressed. "Hope he keeps his promise? What if he doesn't?"

She shrugged. "I'll think of something. I always do."

"There is no way you'll return with that money, and he'll just hand Payton over and let you go. You may not want to admit it, but you know it's the truth."

"Then I'll at least ask for Payton's freedom."

Jace shook his head. "She's his leverage against you. They won't do it. Besides, if Boyd doesn't release you, I'll have to come and get you. Which means we're right back to where we are now."

"There has to be something."

"There is," he said. "Me."

Her face crumpled. "The only thing that's kept me going was the thought of coming back here to you. You. Only you. I can't lose you."

Jace cupped her face in his hands. "I'd walk through Hell itself for you. I know what I'm doing. Trust me."

"I do," she whispered.

He thought about her sleeping beside him last night Of how often he'd woken just to make sure she was still there. He thought of the lonely nights he'd spent and how he'd hungered for her all those years. And now, she was here with him.

His eyes dropped to her sensual lips. He started to lower his head for another taste of her mouth—

"Jace!" Cooper shouted as he came in the back door.

Chapter 15

Taryn sighed at Jace's kiss. It wasn't the long one she craved, but it was still a kiss. Jace jumped to his feet. Tears stung her eyes as she gazed up at the man she loved. She wanted to kiss him, hold him, run her hands all over his body, and feel him inside her every day for the rest of her life. She craved him.

Hungered for him like no other.

She drew in a breath and brought her heated body under some semblance of control. They had one more night together, and she planned to make use of it.

"Hey," Cooper said as he came into view.

Jace's voice was tight as he asked, "What are you doing here?"

"I was hoping to talk to Taryn," Marlee said.

Taryn turned her head to look at the couple. Marlee seemed nice, and at any other time, they probably would have become close friends. But right now, Taryn didn't want to see anyone but Jace—so she could strip him and spend hours enjoying his hard body.

"Ah," Cooper said as he looked between Taryn and Jace. "I think we interrupted something."

Taryn got to her feet. No matter how much she wished she didn't have to consider the hours slipping away, the fact was that she had no other choice. "It's fine. What can I help you with?"

Marlee's bourbon-colored eyes studied Taryn for a moment. "We saw Clayton as he was pulling out. He told us you gave him some information."

"You mean Clayton said that Taryn gave a name," Jace corrected.

Taryn watched as Jace strode to the kitchen and moved out of sight. She pulled her eyes away and focused on Marlee. "I refused to speak any names or locations to Danny or Ryan because there's a very real possibility someone will leak the information. It was only after they left that I told Jace and Clayton."

"Will you share it with us?" Marlee asked, her gaze intense.

For the first time, Taryn recognized that Marlee was excited about the case. And with Marlee's PI skills, there was a good chance she could help.

"We're trustworthy," Cooper said with a smile. "Just ask Jace."

Taryn smiled, happy that it came so easily. "Coop, I know how close you and Jace are. And if you love Marlee, then she is just as honorable. I'll tell you, but I will ask that neither of you share the information with Danny or Ryan."

"We won't," Cooper and Marlee said in unison.

"The man who took us is Boyd Walters."

"Shit." Marlee's face paled as she looked at Cooper. "I'm not from Texas, and even *I've* heard that name."

Cooper frowned as he looked over his shoulder

toward the kitchen. "It sounds familiar, but I'm not sure why. Jace?" he asked and turned on his heel to follow his friend.

"Sorry. I told Cooper to knock before barging in," Marlee said as she walked into the living area.

Taryn motioned for her to take a seat. "It's fine. Really. Don't worry about it."

Marlee quirked an auburn brow as she lowered herself onto the couch. "You didn't see your face. Or Jace's. I'd say you two definitely need some alone time."

"We had a little, but it just doesn't seem to be enough."

"I understand. Believe me," Marlee said with a small laugh.

Taryn shrugged. "I'm happy with any time I get with Jace."

"If I've learned anything since coming to Texas, it's that there's always time for those you love. What's another thirty minutes or an hour? There are things the rest of us can do while you two have some time together."

Taryn had to admit, that sounded nice. "Maybe."

"At least you had last night."

Taryn smiled, recalling every second of it. "Yes."

"Ah." Marlee sighed wistfully. "I know that look."

Taryn continued smiling.

Marlee glanced into the kitchen, where they could hear the guys talking. "I know we don't really know each other, and you've known Jace and Cooper much longer than I've been around, but can I say something?"

Taryn issued a firm nod. "Absolutely."

"Jace loves you. It's written all over his face. It's in his voice, in his actions. None of us know what you've been through, but I think Jace might have a clue."

"He does."

Marlee grinned and leaned closer. "You might have to remind him that he doesn't have to be a gentleman all the time."

A giggle escaped Taryn. She nodded to Marlee. "Thank you for that."

"Anytime." Her expression grew serious. "How are you holding up?"

Taryn briefly thought about lying but decided on the truth. "I'm barely holding it together."

"I've personally seen what those guys are capable of. Trust them. They'll figure something out."

Taryn's stomach churned when she thought about what could happen. "And when one or more are injured or killed? Everyone will blame me."

"Not going to happen," Jace stated as he walked into the room.

Taryn rolled her eyes. "You keep saying that, but words don't make it true."

"He's saying that no one will blame you," Cooper replied. "We make our own decisions."

Marlee shrugged and nodded. "If something happens to Cooper, I won't be angry with you. I'll be furious with Boyd and his men, who are to blame."

"That's right." Jace sat beside Taryn and offered her a glass of sweet tea. "None of this is your fault."

She wanted to argue, but it would take too much energy she needed to use elsewhere. Taryn accepted the glass and drank deeply. When Jace put his arm around her and drew her close, she and Marlee exchanged glances.

"All right. Since I'm apparently behind the times on this Boyd character, someone fill me in," Cooper said.

Jace twisted his lips. "The guy is a millionaire. He owns several businesses and is known for giving huge sums of money to charities all over Texas."

"That's his public persona," Marlee said. "I still have friends on the police force. They made mention of Boyd Walters being named in some drug dealings, even out in California. He might be trying to expand his territory."

Cooper shrugged. "People are named in drug dealings all the time. That doesn't mean they're part of it."

"He is," Taryn said. "He runs the largest drug operation in Texas and most of the south."

Cooper sat back in the chair and stretched out his legs. "Well, shit. That means it's a massive organization."

"It is." Taryn rubbed her finger through the condensation on the outside of her glass. "In the years I spent working for Boyd, they kept many of the specifics of the operation from me. I also had very little contact with others working for him."

Marlee's gaze was steady as she asked, "I gather they kept you around the same individuals?"

"Yes. Two guards rotated watching me. And they rarely spoke to me. They were there to make sure I didn't follow in my family's footsteps and do anything stupid." Taryn twisted her lips, thinking back to everything. "My main contact was Brick, Boyd's go-to man. Brick answers only to Boyd. If something needs to be done, Boyd sends Brick to do it."

Jace glanced down at their joined hands. "But did you see anything?"

"Oh, yeah. Once I had finished for the day and they escorted me to the accountant."

"He has an accountant?" Cooper asked with a frown.

Jace scratched his temple and shrugged. "Makes sense. It isn't as if Boyd handles the money himself."

"Boyd goes to great lengths to conceal his involvement in that side of his business," Taryn told them. "He's never been caught or had charges brought against him, mainly because they haven't caught him on camera or even recorded his voice. He's smart. He learned from others what kept them out of jail and uses it. He has a massive empire, but it was built on drugs, all starting when he was in school."

Cooper made a sound in the back of his throat. "Sounds like a nice guy."

"When I go out to sell, I have at least one watcher with me at all times. They're hidden to the point where I sometimes have to search to locate them, but they're always there. I didn't know that at first, but I still assumed because it made sense. My dad and brother didn't take my advice no matter how many times I told them they were being watched, and that's how they got caught. I always presume I'm being followed. I know exactly how much I have to sell and how much I should return with. It always balances at the end of the day when I see the accountant and turn over the money," Taryn explained.

She paused long enough to take a drink. "Anyway, that night with the accountant, I heard yelling from a building nearby. I instantly recognized Boyd's voice. When he's like that, it's wise to get out of the way, so I hoped the accountant would finish with me quickly. None of the guards watching me, nor the accountant, wanted anything to do with Boyd then either. I had been there for over a year by then, so I knew exactly what was expected of me. I never looked at anyone but the guards and those I interacted with. If other people were about, I never spoke to them or saw their faces.

"Boyd's voice got louder and louder. Out of the corner of my eye, I saw him as he came out of another building. It was dark, but the outside lights illuminated another man on the ground, lying in a fetal position. Boyd was so furious as he yelled that I couldn't make out his words, but he kicked the man over and over. That's when Brick came out of the shadows. Brick pulled a gun and looked at Boyd. At first, Boyd pointed at the man as if telling Brick to kill him. Then Boyd took the gun from Brick and slammed it into the man's head before pointing the weapon at him. Boyd leaned down and whispered something to the man. A second later, Boyd straightened and gave the gun back to Brick before walking away."

There was a frown on Jace's face as he asked, "I get that Boyd was showing his dominance, but weaker ones will always crumble beneath someone stronger."

Taryn shrugged. "Maybe. Once Boyd was gone, the man on the ground got to his feet with Brick's help. That's when the man turned, and I got a look at his face. I didn't know him, but the other guards in the room did. I heard them mumble a name. The guy was some UFC champion."

"UFC, as in Ultimate Fighting Championships?" Cooper asked as he sat up in shock. "Those are some tough bastards."

Jace's frown deepened. "You can't tell me Boyd was stronger than this UFC fighter."

"He wasn't," Taryn said. "But the guy was so terrified of Boyd that he didn't block a single punch or kick."

Jace and Cooper exchanged looks.

"Is it because of how many men Boyd employs? Intimidation with force works," Jace said.

Taryn nodded. "That's part of it, I'm sure. Boyd's operation is huge. Men with guns are always walking around."

"I think you should tell us where this operation is located," Marlee said.

Cooper's brows shot up on his forehead. "That would be good to know. We can get the building plans of the facility and begin sorting out how we'll get in."

When everyone looked her way, Taryn tried not to fidget. "I don't know where the drugs are kept or anything like that. I only know where they held me. The accountant came every night, and I heard him mumble something about some other locations once."

"Striking at one location could mean we miss Boyd altogether," Cooper said.

"Good thing Boyd has a reason to be there." Jace swung his gaze to Taryn. "You."

Chapter 16

"I don't like it, though," Jace grumbled.

Taryn put a hand on his thigh and said, "I've been in danger for years."

"I wish there was another way. I don't like you being in that position."

She smiled sadly. "I have to get my sister out. If there's even a chance at that, I have to be there. I can do this. Especially with you there."

Cooper sat forward in the chair. "You'll have a much better chance of freedom with us along."

"It's a good plan," Marlee added.

Jace ran a hand down his face and rose to his feet. "So much can go wrong."

"Which is why I didn't want you to do anything at all," Taryn said. "Now do you understand why I tried to leave?"

He turned back to her and looked into her green eyes, then lowered himself to the couch and took her hand in his. "I do."

"Good," Cooper said as he clapped his hands together once. "We need to get a plan going."

Marlee asked, "Taryn, do you know the address of where you were held? We need the schematics of the structure."

Taryn rattled off an address that the other woman quickly wrote down in the pad of paper she pulled from her purse. Then Marlee ran to the kitchen, returned with a laptop, and began working.

"We're going to need more than just the two of us," Cooper said.

Jace pinched the bridge of his nose with his thumb and forefinger. "Brice has a kid now. I don't want to include him."

"As if he would stay back," Cooper replied with a snort.

Jace looked up at his friend. "Frankly, I don't want you to go, either."

There was a pause as Cooper glared at him. "If you tell me it's because you're afraid I'll get hurt, I'm going to punch you in the face."

"You've got Marlee," Jace began.

"Who will be right in the middle of this," Marlee declared in a no-nonsense tone.

When Jace looked at Taryn, she shrugged as if to say that he was on his own.

"Stop being an idiot," Cooper told him. "You need me. And you know it."

Jace blew out a breath and threw up his hands in surrender.

"You better call Caleb and Brice," Marlee warned as she glanced up from the keyboard.

Jace's and Cooper's phones went off simultaneously. Jace pulled his out of his pocket and saw that Caleb had sent a message through their group text, saying that he and Brice would be over shortly. Obviously, Clayton had spoken to them, as well.

"There's someone else I think we should call," Cooper said.

Jace had already thought of it. "Cash."

"Yep," Cooper replied with a smile.

Jace nodded. "Get ahold of him. I've got a couple of guys I can call."

"Hold up," Taryn said. "Both of you are acting like you're putting together an army."

"What do you think Clayton is doing?" Jace asked her. "He's getting men."

Cooper shot her a wry grin. "It's either us or the authorities. We're trained in stealth and special reconnaissance, and we have no ties to Boyd, so nothing will get leaked to him."

Taryn shook her head as she looked at the ceiling. "I just want to be free of all of this. I want to make my own decisions and go where I want. I want the same for my sister."

"Then trust me," Jace urged her. "I know it's scary, but this isn't far removed from what Cooper, Brice, Caleb, Clayton, or I did for the military."

Cooper shrugged and said, "Only this isn't sanctioned by our government."

"If any of you get caught by the authorities, things will be bad," Marlee told them.

Jace didn't look away from Taryn's face. "We aren't going to get caught by Boyd, his men, or the authorities."

"You're very cocky," Taryn said, but there was a smile on her face.

Jace shrugged as he returned her grin. "Our government spent a great deal of money to train us. They used us for their operations for years. So what if we use it to our benefit? Especially when someone we care about is in serious trouble."

"Most people would've told me to go to the police or the FBI," Taryn said.

Jace reached up and tucked a strand of her dark hair behind her ear. "It's a good thing you don't talk to those people."

Taryn chuckled and touched his face. Once more, Jace felt her pull. He didn't care that they weren't alone. The woman who had stolen his heart was back in his life, and he didn't want to waste another moment not kissing her.

"We've got company," Cooper said as he got to his feet and went to the side door.

Jace didn't move. He lowered his head to Taryn's and pressed his mouth to hers. For a heartbeat, he didn't move. Then he began slowly moving his lips over hers, nipping and kissing. He pulled her closer, wrapping his arms around her as his tongue moved past her lips to tangle with hers.

She sighed, the sound going straight to his cock that had already begun thickening with arousal. The world fell away as he deepened the kiss, giving in to the hunger, the temptation that was Taryn. The feel of her soft body against his was everything he remembered and more. Now that she was back in his arms, he was never letting her go again.

He had lived without her, and he had been miserable. She made life better, brighter. She was the other half of his soul. He'd known it the day he first saw her—the day he fell in love with her. People didn't believe in love at first sight, but he did. Because he'd experienced it with Taryn.

She ended the kiss, then pulled back and smiled up at him. "We're being watched."

"I don't care," he told her. "I've wanted to kiss you for too long."

Caleb said, "Don't stop on our account."

Taryn laughed, and Jace briefly closed his eyes. Now wasn't the time to do everything he wanted with Taryn. It would have to wait until this nightmare with Boyd was over. Jace made his arms loosen so he could release her. Then he looked over to find Brice, Caleb, and Clayton watching him.

Clayton slapped a hand on Brice's shoulder as he walked past to enter the living room. He took the vacant chair and stretched out his long legs. "What's the time limit on this mission?"

"I have to be back by midnight tomorrow," Taryn said.

Brice took off his Stetson and laid it on a table before running his hands through his dark brown hair. "That leaves us thirty-eight hours from right now."

"And where are we going?" Caleb asked.

Jace inwardly smiled when Taryn took his hand. "Fort Worth."

"Add in travel time, and we've got about thirty-six hours to formulate a plan," Brice said.

Clayton popped his fingers. "I've made some calls."

"I'm getting ready to," Cooper said as he held up his phone and stood to walk out of the room.

Jace met Clayton's gaze. "I've got a couple of calls to make, as well."

"Then go do it," Clayton said.

Jace hesitated as he licked his lips. "Clayton, you've been a brother to all of us. You've gotten us out of trouble, guided us, and led us more times than I can count. But you have a wife and kids. A ranch."

"You telling me I'm old?" Clayton asked without any emotion on his face.

Jace looked at Caleb and Brice, but both shook their heads, telling him he was on his own. Jace took a deep breath and tried to find the words, but he couldn't. "Never mind."

"I'm not an idiot," Clayton said. "I'm nearing fifty, and while I still train, I've not been out in the field for some time. I'd like nothing more than to join all of you on this mission, but my skills are being put to another use. The calls I made are favors that could mean the difference between life and death for all of you."

Jace didn't know what to say. Fortunately, Taryn didn't have that problem. She smiled at Clayton with tears in her eyes. "Thank you. For everything you're doing. All of you," she said as she looked around.

"You're making Brice tear up," Caleb said.

Brice gaped at him. "What? I'm not crying."

Caleb rolled his eyes. "I saw you wipe at the corner."

"I had an eyelash in my eye."

"Whatever. Let's get to planning. Time is ticking," Caleb said.

Chapter 17

The neighborhood allowed Brick to hide in plain sight as he watched the house. Three vehicles had arrived, with four men and one woman entering the residence. He drank the rest of his coffee before reaching for his cell phone.

"What's the update?" Boyd asked when the call connected.

Brick didn't take his eyes from the house. "Based on the two men we had watching her, Taryn worked diligently to attain the money."

"But did she get it? Since she isn't here, I assume the answer is no."

"She had it. A small player in town named Big Pete agreed to give it to her."

Boyd paused a moment. "How did she lose it?"

"There was . . . an issue. Pete wanted her to do a deal with one of his top buyers. Things didn't go well."

"I don't believe that," Boyd said. "Taryn always closes her deals."

"From what I hear, it wasn't entirely her fault. The

man, a prominent businessman in the area, found her exceedingly attractive and offered her more money if she agreed to be his."

Boyd chuckled. "I can guess how that went."

"Not as you'd expect. I think Taryn actually tried to negotiate with him. However, the moment he heard your name, he wanted nothing to do with her. He wouldn't even buy his regular. When she couldn't complete the deal for Pete, he withdrew his offer for the money."

"No doubt Pete learned of me, as well."

"No doubt," Brick agreed.

The sound of clinking ice came through the phone as if Boyd had taken a drink. "I told you Taryn would come through. She always does."

"She doesn't have the money."

Boyd chuckled. "Yet. Taryn will do anything for Payton. We've seen it time and again."

"I agree, but I've got a feeling this time will be different."

"You worry too much," Boyd admonished. "She knows I've got Payton's life in my hands. Taryn won't run or go to the police."

"She returned to her hometown. She has friends here. That could mean trouble."

Boyd laughed again. "You can't honestly believe that anyone from that town—or anywhere, for that matter—can go up against me and win. I've too many men, too many guns at my disposal. If Taryn is stupid enough to try anything, then we'll take care of the problem. I've proven to Taryn that I'm a man of my word. Her father and brother are proof of that."

"You trust me to carry out your orders and to be honest. I think you should call Taryn home. Immediately."

There was a beat of silence before Boyd asked, "What aren't you telling me?"

"Taryn is desperate for the money to save herself and Payton. It could lead her to turn to old friends."

Boyd made a sound in the back of his throat. "Let her have a little time with them. She'll come back."

The call disconnected. Brick set the phone in the cupholder beside him and rested a hand on the steering wheel. He'd been watching the house for hours, and so far, there had been no movement. The sky was darkening, and his stomach rumbled with hunger. At that moment, the passenger door opened, and a man sat beside him, a bag in hand.

Brick stared into green eyes as the smell of food filled the vehicle. "You shouldn't be here."

Ryan Wells shrugged his shoulders. "Neither should you."

"I go where the job takes me."

The police chief slid his gaze to the house. "Ditto. You aren't going to sit out here all night, are you?"

"I am."

"Then I'll join you."

Brick sighed loudly. "Get your ass out of my car. If your friends see you, they won't understand. And you can't tell them the truth."

"They're smart. And they'll believe me."

"I can't chance it. I've been embedded with Boyd for too long to have everything ruined now."

Ryan opened the bag and pulled out a hamburger that he passed to Brick. "You're the one who had me call off the deputies about to detain Taryn. You didn't have to let me know you were in town."

Brick didn't answer as he unwrapped the burger and took a bite. He closed his eyes and chewed, savoring the amazing taste. He took two more bites before he said, "You would've found me eventually."

"Bullshit," Ryan said around a mouthful of his grilled tuna sandwich. "You're too damn good for that. Which means you told me for a reason."

"You're reading too much into things."

"I don't think so."

Brick looked at Ryan, their gazes meeting in the darkened interior of the car. "Taryn is inside with Jace Wilder and his friends."

"Since you've been watching Jace's house since Taryn returned, you already know the answer."

"You've got to stop them from attempting anything."

"I already tried. So did Danny."

Brick's eyes widened. "The sheriff? Did you tell him?"

"He knows nothing. Danny is a good man who toes the line just as I do with our friends. Those men have military training, just as we do. I've seen them in action. They're more than qualified to handle themselves."

"Which is why you need to put a stop to any plans they have. I know Jace wants to protect Taryn, but there won't be a happy ending for them."

Ryan tossed the rest of his sandwich into the bag and wiped his hands. "And you think making Taryn return to Boyd to continue working for him is what she should do?"

"It'll take some time, but I can use Taryn. It might take another five to ten years, but with her help, we can bring Boyd down."

Ryan shook his head, anger filling his gaze. "You son of a bitch. Have you forgotten what it was like to be forced to do things against your will? Have you forgotten what you had to do to get away from that? You went from having one asshole controlling you to Boyd."

"I told you I was going to do great things. I infiltrated the organization of the most feared kingpin in Texas, and I'll be the one to end his reign."

"And waste years of your life in the process."

Brick snorted, his appetite now gone. He folded up the hamburger wrapper and set it gently on his leg. "Your life is so much better? Talk about being told what to do. And let's not forget that ex-wife of yours."

"Enough," Ryan said in a low tone that he always used when he was furious.

Brick chuckled, though he didn't feel any humor. "You sound just like him."

"You're the last person who should be giving me any sort of advice. You work for a maniac. How many people have you killed to keep up the disguise?"

Brick quirked a brow. "How many people did you kill while in the military?"

"That's different. I was under orders."

"So am I," Brick retorted.

Ryan rolled his eyes. "You can't compare my being a SEAL to you working for a drug lord."

"The hell I can't. We're both fighting against evil."

"Keep telling yourself that."

Brick fought the urge to slam his fist into Ryan's nose. "I was never good enough, and nothing I do will ever be enough."

"I'm still not sure how you convinced them to make you an agent after you were dishonorably discharged from the military. Do you know what others have to go through before they become FBI agents?"

"I don't give a shit what anyone else does."

Ryan snorted and looked out the window. "Yeah,

you've never cared about anyone but yourself." He
swung his head back to Brick. "You want to make a
name for yourself, go right ahead. More than likely,
you'll be killed. Probably by Boyd. He'll find out you're
undercover. I can't believe you've survived this long.
But those people in that house are my friends. Hell, you
might even say they're family. Jace and Taryn love each
other. Boyd ripped her away from him, away from
her life, and forced her into servitude for the last five
years. And you want to keep her there? What the fuck
is wrong with you? Have you forgotten all sense of
family and love, that you'll sacrifice anyone and everyone to get your glory?"

There was so much Brick wanted to say in response.
Instead, he kept his mouth shut. Ryan wouldn't listen
to anything he had to say anyway.

"Figures," Ryan said as he shook his head. "When
you contacted me, I thought things had changed. But
they haven't. Don't try to stop my friends. I won't let
you."

Brick remained still as Ryan slammed the car door
and walked to his vehicle before driving away. Only
when the taillights disappeared did Brick slam his hand
against the steering wheel.

His stomach churned from the memories Ryan had
tugged free of their hiding place. And to think, Brick
had actually looked forward to seeing Ryan. Now, he
wished he hadn't contacted him. But it was too late to
change that now.

Brick drew in a deep breath and closed his eyes, then
slowly released it, seeking the calm that had gotten him
through much in his life. Bad things happened to others
when he lost control. Too much rode on him keeping a
firm hand on his emotions.

Ten minutes later, the anger and resentment from Ryan's visit had been firmly addressed. Brick reopened his burger and went back to eating. He was on his third bite when the lights of a car flashed over him as it turned onto the street. He watched a Jaguar F-type in British racing green pull into Jace Wilder's driveway.

The moment the tall, muscular man with thick, black hair unfolded himself from the sports car, Brick realized two things: the man was former military. And he was most likely here to help the others cause a lot of trouble.

Chapter 18

Taryn's eyes could no longer focus. She had looked at so many maps and drawings that she couldn't see straight. Everyone else was downing coffee to help themselves stay awake, but after three cups, her stomach refused to let her have any more.

She rubbed her eyes and stifled a yawn, hoping that no one saw. They were all there for her. Taking time away from their loved ones and family to help her out of a very sticky situation. The least she could do was be a part of the conversation and stay awake. She was just so tired.

The yawn came upon her too quickly to hide it. When she opened her eyes, she found Jace smiling at her. He moved his hand under the table and put it on her leg, giving it a little squeeze.

"Go to bed," he whispered.

She shook her head. "I can't."

"You can. We have the plans to the warehouse complex where you were. We're still coming up with ideas for how to get inside. At least go lay on the sofa."

"I'll be fine," she assured him.

He squeezed her leg again before turning his attention back to the others. Taryn forced herself to pay attention as she listened to the guys tossing out ideas regarding different ways to get into the compound as quietly as possible. She couldn't tell them where all the guards were stationed since she had been kept to a specific area. But she was able to give details on how many men were where she was housed, and the building where she went to see the accountant and Boyd on occasion, as well as give suggestions on the best hiding places.

Not long after, her eyes became heavy. She closed them for just a moment, but that's all it took for her to fall asleep. Taryn jerked awake when she heard someone come into the house. She leaned to the side to look around bodies. Her gaze landed on a tall man in a dark gray button-down and black slacks. He dressed like a businessman, but given the way he carried himself, he was anything but.

She took in his long, black hair pulled into a queue at the back of his neck when the man turned his head to her. Cooper brought the stranger to the table. Jace smiled and rose to shake hands with him.

"This is Taryn," Cooper said. "Taryn, this is Cash. We served in the Air Force together, but now he works as a private investigator."

Cash's light gray eyes landed on her. They crinkled slightly at the corners as he smiled and nodded. "Nice to meet you."

"Likewise," she replied, shaking off the sleep.

Cash then looked around as he unbuttoned the cuffs on his shirt and rolled up the sleeves. "Shall we get started?"

As if on cue, the men moved to the living area, where Cash had a pad of paper and pencil at the ready. Taryn and Marlee remained at the table and listened as they began listing off weapons and tactical gear.

"Is that what they have or what they need?" Marlee leaned over and whispered.

Taryn shrugged. "I was hoping you knew."

The two shared a smile. Then they went back to listening to the guys. A half hour later, the men rose in unison and bid each other goodnight before they filed out of the house. Marlee waved to Taryn as she got to her feet and hurried to Cooper, who waited for her.

When Taryn and Jace were finally alone, she asked, "What's going on?"

"Cash and Cooper are going to see about getting the supplies we want. With the plan now formed, Clayton is calling one of his Navy buddies who owns a helicopter business in the hopes he can drop us in Fort Worth that way. Brice and Caleb are sorting through the supplies we listed as having so we can figure out if it's enough or if we need to add more to the other list."

Taryn nodded as he spoke. "What do we need to be doing?"

"Nothing."

She got to her feet, frowning. "There must be more that needs to be done. Tell me. I can handle it."

"My job is to make sure you're safe until we put our plan into motion," he said and pulled her toward him.

She recognized the darkening of his hazel eyes. It caused her stomach to flutter in anticipation. She couldn't wait to have his hands on her again. It was a simple fact that she couldn't get enough of Jace. Taryn pulled his head down and gave him a lingering kiss.

"Mmmm. I take that to mean you're just fine with the arrangements?" he asked with a sexy grin.

"More than fine."

"Good." He took her hand and led her to his bedroom.

Jace paused and set the house alarm before he turned to her. Taryn barely had time to react as his mouth came down on hers. His tongue swept into her mouth as his arms tightened around her, holding her firmly.

The kiss started soft and slow, but it wasn't long before it became intense and fiery. They began clawing at each other's clothes, yanking—and tearing—them off. They broke the kiss only long enough to remove an item of clothing, then their mouths were meshed together again.

Taryn welcomed the hunger, such craving. Her body knew what it was to be pleasured by Jace, and she needed it now more than ever. When they were finally devoid of all clothing, she sighed at the feeling of his heated flesh against hers. The way she fit in his arms, the way he held her. It was like they had been created especially for each other—they fit so perfectly.

Jace fisted his hands in her hair and pulled her head back as he ended the kiss. His hazel eyes were intense as he looked down at her. "I'm not whole without you."

She put a hand to his face. "I love you, too."

He released a shuddering breath and loosened his hold on her hair so he could rest his forehead against hers. "I'm sorry. If I had known where you were, I would've come for you. I don't know what all you've endured—"

"Stop," she said gently as she put her fingers against his lips to hush him. "I don't want to think about that time right now. I need to be in your arms. I need you to make me forget all of it. Even if it's just for a short while."

Without another word, he slid his hand around to the back of her neck and ravaged her lips so completely that she wasn't sure where she ended, and he began. She clung to him, sinking into everything that was Jace, everything that was *them*.

Then he lifted her and swung her around to the bed. They fell together, a tangle of arms and legs. She ran her hands down his back, feeling the many scars she knew so well. But he quickly trapped her hands and held them above her head. His lips trailed from her mouth, down her neck, and over her chest to her breasts. When his mouth closed over a hard nipple, she moaned.

How he loved the sound of her moans. Jace continued suckling until Taryn squirmed beneath him, her hips seeking contact. He desperately wanted to be inside her, and he knew she wanted the same thing, but he was making them wait—for both of them.

He moved to her other nipple and teased that dark peak as he used his free hand to cup her full breast and massage it. She had the most amazing curves that made his mouth water and his body yearn to have her. He didn't know why she loved him, but he was glad that she did. Because together, they were amazing.

His mouth moved down her stomach, his tongue flicking at her navel. As he moved down farther, he released her hands so he could settle between her legs and hold her hips. He slowly licked her before swirling his tongue around her clit.

Her back arched as she sucked in a breath. Jace

inwardly smiled. He knew just what to do to bring her the most pleasure.

It was too much.

It wasn't enough.

Taryn cried out from the incredible feelings that rushed through her body as Jace's tongue worked its magic on her. It had been so long since she had felt any pleasure that she found herself on the precipice of an orgasm within moments.

She clutched at the sheets and pulled on them as the climax overtook her. Her lips parted to scream, but the sound got trapped in her throat as her body convulsed from ecstasy. Before the orgasm finished, Jace moved on top of her. Taryn opened her eyes to meet his as he slid deep inside her.

"Oh, yes," she whispered.

In between kisses on her neck, he said, "I've dreamed of this every night."

"Yes," she replied, her hands sinking into his thick golden locks.

He began rocking his hips, sliding in and out of her in the most decadent fashion. Just like his kiss earlier, he began slow and easy, gradually increasing his tempo until he was driving into her hard and deep.

Taryn wrapped her legs around him as she found herself careening toward another climax.

None of his dreams could compare to actually being inside Taryn. Her wet heat clutched him perfectly, sending him spiraling into pleasure as only she could. He looked down to find her watching him. As their eyes met, he knew that he would gladly give his life for hers. She was his everything.

And she had somehow found her way back to him.

"I love you," she said.

He saw a tear fall from her eye to roll across her temple into her dark locks. Then pleasure filled her face a heartbeat before he felt her body spasm around his cock. That's all it took to bring on his own orgasm.

Jace pumped his hips as he spilled his seed inside her. When he was spent, he lowered himself, and she wrapped her arms around him, holding him. They remained that way for several minutes before he rose and pulled out of her.

When he rolled onto his back, she followed him to curl against his chest. He wrapped an arm around her and put his other behind his head as he closed his eyes, a smile on his face. Nothing could ruin this night.

"Um . . . I probably should've told you last night that I'm no longer on birth control."

Jace's eyes snapped open.

Chapter 19

"Shit."

Taryn kissed Jace's chest. "There is still time for me to get a morning-after pill."

"I should've thought about that."

"Passion took us last night and today." She returned her head to his chest and looked into the darkened room. "And if I get pregnant, then it was meant to be."

He rubbed his hand up and down her back. "I once thought we would have had a child by now."

That made her smile. "We probably would have."

"Sounds like a nice idea, doesn't it?"

"Very."

"Marry me, Taryn."

She frowned and rose up on her elbow to look at him. "You can't be serious. Not now."

"I'm very serious. I had planned to propose the day I woke to find you gone."

Taryn didn't know what to say. Her heart broke all over again. That's when she had to remind herself that she was with Jace now.

He pulled her back down and kissed the top of her head. "You had to have known."

"I didn't," she whispered. She didn't even try to stop the tears from coming. "You're such a romantic."

"Shhh. Don't tell anyone."

"It'll be our secret."

Jace drew in a breath and released it. "I mean it. I want to marry you. I don't care if I have one minute with you or a hundred years. I want to be with you."

"I want that, too."

"Then let's get married before we go on this mission."

Taryn shifted her head to look at him. "If something goes wrong and Boyd finds out about you, he'll torture you in front of me. He'll bring you untold pain before he kills you."

"He might. Or he may not. The fact is, I don't care about him right now."

"You should. He's dangerous. I went out of my way to ensure that he thought we had broken up that night so he didn't try to drag you into this."

Jace's lips twisted. "I have a hard time believing a man like him wouldn't have had spies in Clearview before they came for your father and brother. I'm betting he knows all about me. And that you'd come to me this time."

Taryn's stomach dropped to her feet as she sat up. "Shit. If he knows, then—"

"It doesn't matter," Jace said calmly as he pulled her back down and wrapped his arms around her. "We're safe now. We've got this time. Let's not have him intrude on things."

"You're right. He's already taken so much from us."

Jace rested his cheek atop her head. "Exactly. I'd much rather talk about you agreeing to marry me."

She chuckled, unable to help herself. "Of course, I want to be your wife. I've loved you from the first moment I saw you."

"Then what's stopping us from getting married before this mission? We can go down to the courthouse and get it done quickly and quietly. No one else needs to know."

Taryn looked up at him. "Is that what you really want?"

"It is."

She grinned, happiness filling her. "Then let's do it."

"And keep it a secret?"

"Our secret until we've succeeded in this mission."

A smile broke out over his face. "There's that fire I've always loved."

"I'm not the same person I was."

"No one ever stays the same."

"Jace, I've . . ."

He nodded solemnly. "I understand. If you want to talk about it, I'm here. If you don't, you don't ever have to share a word. But understand that I love you no matter what. I loved you before I met you. I've loved you all these years you were away. And I will love you from this life into the next."

She held onto him. When his arms tightened around her, she closed her eyes. Never in her wildest dreams had she thought that Jace would be single if she ever managed to get back to Clearview. The fact that he still loved her and wanted a life with her despite everything that had happened was proof that they were meant to be together.

"I love you so much," she whispered.

He ran his hand down her hair. "It's going to be all right. I've got you now."

A tear fell from the corner of her eye. It was far from okay, but she appreciated that he wasn't only willing, he *wanted* to stand by her against such a man as Boyd. Taryn had known that Jace was a different sort of breed from the other men she knew. He had been through Hell and back, and yet he hadn't allowed that horrible time to define him.

It hadn't been an easy road. She had been there during the nightmares and occasions when the memories were too much for him to endure. Somehow, Jace always managed to pull himself back from the brink. Partly because he was that strong mentally, but it also had a lot to do with the close connection he had to his family and friends.

Jace was the driving force for her to keep fighting every day that Boyd held her. There had been decent days, and there had been bad days. But every night when she closed her eyes, she thought about Jace and the life they had shared together—however briefly.

Now that she had returned to Clearview and Jace, there was no way she could go back to the life she'd led the last few years. She wished she could say that she was done with Boyd and his demands one way or the other, but that wasn't an option. Not as long as Boyd held Payton. Her sister was the only thing that kept Taryn doing whatever Boyd wanted.

And it made her hate him all the more.

"You're shaking," Jace whispered.

"I'm thinking about how Boyd has used Payton against me. I don't know if she's been raped or abused.

He assured me that isn't the case, but I've never believed him."

Jace's chest rose as he pulled in a long breath. "We'll be able to get to Boyd because he's going to want to be there to take the money."

"Oh, he will."

"We don't want to alert him that you're planning something, but we need to ensure that Payton is there so we can get her out with you."

Taryn rolled onto her back and looked at the ceiling. "I always ask to speak to Payton, and he always refuses. I need to push more this time."

"Don't be too aggressive. It'll raise suspicions. Are you supposed to call in before you return?"

She turned her head to look at him. "Yes."

"When you do, tell him that you've got the money, but you want to have your sister there to finish the transaction. He shouldn't object because he did agree to your deal."

Taryn nodded. "I know exactly what I'll say to him."

"He's kept a tight hold on you. If you suddenly begin acting strangely, he'll know something is up. That could make him bolt and take Payton."

"I'd be free then, but my sister wouldn't." She blew out a frustrated breath.

Jace rolled onto his side to face her. "There are five of us, and another that I've asked to help. I know how good a small team of highly skilled men can be."

"It won't be enough. You saw the schematics of the warehouse. It's a huge area. And he has men everywhere."

"It won't be the first time we've gone in outnumbered. It's how we operate. You saw the plan. Two teams of three coming in at different points. The main goal is to get you and Payton out."

She frowned. "And what of Boyd? If something isn't done about him, he'll come after us."

"Don't worry about him. We've got that covered."

Taryn wished she knew what they planned for Boyd, but perhaps it was better she didn't. The more she knew, the more she would worry about Jace. In order for this to work, she had to trust him completely.

She threaded her fingers with his. "I know all of you are trained, but that doesn't stop my concern."

"I need you to concentrate on two things," he told her. "Yourself, and your sister. Get to her and get somewhere safe. That's all I need you to do."

"I could help with Boyd and his men."

Jace shook his head and gripped her fingers tightly. "Just get Payton and take her out of the line of fire. You need to think up two places you could go to and wait for me to find you and Payton."

"I can do that. Talking now, everything sounds so easy, so simple. But it won't be."

His lips curved into a grin. "It'll be far from easy. It'll be loud, chaotic, and scary. It's easy to get disoriented, which is why you need to be the one to choose the places in the compound you can get to without too much difficulty."

"Why not just one?"

"Because something may prevent you from getting to that spot. You always need at least one backup."

She licked her lips, trying to take it all in. "I never would've thought of that."

"That's my skill set," he replied with a wink. "Yours is making Boyd think you're coming back to him for your sister's sake like you always have."

"I wish I never had to set eyes on him again."

Jace brought her hand to his lips and kissed her knuckles. "I know, darlin'. We're going to get there. Promise."

"Do you think I made a mistake not going to the authorities?"

"Don't do that. Don't second-guess yourself. You made a decision—which was valid, by the way. Stick with that and look forward. If you start wondering about things or changing your mind, it only confuses the issue."

She knew he was right. Her gaze briefly lowered to their hands. "What if I can't get to Payton?"

"Then you get safe. I can't do what needs to be done if I'm worried about you. It's bad enough you'll be there at all. Frankly, that scares the hell out of me. But I know that none of this will work unless you're there." A frown pulled his brows together for a heartbeat. "There's a good chance you won't be able to get to Payton. We talked about that last night when you were dozing. Our plan factors in that Boyd will have her held, possibly by that Brick you spoke about. We'll extract her like we would any high-value target."

She swallowed loudly. "As long as I'm out of the way."

"When the attack starts, Boyd will likely have one of his men try to take you."

"No."

"Sweetheart, I'm not going to let that happen," he assured her before he pressed his lips to her mouth.

Chapter 20

Ryan stared out his office window as the sun came up. He'd decided to come in early and get some paperwork done, but he couldn't stop thinking about his conversation with Brick.

Or what he knew his friends were planning.

He was being pulled in too many different directions, and he didn't like it. Helping Jace and Taryn seemed like a no-brainer, and yet his position as the police chief put a halt to that. Then there was Brick. While his friends knew an undercover agent had infiltrated Boyd's organization, they didn't know it was Brick. And they didn't realize that Ryan knew about Brick, or that Boyd was the man who had Taryn's sister.

"Fuck," Ryan said and slammed his hand on the desk as his frustrations continued to mount.

There was a rap on his door. He didn't want to talk to anyone. If he came in early, he was usually left alone. Didn't seem like he would get that this time.

"Enter."

The door swung open, and Clayton filled the doorway. "Mornin'."

"What can I do for you?" Ryan said as he forced a smile and looked into pale green eyes that regarded him solemnly.

Clayton walked into the office and softly closed the door behind him. He settled himself in a chair before Ryan's desk and crossed an ankle over his opposite knee. There might be gray at his temples, partially hidden by his Stetson, and a few more wrinkles around his eyes, but those were the only things that showed Clayton's age. He kept his body and mind in top shape as only an ex-special ops would.

When he didn't speak, Ryan leaned back in his chair and folded his hands over his stomach as he returned Clayton's stare. Clayton was a man of few words. He was observant, and just because he didn't mention something, didn't mean he hadn't noticed it.

"You've been here several hours already today," Clayton remarked.

Ryan shrugged nonchalantly. "I work a lot. You know that."

"That you do."

"I've got a lot on my mind. I don't mean to offend, but if you have something to say, please say it."

Without missing a beat, Clayton said, "This isn't the first time I've seen you today."

Ryan looked at the clock and saw that it was just after six. His gaze slid back to Clayton. "I didn't see you."

"I know. I saw you at four at the corner of Magnolia and Main as we pulled up next to each other. I waved. You had a peculiar look on your face. After I picked up some medicine for Hope's allergies, I saw your truck at Velma's Café."

Ryan glanced at the cup of coffee with Velma's logo on it. He had bought it, but he hadn't drunk any of it. Nor had he touched the ham and cheese croissant he had ordered that still sat in the bag on the corner of his desk.

"Since the kids love Velma's pastries, I pulled in to get some as a surprise for breakfast. I walked right up beside you and called your name. You didn't even look my way. I went home and helped Abby get Hope settled then drove back into town. To see you."

Ryan ran a hand down his face. "Shit."

"I'm not here to pry. I'm here to make sure you're all right."

"Yeah. No." Ryan scrunched up his face. "Hell. I don't know anymore. I'm so fucking twisted in knots that I'm not sure if I'm coming or going."

Clayton pursed his lips. "That's what I figured. You usually handle stressful situations like a pro, which is why you've got me concerned."

"I'm stuck." The moment the words were out, Ryan sighed in relief.

That caused Clayton's blond brows to shoot up on his forehead. "Women problems?"

"Oh, hell no." Ryan had been down that road once before. He wasn't going to travel that path again. Ever.

Clayton chuckled and held up his hands. "All right." His smile died. "I take it this is about Jace and the others?"

Ryan squeezed his eyes closed for a heartbeat. "Have you ever known what you should do but were unable to do it because of obligations?"

"A few times."

"What did you do?"

"I followed my gut."

Ryan looked out his office window. "It isn't that easy. If it was, I'd resign and join my friends."

"I see."

Silence stretched. It would be easier if Clayton asked questions, but he wasn't that type of man. When he'd said he wouldn't pry, he'd meant it. But his appearance in Ryan's office spoke to his willingness to listen and offer any advice that was requested.

Ryan slid his gaze back to Clayton. "There's another factor."

"The undercover agent."

It never failed to amaze him how intelligent Clayton was. The man never missed anything. Ryan nodded in reply.

Clayton removed his hat and set it on his knee before running his hands through his thick blond locks. "When you're in a position of authority, things are always pushing and pulling at you. Sometimes, we do what we have to do. Other times, we do what we want to do. But there are rare times when those two are one and the same. You have an obligation as chief and to the men and women who work for you."

"I also have an obligation to my friends," Ryan added.

"Yes, and no. You and Danny offered aid, and Taryn refused it. You've done all you can as chief."

Ryan leaned forward and rested his arms on the desk. "And if I have information?"

"If it was something that put them in danger, you would've already picked up the phone or gone to see them. Since you're sitting here talking to me, that means it's something else entirely. And I'm guessing it once more goes back to the undercover agent."

Ryan didn't respond, which was answer enough.

Clayton released a long breath. "Then you also have an obligation to this agent to keep him or her out of danger and continuing in their duties for the FBI. Seems pretty cut and dried to me."

"If only it was."

Clayton said nothing, though if the shrewd way his pale green eyes studied Ryan was any indication, his friend might have already pieced together the puzzle.

"And so your dilemma," Clayton replied.

Ryan nodded once. "Yes."

"Sounds like a tough one."

"The toughest."

Clayton lifted one shoulder in a shrug. "I'm sure you thought that not too long ago when the rest of us went after the people who nearly killed Jace, kidnapped Brice, and attempted to kill Marlee. You and Danny warned us to stay out of the way."

"If y'all had listened, Marlee would most likely be dead, and those responsible would still be on the loose."

"I have the utmost respect for law enforcement of any kind. Numerous rules have to be followed, but it sometimes hinders you in getting the job done."

Ryan quirked a brow. "There's a *but* in there."

Clayton grinned. "But . . . things are never black and white. Those who believe that are either naïve or stupid. Of which, you are neither. You're a smart man, Ryan. Otherwise, you wouldn't be the chief of police, and the Texas Rangers wouldn't still be trying to get you to join their ranks."

"You know about that?" Ryan asked in shock.

Clayton chuckled and lowered his foot to the floor. "I could tell you that it's a small town, but the truth is, I've got some friends who are Rangers. They speak very highly of you."

"As a little kid growing up on the outskirts of Houston, all I wanted to be was a Ranger. My path took me on a different route."

"You became a SEAL and then a cop. I'd say that's a good road," Clayton replied.

Ryan thought back to his difficult childhood. "There are a lot of other—hazardous—roads I could've taken."

"What's holding you back from joining the Rangers now? I think you'd fit in well there, but I'd sure hate to lose you. It's been a long while since a Clearview police chief and our county sheriff got along."

Ryan shared a smile with Clayton. "I like my job. A lot. I like the people I work with, I like Clearview, and I've made some incredible friends." He nodded to Clayton. "Like you. It's not an easy thing to find people you trust with your life. I had it with my SEAL teammates, and I've found it again."

"No matter where you live or what you do, we'll still be your friends."

"I know. But the dream I once had doesn't mean as much anymore."

"I think it means more than you think. It shifted without you realizing it."

Ryan chuckled as he looked at the floor and realized that his friend was absolutely right. He met Clayton's gaze. "If I joined the Rangers, who the hell would keep all of you in line? Danny can't handle it by himself."

Clayton let out a loud laugh. He had a smile on his face when he said, "I'll tell you what I told Brice, Caleb, Cooper, and Jace—as well as my own kids. Follow your gut. It'll never lead you wrong. In anything."

"Thank you."

Ryan stood when Clayton got to his feet. They clasped hands and shook. Clayton flashed him a smile and walked out after putting the Stetson back on his head. When Ryan took his seat once more, he didn't feel as if he carried the weight of the world any longer. He still hadn't made a decision, but the path to it was clearing.

He hadn't lied to Clayton. He loved his job, and if he joined Jace and the others on an unsanctioned raid on one of the businessmen in Fort Worth and things went badly, Ryan's life as he knew it would be over. He would no longer be a cop, much less the chief. The Rangers would no longer want him. Everything he held dear would vanish.

But if he didn't help his friends . . . he'd never forgive himself.

Chapter 21

The dream was always the same. She tried to wake herself, but just like the many times before, she couldn't. Ice filled her veins when Boyd's man Brick bound her hands behind her and motioned for two men to take her.

Taryn struggled to get away, but it did no good. No matter how many times her feet connected with them, they didn't so much as flinch. She knew she was being brought to her execution. This wasn't supposed to happen. Her life was supposed to be with Jace. She wasn't supposed to end up selling drugs to help her father and brother pay back a debt that shouldn't have become hers.

Lightning flashed in the sky, followed immediately by a long rumble of thunder. The warehouse loomed before her as the men hauled her inside the darkened building. Her rapid heartbeat slamming against her ribs drowned out the sound of Brick's boots on the concrete.

Brick looked back at her, his dark brown eyes meeting hers briefly as he walked beneath a couple of lights. Then he halted and turned to face her. She tried to catch his attention again, hoping that she might convince him to help her. A form took shape out of the darkness behind Brick. Then the men holding her stopped.

And Boyd came into view.

He had his hands behind his back as he stopped beside Brick, and the two of them exchanged whispers. Taryn tried to hear what they said, but she couldn't make out anything. Her once easy life had turned into one of fear and dread.

"If you're going to kill me, get it over with," she told them.

Boyd's head snapped to her as he halted midsentence. Brick's look of shock made her wonder if she had lost her sanity. Only a fool would bring attention to themselves in this scenario. Maybe she had gone mad. All she knew was that she couldn't live like this any longer. If she couldn't be free, then there was no reason to keep living.

"I'll get to you," Boyd replied.

Taryn heard a sound behind her. She twisted to see two others being dragged in, though they weren't fighting like she had been. Her curiosity turned to shock when she realized that the other two were her brother and father. They were shoved to their knees on either side of her.

"Dad," she whispered when he and Ben were settled.

One of the men holding her yanked down on her arm. She fell to her knees so hard she feared she had cracked her kneecap. Her father wouldn't look at her. His head hung so low, his chin touched his chest as tears ran down his face.

Taryn then looked at Ben. He glanced at her, and the

terror in his eyes sent her into an all-out panic situa-
tion. That's when she knew. Boyd was going to kill all
three of them. All Taryn could hope for was that they'd
spare Payton. She was the most innocent of all of them.
The more time that passed without her arrival, the
more Taryn hoped that her prayers might be answered.

"Someone has betrayed me," Boyd said.

Taryn squeezed her eyes closed. She knew this part.
This was where Boyd killed her father in front of her. She
couldn't watch it again. She wouldn't. She kept telling
herself to wake up, that she was reliving a nightmare.
But nothing she did untangled her from the dream.

"Haven't you, Taryn?"

Her heart dropped to her feet as her eyes snapped
open. She found herself looking into Boyd's blue eyes
as he aimed the gun at her face. This wasn't the usual
nightmare. And that alarmed her even more. "No."

"You went to Jace. You told him who I was. I warned
you what would happen if you betrayed me."

She shook her head furiously, unable to comprehend
what was going on. "No. No, please. I-I didn't do any-
thing."

"You think you can be free of me? Never. For this
betrayal, I'm going to take your sister's life."

He swung the gun to the side. Her father no lon-
ger kneeled beside her. Instead, it was Payton, tears
coursing down her face.

"Taryn? Help me. You said you would protect me."

Taryn swung her head to Boyd, trying to think of
something to say, when he fired the gun.

Taryn jerked upright as she came awake at the sound of
the gunshot in her dreams. She was breathing heavily,
her heart racing.

"Easy," Jace said as he sat up. "You're safe, darlin'. Everything is fine."

Taryn dropped her head into her hands. Nothing was fine. She might be safe, but her sister wasn't.

"It was just a dream," Jace said as he pulled her into his arms.

She crumpled against him and let the tears flow. A long time passed before she stopped crying. He held her through it all. When she finally raised her head and wiped at the tear streaks on her cheeks, Jace didn't ask her to tell him what had happened. He offered her a smile and a box of tissues. Taryn found herself grinning as she took a tissue to wipe her nose.

"It's dawn. You hungry?" Jace asked.

She shrugged. "A little."

"How about one of Velma's blueberry donuts?"

They were her favorite, but of course, he would remember that. "I've not had one in forever."

"I'm craving one of her cinnamon rolls myself." He tugged on her hand. "Come on. Let's treat ourselves."

She let him pull her from the bed. "I need to stop by the drugstore."

"No problem." He kissed her before turning to get dressed.

The dream began to fade, and with it, her fear. At least, for now. She pulled on her jeans and a sleeveless shirt before she wound her hair up in a messy bun. Then she went into the living room to find her shoes she had kicked off the previous night. Jace was waiting for her near the garage door by the time she grabbed her purse.

The drive into town was done in comfortable silence as the radio played. She looked at everything as they passed, noting what had changed and what hadn't. All too soon, they pulled up to the drugstore.

They got out and walked inside, hand in hand. Everything felt like it had before Boyd had taken her away. She could almost believe the last years hadn't happened. When Jace stopped to look at a cat toy, Taryn continued on to the pharmacy to get the morning-after pill.

As she stood in line, she realized that someone had walked up near her. She moved over, thinking they needed room to reach something on the shelf next to her. She glanced at them. Then quickly did a double-take when she recognized the face.

Brick's dark brown eyes met hers. "Picking up something for yourself? Or someone else?"

Her heart skipped a beat.

He nodded to the pharmacy desk. "You're up."

Taryn glanced at the clerk and woodenly walked up to the counter. She asked for the pill and waited as the employee found it and brought it back. Her hands shook as she pulled out cash to pay. She glanced behind her to see if Brick was still there, but he was gone. And that worried her more than if he were still standing there.

The fact that he was in town could only mean bad things. Brick was completely loyal to Boyd. Was he here for her? Or was Brick in town for the undercover agent? She got her receipt and put her change in her wallet.

"Hey."

Taryn jumped, dropping her purse and the bag with her purchase when Jace touched her arm.

He studied her for a moment before picking up the

items and putting his hand on her back. "What happened?"

"One of Boyd's men was in the store."

"Who? Where?"

She looked around as they walked through the aisles, but she could no longer find him. "Brick. He's gone."

"And you're sure it was him?"

"Yes."

Jace didn't say another word as they hurried from the store and got into his truck. "Do you know what he drives?"

"I . . . no," she said with a shake of her head. She studied the cars in the lot, trying to see inside the vehicles. "I don't see him out here either."

Jace looked at her. "What did he say to you?"

"He asked if I was getting something for myself or someone else. Then he told me it was my turn at the counter."

"That's it?" Jace asked with a frown.

Taryn shrugged. "That's it."

"Did he try to take you? Did he ask if you had the money?"

She shook her head. "All he said was what I told you."

"Well, looks like he just wanted to remind you that you were being watched."

"What do we do?"

"Nothing. You've got time before you have to be in Fort Worth. For all he knows, you're just catching up with an old friend."

Taryn's hands shook as she fastened her seat belt. "Yeah."

"We can go home," Jace offered.

She turned her head to look at him. "Boyd has

already taken so much from us. I'm not going to let them take another second. Let's have breakfast."

"I agree completely," he said with a sexy grin.

But as he backed out of the parking spot, Taryn noticed that Jace scanned faces and vehicles, looking for threats. And so was she.

When they reached Velma's, they decided to eat there. Taryn scarfed her blueberry donut down so fast that she wanted another. Jace happily ordered a second as he devoured the huge cinnamon roll and drank a mug of coffee. Taryn opted for a latte.

It wasn't long before Jace had her laughing as he filled her in on stories from the time she had been gone. When she was with Jace, it was easy to forget the trouble that awaited them. He'd always had that ability. Not only was he likeable, but there was also something about him that drew others. Women, especially.

When he had been with her, he never gave any other women even a glance. Taryn never worried about him cheating. But it was also why she was surprised he was single.

"How are your parents?" she asked.

Jace smiled as he swallowed his bite of food. "The same. They're going to be so happy you've returned. I haven't told them yet because they'd want to see you."

"And they don't need to know about all of this while it's going on," she finished.

He reached across the table and took her hand. "They'd want to help."

"I wouldn't let them. I'm barely allowing you."

"I know," he said with a chuckle. "But as soon as we get back, we'll head there for some dinner and a ride to the river."

"Oh, that sounds heavenly," Taryn said. "Both the

horse ride to the river as well as your dad's amazing steaks and your mother's cherry pie."

Jace chuckled.

She pushed away her empty plate. "I hope you aren't going to leave without letting them know where you're going."

"Clayton and Abby will tell my parents and Cooper's mom after we leave. We know better than to take off and not let someone have information to tell our families."

"Good."

Jace held her gaze. "I think Boyd's idiotic for allowing you to return to your hometown to do what he ordered. But I'm glad he did. Otherwise, we wouldn't be together now."

"He doesn't care about the money. It's about controlling me."

"That's right, but it's all about to change." Jace cleared his throat, a smile on his face. "So, when do you want to go down to the courthouse?"

She laughed, loving how he always knew when to change the subject. "You do know there's a seventy-two-hour waiting period after we apply for a marriage license before we can get married, right?"

"And you know that I have connections, right? It can be waived with a court order."

Her eyes widened. "You're serious? I thought you wanted to keep it secret."

"What I want is to marry you. What do you say?"

She hesitated for just a moment before she nodded. "I told you last night I wanted to be your wife. That hasn't changed."

"Then let's go see what we can do about that."

She scooted from the bench as they walked out

together and drove to the courthouse. Taryn waited in the lobby as Jace spoke to the front desk. A moment later, he was shown into an office. She used that time to freshen up in the bathroom. She took her hair down, ran her hands through the strands, and dug into her purse for some lip gloss. Fifteen minutes later, Jace returned with a piece of paper in his hand.

"You got it?" she asked as she rose to her feet.

He looked shocked. "You doubted me?"

"I wasn't sure there would be time."

"The benefits of living in the same town all my life. Come on. They're waiting for us. Unless you want to change. We can come back."

She glanced down at her jeans and shirt. "We can have another celebration later if we want to. A fancy dress doesn't matter right now. You do."

Chapter 22

Jace caught Taryn looking down at the bouquet of white anemones as they drove back to his house. The priceless look of surprise and love on her face when she saw the flowers made him glad that he asked a woman to go across the street for them as he settled the paperwork. The florist had put some eucalyptus into the small bouquet and tied it with a white ribbon.

Taryn looked up and grinned at him. "We're married."

"I know," he said and reached over to cover her hand with his. His finger slid over the ring on her hand, proclaiming her as his.

Because Taryn was such a unique and singularly incredible person, a regular wedding ring just wouldn't work, at least in his opinion. The moment he'd found the ring, he'd known it had been designed for her. Three golden twig branches had been woven in an asymmetrical design that symbolized unity and strength. The ring was as exceptional as the woman who had stolen his heart.

"I love it," Taryn said with a smile as he continued running his finger over the ring.

He squeezed her hand. "I'm glad. If you want a diamond—"

"I don't need a diamond. I didn't even need this. My heart has been yours for years. I didn't need a ring or a piece of paper to tell me that."

Jace slowed the truck and pulled into the drive. He shut off the engine and turned his head to her. "That is one of the many reasons I love you."

She leaned over, and they pressed their lips together. When she moved back, she said, "What about you? Do you want a ring?"

"Do you want me to wear one?"

"Do you want to wear one?"

They both laughed. Jace shook his head. "I'd be happy to wear a ring, but like you said, I've been yours for years. This just makes it all official. When all this is done, we'll go get me a ring, and we'll plan a big event to celebrate with everyone."

"How about a small event? Something casual."

"Whatever you'd like, darlin'. I know women think about their weddings for years."

She shrugged and glanced away. "I witnessed the stress of a couple of my friends during their weddings. I'd rather the event be special. Like it was today."

"At the courthouse?" he asked with a frown.

Taryn smiled, her eyes lighting up. "Yes. Because it was about us and our love."

"You're a special one, do you know that?"

"Of course. I just want you to realize that," she replied sassily.

They shared another laugh until Jace saw her look nervously at the house. "What is it?"

"This has to come off," she said and moved the fingers on her left hand to bring attention to the ring.

"It doesn't have to. Not until you leave for Fort Worth, at least."

Her beautiful green eyes lifted to his. "We agreed not to tell anyone until after everything."

"Those helping us won't tell a soul. Leave the ring on."

Jace saw movement in his rearview mirror and looked up to see Cooper and Marlee park behind him.

"Come on," Taryn said with a wink. "Our quiet morning is over."

He didn't want to leave the truck. He wasn't ready for the others to arrive because that meant the countdown to their mission had begun. He knew it was silly. The countdown had begun the moment Taryn asked for help. That didn't mean he was ready for any of it.

Jace told Taryn what she needed to hear to feel safe, but he, like his friends, knew all too well the many things that could go wrong. They were professionals, and Jace trusted each of them with his life. Every one of them had been in a bad situation and had gotten out of it.

But this was the first time it was truly personal for him.

He'd helped his friends when they needed it, but this was about the woman he loved. His wife. He couldn't lose her. Not again.

"Jace?"

He swallowed and tried to smile, but as he looked at Taryn, he failed. "You're beautiful. Your soul is beautiful. Your body and face are stunning. You are simply amazing. I'm lucky to have your love."

Her lips curved into a smile as she cupped her hand

on his cheek. "You've got that backward, handsome. I'm the lucky one."

"We have years to debate this," Jace said with a wink.

Taryn chuckled. "Exactly. More people are pulling up. I think we should go in."

Jace could no longer put it off. He released Taryn's hand, and they climbed out of the truck and walked to the house together, Clayton and Caleb not far behind. Inside the house, Cooper had already opened the schematics of the warehouse complex while Marlee talked on her phone in the kitchen.

Taryn set down her purse and put the flowers in water before she stood with Jace as Caleb went to Cooper. Clayton nodded to Taryn as he removed his hat and hung it on a hook near the kitchen's side door. Jace watched her looking at the others. About that time, Brice and Cash walked in. The conversations grew loud as everyone talked over one another. That's when Jace noticed that Clayton stood to the side, watching him and Taryn. She turned her head to Jace and gave him a small nod.

Jace cleared his throat. "Hey, everyone! We've got something to say."

Marlee ended her call, and the others turned to face them, waiting patiently.

Jace glanced at Taryn as he put his arm around her. "I honestly didn't think I would ever see Taryn again. We both realize that we got a second chance, and while there's a rather large obstacle in the way, it will soon be remedied thanks to the help of all of you."

"Which I'll never be able to repay," Taryn said.

Cooper crossed his arms over his chest. "There's no need to repay us. This is what friends do for each other."

Jace couldn't stop the smile from spreading over his face. "We wanted all of you to be the first to know that less than thirty minutes ago, we got married at the courthouse."

The room erupted with chatter—questions and congratulations.

Finally, it died down enough for Taryn to say, "We were going to wait and tell everyone after we returned from Fort Worth, but that didn't seem right. Y'all are risking your lives for my sister and me."

"We're asking that the news not get back to my parents, though," Jace said. He then looked at Cooper. "Or your mother. Not yet. We plan to have a celebration when we get back, but for now, this needs to stay between us."

Clayton nodded as he pushed away from the wall. "A wise decision. I'm not sure what Boyd would do if he learned of this."

Jace felt Taryn shiver at Clayton's words. "He's not going to find out."

"No, he isn't," Caleb said.

Brice looked around. "Where's the champagne? Beer? Wine? Something. We need to toast."

"We will," Jace told him.

Cooper walked to Taryn and hugged her before he slapped Jace on the back. "Jace is right. There's work to do. We'll celebrate after."

That seemed to put everyone in gear. Jace went with the guys to go over details once again before they began checking their equipment. He saw Taryn with Marlee as the two looked at Taryn's ring. This was the first day of their married lives, and if Jace had any say in it, it wouldn't be the last.

"There's still time to bring in the authorities," Clayton said in a low voice near Jace's ear.

Jace glanced at the man who had been a father figure, brother, and friend. "If our situations were reversed, and Abby was in Taryn's place, what would you do?"

Clayton's lips twisted as he shrugged. "That's a tough call. But if I'm being honest, I'd probably do exactly what you're doing. Especially with the intel that Taryn gave about the connections Boyd has. Y'all have one shot to get Payton out and Taryn free once and for all. But do you understand what that's going to entail?"

"Boyd either in custody . . . or dead," Jace replied.

Clayton glanced at Taryn. "And with how the authorities have tried to get him for some crime, the likelihood of him actually being prosecuted is slim."

"Taryn would testify against him. I'm sure Payton would, as well."

Clayton shot him a surprised look. "You understand that even if Boyd does get arrested, his organization won't stop. His men know what to do in that instance. And they'll be gunning for one person."

"Taryn," Jace said, his stomach knotting.

"She'll have to go into witness protection to stand any chance of surviving until the trial."

Jace ran a hand down his face. "She's already lost so many years. I don't want to put her through that."

"It might not be your call to make. However, it is something you should talk to her about. She may want him to pay for his crimes."

Jace knew it would be easier if Boyd just stopped existing. Would that be enough to halt his men from going after Taryn? Jace wasn't sure.

"You've not even thought of Payton," Clayton added.

Jace grimaced. He was so focused on Taryn that he kept forgetting her sister. "She's been held as a prisoner this entire time. Taryn said the few times she saw her, Payton looked well. But that doesn't mean anything."

"You know better than most what it's like to be a prisoner."

It was something Jace wished he could forget, but he understood what Clayton was trying to say. Payton might be so damaged psychologically and emotionally that she won't be able to testify. Or may would refuse to. That would put the burden on Taryn.

Clayton caught his gaze. "It's something to think about."

Jace nodded his thanks as he turned his head to look at his wife, who beamed. Taryn wouldn't live in fear anymore. She wouldn't be ruled by Boyd any longer.

And Jace was prepared to do whatever it took to ensure that happened.

Chapter 23

All too quickly, the day was gone. Before Taryn knew it, Jace had carried the duffle of cash to her car. He was the only one who wasn't already dressed in the all-black tactical gear, including bulletproof vests and helmets. After hours of going over every detail of the plan, watching Jace and the others clean their weapons and load ammunition, check their equipment three different times, and hearing Marlee and Clayton finalizing the last arrangements for additional help, it was time for the mission to begin.

This could be the beginning of a new life for her.

Or it could all end in a few hours.

Taryn was both scared and excited at the prospect of regaining her and Payton's freedom. Not to mention her new marriage to Jace. She had never been so happy. Or so terrified.

She followed Jace under cover of night to her car. As each minute passed, bringing her closer and closer to the time she had to leave, she found it more and more difficult to do it. So many things could go wrong. But what choice did she have? Her sister was at the mercy of a lunatic, and the only way Payton would get free was if Taryn did something.

But she was also being selfish because she no longer wanted to be beholden to Boyd.

Jace put the bag in the back seat and closed the door. Then he faced her. He cupped her face with his hands. "Baby? What is it?"

"I don't know if I can do this."

He smiled as his hands dropped to her shoulders and skimmed down her arms to take her hands in his. "If anyone can do this, it's you. Look what you've already done without anyone's help."

"I've been balanced on the edge of a cliff for years. I'm not sure how I didn't fall off before, but I know it's going to happen tonight."

"It isn't," Jace insisted. He caught her gaze and held it. "I won't let you down."

She glanced at the sky, not seeing the thick clouds rolling past the full moon. "I know you won't. It's Boyd and his men."

"Don't think about that. You need to keep going over the plan. You know the area where you'll be. You remember the two locations to go for me to find you, right?"

Taryn nodded woodenly.

"Just go over everything again and again. You know the plan. You know the backup plan. You know all the contingencies."

"If something happens and I'm not able to get away, I won't work for him anymore. I can't. I'd rather die."

Jace grabbed her shoulders and gave her a slight shake. "Stay alive. No matter what. Do you hear me? Because nothing will keep me from getting to you.

Nothing. If I have to traverse Hell itself to find you, I will."

She threw her arms around him. Jace sighed and held her tightly. Taryn knew how organized Jace and his friends were. She knew the plan was good. The contingencies were solid. Yet, she couldn't shake the feeling that something was going to go wrong.

"It's going to be all right. I promise," Jace whispered. "We have the rest of our lives together."

Taryn squeezed her eyes closed as she fought against the flood of tears. She wasn't strong. Fear had gotten her through each and every day. Fear of being killed, of losing her sister. That's what drove her to work harder than anyone else. If she had been as strong as everyone thought, she would've found a way to free herself and Payton a long time ago.

And she would've come to Jace the moment she drove to Clearview.

No, she wasn't strong. She was a coward. The last thing she wanted to do was return to Boyd. But she didn't have any other choice.

"I need you to stay to the course you've been on these last years," Jace told her. "Do that just a little while longer, darlin', so I and the others can get to Fort Worth and end this nightmare you and your sister have been living. Can you do that for me?"

Taryn nodded as she pulled back and opened her eyes to look at him. "I can."

"All of this will be over soon."

Yes, it would. One way or another. Taryn forced a smile when Jace continued staring at her. He made a sound in the back of his throat and pulled her against him for another hug. Then he kissed her—a long, slow kiss full of promises. A display of his unending love.

When he finally ended it, all she could think about was going to their room and taking off his clothes.

Instead, she got into her car and fastened her seatbelt—and everything came rushing back. Jace stopped at the front of the hood when she started the engine. To anyone watching, it would look as if they were saying goodbye. She waved at him. Jace blew her a kiss. Taryn smiled and blew him a kiss in return.

Then she put the car in reverse and backed out of the driveway. She gave Jace one more look before she drove away. He stood in the same spot and lifted a hand in farewell. Then he was out of sight, swallowed by the darkness.

The lines on the road passed in a blur as Taryn pointed her car northwest and headed toward Fort Worth. Fifteen minutes on the highway, she phoned Boyd as planned.

"I wondered if you were going to call. You're cutting it close," he said when he answered the phone.

Taryn gripped the steering wheel tightly and kept her eyes on the road. "I have the money."

"I had no doubt."

Just the sound of his voice made her want to hit something. "We both know you had me followed."

"Well, I couldn't exactly let my best seller get away, now could I?" he asked with a chuckle.

"You have my sister. You know I'll do whatever you want."

Boyd made a sound, and she heard the rattle of ice cubes as if he were taking a drink. "I do hope there will come a day when I don't have to use Payton to get you to do what I want. You could make a fine living working for me. I treat my people well."

"I would disagree."

"Now, Taryn," he admonished with a click of his tongue. "You know that isn't true. Have any of my men laid a hand on you? Have you been raped? The answer is no. Trust me, I could make your life so much worse than it is."

She didn't think she could hate anyone as much as she did Boyd. "You kidnapped my family and me. Took Payton away and made me work to pay off my father's and brother's debts. And you want me to be *thankful*? I can't. I won't."

"You and Payton have been treated well."

"I need your word that you'll have Payton there as agreed. I'm returning with five hundred thousand dollars in exchange for my and Payton's release."

"I gave you my word. I won't go back on that. Your sister will be here, and you'll get to talk to her like you've longed to do."

Taryn shook her head, even though he couldn't see it. "You're going to have my sister beside you, right? Not have me looking at her through a window. I want to see Payton. I want to hug her, touch her. She's all I have left."

Boyd sighed dramatically. "You want to make sure she's still here, and you haven't been doing all of this for a sister that's been dead. Admit it."

"Of course, that's what I want!" The minute the outburst happened, Taryn regretted it. She winced and drew in a steadying breath. "I watched my father and brother be killed right before me. I just want to make sure Payton is fine."

"She is."

"Can I talk to her now?"

"I would absolutely allow that, but I'm not near her right now. You'll have to take my word for it. She's hale and hearty. Shortly, you'll get to see for yourself."

Taryn went to hit the steering wheel but stopped short of doing it. She was worried that she had gone too far with him, and he wouldn't bring Payton tonight. "I'm only a few hours out. I'm really looking forward to seeing my sister."

"Then you'd better hurry."

The call disconnected. Taryn blew out a breath. She didn't call Jace. There was no need. Cash had put a tracker on her phone that let them know where she was and allowed them to hear any calls she made and see any texts. She *wanted* to call him, to hear his voice, but she didn't. He was likely loading up and heading out.

Taryn sat up straighter in the seat. "I can do this. I will do this. Because I don't have a choice. But also because my husband"—she paused and smiled at the word—"my husband and his friends are risking every-thing for Payton and me. So, yes, I will face the man who killed off my family one by one and held me against my will. I will face the man who forced me to sell drugs to keep my sister safe. Hold on, Payton. I'm coming. We're going to be free of Boyd this night."

The words helped greatly, but as she drove, her mind began to wander. It thought up dozens of differ-ent scenarios where Brick killed Jace and the others. It wasn't until her imagination created a scene where Boyd killed Payton that Taryn reached over and turned up the radio. She searched until she found a song she liked, then she turned it up even more and sang along. If she didn't, she would drive herself insane, thinking of all the different ways things could go wrong instead of going over the plan like Jace had told her to do.

The drive seemed to take an eternity. Forty-five minutes from the city, Taryn turned down the music and began saying the plan out loud over and over again. She went through it in her mind as if she were already at the warehouse. She even went through the backup plans and locations they'd discussed. She was calm and ready.

Or so she thought until she slowed the car and pulled into the gated drive for the warehouses. A fence encircled the entire property. It had five entrances, and each of them had a guard shack with at least one man on duty—all armed. These weren't your everyday rent-a-cops. They were ex-military. But Taryn wasn't worried about Jace and the others running into them. They were getting onto the property another way.

She pulled up at the guard post and rolled down her window so he could see her face. Taryn recognized him, though she didn't know his name. He was of Polynesian descent with dark skin, eyes, and hair. Tall with bulging muscles. Not someone anyone messed with, which was why he stood guard.

He jerked his head toward the back seat.

Taryn rolled her eyes. "It's a bag of money. As I'm sure you know, Boyd is waiting for me. Open the gate so I can go in."

He stared at her for a long minute before he jerked his head to the bag again.

Taryn unbuckled and twisted around to grab the bag. She dragged it into the front with her and opened it to show him the cash.

"The other," he bit out.

She went through the bag for him. He even made her go through the bag she had left with. Once she had, Taryn dumped everything in the back seat again and then faced forward to put the vehicle in gear.

"Open the trunk."

Her head snapped to him. "Excuse me?"

Instead of replying, he quirked a brow.

Taryn blew out a breath and put the car in park again before pressing a button on the door to pop the trunk. That's when she saw something out of the corner of her eye. She turned her head to see a man walking around her car with a mirror attached to a long pole, the kind they used to look for bombs. She chuckled to herself. If she had actually thought that would work, she would've done it a long time ago.

"Clear!" the guard said after he closed her trunk.

This time when she put the car in gear, the guard opened the gate. Taryn didn't look at him as she drove away. Once through, she glanced in the rearview mirror to see the guard speaking into a phone. No doubt he was alerting everyone that she had arrived.

The closer she got to the warehouse, the more her hands shook, and her heart raced. When she finally parked the car and turned off the ignition, she was breathing as if she had run a marathon.

"I can do this," she told herself as she closed her eyes.

When she opened them, Boyd stood in front of her car, wearing a smile. And beside him was Brick.

Chapter 24

By the time the helicopter with Jace, Cooper, and Cash
flew to Fort Worth, Jace was ready to get boots on the
ground. After the chopper landed atop the building and
they'd disembarked, the three of them gave a wave of
thanks to the pilot—Clayton's friend Doc. He would
remain on standby in case there was trouble, and they
needed out of the city quickly.

Marlee and Audrey had followed Taryn to Fort
Worth in different vehicles to keep an eye on her and
make sure Boyd didn't have some trick up his sleeve.
Jace knew from the tracker that Taryn was at Boyd's
compound in the city, and both Marlee and Audrey had
confirmed that, as well. The girls wouldn't go too far,
however. They were meeting up with another of Clayton's military friends who happened to be a retired
Texas Ranger. He would call in the Rangers if things
went sideways.

Caleb and Brice were coming in on another chopper
with Myles, one of Jace's Marine buddies, and planned
to hit the warehouses from the opposite direction. They

were all going in quietly, taking out anyone they saw so as not to cause a ruckus of any kind. This was the kind of mission they had all been trained for.

Some believed that in order for them to win, their team needed more men. That wasn't always the case, especially in a situation like this with two small teams used to gain the advantage by getting inside the compound and taking up positions that would put Boyd and anyone near him in their crosshairs.

Jace, Cash, and Cooper headed for the door leading down the skyscraper. The building had been chosen because Clayton knew who owned it and had called in yet another favor. Just as they reached the entrance, the door opened, and a security guard gave them a nod and stepped aside. Cash took the lead inside with Jace bringing up the rear. After descending some stairs, they made their way to the service elevator, which stood open and waiting, just as Clayton had said it would be. The three of them climbed inside as Cooper pressed the button for the basement. The ride down was silent as they pulled out their night-vision goggles and set them atop their heads.

The elevator had just reached the bottom when they heard static over the COMs in their ears. Then Brice's voice reached them. "Stingray."

"Heard," Cooper replied, noting that the second team had landed.

The elevator door opened, and the three of them filed out quietly, moving to the left and down a long corridor to an exit. Jace exchanged looks with Cash and Cooper before opening the door wide enough to slip through. Once outside, they pressed themselves against the building in the shadows.

Jace checked his watch as he waited to execute the

next part of their plan. They had sixteen seconds before the streetlights and power to all the surrounding buildings were set to blink out, giving them time to get across the street and into more shadows without being seen—all thanks to Cash and his connections.

"Now," Cash said.

As one, they pulled down their night vision goggles the same instant the lights went out. They rushed across the deserted street and into an alley, covering ground quickly. With their hands on their weapons, they reached the edge of the next building. Cooper had taken point and held up a fist as he came to a stop and took a knee to peer around the corner. He jerked back almost instantly.

A moment later, a car drove past. Jace became impatient when they remained there. He knew full well that this was a busier street, but that didn't matter when he wanted to get to Taryn. Jace looked ahead to see another grid of lights blink out, giving them cover for as long as possible as they approached Boyd's complex.

Finally, Cooper got to his feet and motioned for them. The warehouses were only half a mile away, and their route was covered for the most part. Still, Jace was on edge. Boyd wasn't a stupid man. He would have people watching the area, especially since he knew that Taryn had been with friends. And if Boyd knew that, then he also knew exactly who Jace was. So, yes, Boyd would be prepared for them. Jace didn't have a doubt in the world.

Jace and the others navigated around building after building, halting only when people or cars passed. With each step Jace got closer to Taryn, his mind became clearer and clearer. It had been a long time since he had been on such a mission. The last one had ended in him being captured by enemy forces, who held him for three months. If any of them were caught this time, there would be no capture. There would only be an execution. So much hinged on their carefully thought-out plan going right.

"Wildcat," Jace said into the COMs when they reached the complex and he removed his goggles.

Several tense seconds passed in silence before Caleb answered with, "Wildcat."

Jace stared at the tall fence around the block and the several warehouses within. Lights were everywhere, ensuring there wasn't a single section of darkness. Guard houses stood at each of the five entrances, and the guards were heavily armed and ex-military. They had cameras posted everywhere, watching the perimeter of the fence.

Cash turned his arm to stare down at his forearm and the small burner phone strapped there. He stared at the blank screen as they all waited.

"Cash," Cooper whispered.

Without looking up, Cash said, "He'll come through. Lane is a master."

Jace kept a lookout from their hiding spot. Lane was another of Cash's employees and could hack into just about anything. Lane's look into the area had alerted them of the many cameras Boyd had installed. And it was Lane who'd promised to disable the cameras to allow them—as well as the other team—access into the compound.

"Done," Cash said and rushed the fence when he got a text from Lane, confirming that he had looped a five-second recording of the area to trick anyone watching the feed.

Cooper and Jace were right behind him. Within seconds, they'd cut through the fence and were inside.

"Firebird," Cooper whispered over the COMs.

A second later, Caleb replied that they were also inside.

The building closest to Jace and his team was a warehouse Taryn had never been in. Cash was the first to enter. He came to a stop and waved Jace and Cooper inside when it was clear. Cash then motioned that he was headed upstairs, leaving Cooper and Jace to take the bottom floor.

They were looking through a room, checking the various crates, when Jace looked up to find a man in the room with a weapon pointed at Cooper. Without hesitation, Jace fired, hitting the man square in the forehead. The guard fell without a sound, but the pop of Jace's M4 was deafening in the silence.

"Got one," Cooper whispered in the COMs to alert the rest of their team.

Neither Cooper nor Jace moved as they listened for anyone approaching. When several moments passed without another gunman appearing, they hurried from the room to the next one. They were nearly finished with their search of the bottom floor when they heard Cash fire his weapon.

"Cash?" Jace asked through the COMs.

Seconds passed in silence before a crackle came over the line, and Cash replied, "I'm good. Came upon a guard. Floor is clear."

"Down here, as well." Jace then asked, "Myles?"

Myles's voice came through the line. "We're good. Three more are down. Moving on to the next building."

Jace motioned to his team as they headed to the next

warehouse. They repeated the entire process, removing more of Boyd's guards. Only one building remained between Jace and Taryn. When they reached it, Jace was the first one in.

"Eldorado," Cooper said into the COMs.

Jace took the stairs and went to the second floor. He glanced out the window and saw the car Taryn had driven parked nearby. His gaze swept the area, searching for her. The moment his eyes landed on her, the band around his chest loosened. Taryn stood talking to Boyd and four other men. Jace wished he could hear what was said, but the team knew there was no way she'd get in wearing a wire.

A grunt sounded behind him. Jace whirled to find a guard on the floor with a knife sticking out of his back. Jace looked at the doorway and saw Cash there. Cash gave a nod, and Jace returned it. He glanced down at the dead man and realized that he had come close to being killed because he had been so worried about Taryn. If this mission was to be a success, he had to set aside emotion. He had to focus on the plan and what needed to be done.

Cash walked to the dead guard and removed his knife from the body. He wiped it on the dead man and slipped it back into its sheath. "We've got your back."

"Thank you," Jace replied.

Cash flashed him a grin. "Let's go get your woman and her sister."

"Guards are on the roof of your building," Caleb said over the COMs.

Cash glanced upward. "I got this."

Jace pressed the COMs button and said, "Likely on yours, as well."

"Myles is headed up there now," Caleb answered.

Jace moved from room to room, keeping an eye on Taryn and Boyd. He gripped his M4 tightly, wanting nothing more than to put a bullet between Boyd's eyes for everything he had done to Taryn and Payton. But he couldn't do anything until they brought Payton out. Jace knew Taryn had to tread carefully in how she pushed Boyd. And everything hinged on Taryn being allowed to see her sister.

What Jace hadn't told Taryn was that if Payton wasn't brought out, he was still getting Taryn away from this nightmare. They didn't want a gunfight in the middle of the city, but if that's what had to happen to get Taryn free and find Payton, then that's what everyone was prepared to do.

"Clear," Myles said through the COMs. "There are two snipers atop other buildings at nine and one o'clock. Their rifles are trained on Taryn."

Jace drew in a deep breath and waited for Cash to tell them that he had taken out the guard on their roof. He didn't have to wait long.

Cash was out of breath when his voice filled the COMs. "Guard is down. I also see the snipers."

"Eldorado," Brice said.

Now that Jace knew the second team was in position, he quickly found his spot and sighted his rifle on Boyd. Everyone was in place. Jace's heart slammed against his ribs. He took a deep breath and shoved all emotion out of the way as he fell back on his training. He looked through the scope at Boyd, who sneered at Taryn.

Jace swiveled the rifle to the left and saw a tall man with black hair and dark brown eyes standing beside Boyd. He didn't see a weapon, but that didn't mean the guy didn't have one. Jace knew that Boyd wouldn't let anyone near him who wasn't capable of protecting him.

Next, Jace looked at the other three guards, all armed, each of them looking around the complex as if they expected an attack.

"I've got the bastard locked in," Myles said through the COMs.

Brice snorted. "We all do."

"Jace?" Cooper asked, wanting to know if he wanted one of them to end Boyd.

Jace's finger curved around the trigger. He briefly thought about taking Boyd out right then. It would be so easy. The son of a bitch was just standing there like he didn't have a care in the world. He was responsible for putting Taryn through hell. For that, Boyd deserved to be wiped from this Earth.

"Jace?" Cash whispered through the COMs.

Jace blinked, remembering that he was no longer in the military and taking orders. "We keep to the plan until we know for certain Boyd isn't bringing out Payton."

They had talked in depth about what would happen if there was a firefight in the middle of the city. Jace was prepared for the consequences. While they had an escape plan that would, hopefully, get them out before the authorities arrived, Jace wouldn't let any of them be detained.

This was something he'd asked for help with. This was his mission, and he would willingly take the fall for everyone.

Chapter 25

Eight hundred meters away, Ryan lay on his stomach and stared through the scope of his sniper rifle as he watched the two teams infiltrate the compound and get into position. They didn't know he was there. No one did. He was too far away for anyone to even know he was watching, and that's just how he wanted it.

This was the only way Ryan could be there for his friends and Brick without betraying his position as chief of police. It wasn't exactly noble, but it was the best compromise he could come up with. He didn't have a spotter, but that was fine. And, hopefully, they wouldn't even need him.

He thought of his badge in his back pocket and knew that if things went sideways and he was caught, he would lose his position. While Ryan loved being a cop, he wouldn't have been able to live with himself if he hadn't come to help. And if that meant he got fired, then so be it. He would find another job somewhere. At least his conscience would be clear.

Ryan had chosen the building because of its location,

but also because it gave him a vantage point where he could look down upon the entire compound. The fact that he'd used his badge to get into the structure and onto the roof was something he had done before. Now, he used the scope to look down at Taryn, Boyd, and Brick as well as the three other guards.

It didn't take Ryan long to find a member of Jace's team atop an adjacent roof. Cash, also wearing all black, was on another roof. Two teams. A good move. One he would've made, as well. Then again, all of them were highly trained ex-military with plenty of experience.

"None of my friends are going to die today," he whispered. Then he moved the scope and looked at Brick. "And neither is my cousin."

Clayton sat at his desk, listening to the COMs with his hands steepled. Abby paced the office, twisting her hands nervously. He didn't bother to tell her to sit down. Her brothers were out there. And though Cooper and Jace weren't blood, they were part of their unit, which meant whoever they gave their hearts to was also part of their ever-growing family.

Abby paused and swung to face him, her big blue eyes meeting his. "They have to pull this off."

"They will. Look what they've done before."

"It wasn't this." She sank onto the sofa and dropped her head into her hands. "I knew they put their lives on the line in the military. It was easier then because I didn't know about their missions and wasn't able to listen in."

Clayton rose and walked to his wife. He sat beside her and put an arm around her as he pulled her against him. "They're good at what they do. I wish I was younger. If I were, I'd be right there with them."

"I know. Part of me wishes you were there to look out for them, but then again, I'm glad you're here." She sniffed. "We've been so lucky. All of us. The closest we came to losing anyone was when Jace was knocked on the head, and Cooper was locked in the building rigged to blow. I'm worried we've run out of luck."

He rubbed his hand up and down her arm. "Do you really think I'd send any of them out there without some kind of backup? Doc is on standby, ready and willing to use his chopper however and whenever necessary."

"Doc is only one man. I don't mean to sound ungrateful, but they need more."

"They have it."

Abby's head jerked to him. "What?" she asked breathlessly.

"I said I called in some favors. What I didn't say was who those requests went out to."

"Honey, please don't keep me in suspense."

"A select group of retired SEALs is in and around the Dallas/Fort Worth area. They're nearby. The moment they hear from me, they'll move in to help the boys."

"Oh, thank God," Abby said as she dropped her forehead against him.

He gave her a squeeze. "They're my family, too. If I can't be there to help them, I'm going to make damn sure someone is."

"I know." She lifted her head. "Thank you."

"Thank me when all of this is over. I just hope it's enough."

Abby released a deep breath. "I wish Ryan and Danny were involved. I know why they aren't, but it doesn't seem right."

"You didn't see Taryn's face. If Jace hadn't backed her up on not telling the authorities, she would've left."

"I realize that. And Jace never would've seen her again. But I also know Danny."

Clayton frowned. "He wouldn't call it in to anyone. He doesn't know when or where. Besides, he wouldn't put his friends in a situation to be arrested."

Abby shook her head. "I've been so worried about them dying that I hadn't thought about them being arrested. Thank goodness we know a good lawyer. Leslie Ross handled Skylar's situation perfectly. She's great at her job, as well."

"Let's not call Leslie just yet," he cautioned.

They looked toward the speaker on his desk when the word *Eldorado* came through. It was the final code, letting both teams—as well as Clayton—know that they were in place and ready. All they were waiting on now was Payton.

Clayton rose and walked to his desk. He glanced up to see Abby pacing the office again. For the first time, he understood what it was for his commanding officers to be at the command center while he and his team were on missions. Frankly, he'd much rather be out in the field. Listening and waiting were worse than being in the midst of the action.

Chapter 26

"When am I going to get to see my sister?" Taryn pressed as she stood before Boyd, fast losing patience. Especially knowing that Jace and his friends were likely in place and waiting to make a move. It was all Taryn could do to stay calm and not tell Boyd how she really felt.

After a beat of silence, Boyd grinned at her. "Right on time, as usual. Something should be said for how punctual you are, Taryn."

Taryn's gaze swung to Brick for a heartbeat. Boyd's bodyguard and personal bulldog held her gaze, and she wondered just what Brick had reported. Taryn returned her attention to Boyd. "I told you I'd be here with the money."

Boyd chuckled. "So you did. Why don't you show it to me?"

"We had a deal. Where's my sister?"

Boyd quirked a brow. "You talk to me as if we're equals, when that's far from the truth. I'm in charge.

You do what I say, when I say it. I thought you understood that."

"I understand it fine. I've done everything you've requested and more. The only thing I asked of you was to see my sister."

"You've seen her," he said without hesitation.

Taryn looked at the concrete as she drew in a steadying breath. "That was six months ago. Before that, it was nine months. And I've only seen her through a window. I'd like to talk to her, see her as close as you and I are now."

"And why would I do that?"

It was difficult for her to remain levelheaded when she hated someone so much. It didn't help that Boyd seemed to know exactly what to say to ratchet up her anger even more. "Because we had a deal. Because I held up my end of the bargain and brought five hundred thousand dollars as promised. Because I've made you a ton of money."

He gave her a look of surprise. "I'm not sure I like your attitude."

"What do you expect?" she asked, throwing up her hands before they slapped back down against her legs. "You killed my father and brother, and you took Payton away. She's all I have left. I'm only asking to talk to her before we move forward with the deal."

"Bring me the money," Boyd demanded.

Taryn briefly thought about refusing. But she knew it wouldn't get her anywhere. Once more, Boyd had put her in a position of helplessness. But he didn't know about Jace and the others.

Still, Taryn needed Payton. She wasn't stupid. She knew that Jace would go through with the plan whether Payton was there or not. He wouldn't leave her behind.

Taryn loved him for that. But she couldn't leave without her sister.

Taryn turned on her heel and walked to the car. She opened the back seat and pulled out the black bag. It was heavy as she carried it to Boyd and tossed it at his feet.

"Open it," he ordered her.

She froze, fury filling her to the point she thought she might explode. Her time of bowing to Boyd's every whim was almost over. She just had to remain calm a little longer. All she needed was Payton.

When she didn't immediately move, Boyd repeated, "Open it."

Taryn bit her tongue to keep from smarting off. She then walked to the bag and bent to unzip it. When it was open, she straightened and looked at him, waiting for his next order.

Boyd's lips curved into a cocky smile that made her want to knee him in the balls. He didn't even look at the money inside the bag. "I still can't believe you came back. You had a chance to escape, but you didn't. That means you like working for me."

"I fucking hate you. I've done everything I had to in order to stay alive and keep my sister alive. I'm here for her."

Boyd started chuckling. "Oh, the irony."

Taryn frowned and glanced at Brick, but the bodyguard's gaze was on something behind her. "What's that supposed to mean?" Taryn asked Boyd.

"This is going to be priceless," Boyd replied.

Taryn was growing more and more confused by the second. The approaching sound of high heels on concrete got her attention. Taryn found her gaze drawn to Brick once more. His black brows were drawn together in a slight frown. But it was Boyd's arrogant smirk that made her blood run cold.

Taryn wanted to turn around and see who it was, but she made herself remain still. The closer the footsteps came, the wider Boyd's smile got. If Taryn hadn't looked at Brick, she wouldn't have seen his face go blank as if he were wiping all expression from his visage. She didn't get a chance to think about that for long as she saw movement out of the corner of her eye.

She turned her head to see who it was. At the sight of her beautiful sister, Taryn's heart leapt. She took in Payton's body-hugging bright blue dress, the large diamonds in her ears and on her fingers, and her blue heels. The smile Taryn had slipped when Payton didn't even look her way as she walked to Boyd and put her arm around him. Taryn's gaze moved from Payton to Boyd and back to her sister.

"She hasn't figured it out, sweetheart," Boyd told Payton.

Payton rolled her large brown eyes that were so like their mother's. "Taryn always did think she was the smartest person in the room. It's nice to finally put her in her place."

Taryn couldn't breathe. The world spun uncontrollably around her. She wasn't sure which way was up and which was down. This had to be some kind of nightmare. She'd wake up any moment. She'd wake up.

Wake up!

Taryn squeezed her eyes closed and then reopened them. Still, Payton stood beside Boyd, her arm around his waist. Maybe this was some trick Payton pulled to fool Boyd into letting his guard down. Yes. That had to be it. "Tell me what's going on."

"Just like Taryn. Always demanding," Payton stated in a voice filled with hatred.

Boyd couldn't contain his glee as he smiled at Taryn. "I've been waiting for this moment for years. I thought you would've figured it out by now, but you couldn't get it out of your head that you were supposed to save your sister. You should've thought about yourself. I even gave you a chance."

"I told you she'd come back with the money," Payton said with a laugh that was as cold as the Arctic. "We should've demanded more."

Taryn's blood ran like ice as uncertainty and rage filled her. The woman standing before her looked like her sister, but Payton would never act like this. Would she? "Payton. Wh-what are you doing?"

"I had to get free of you," her sister spat, resentment and ire contorting her features. "You were so fucking controlling, always telling me what I could and couldn't do."

"I-I was taking care of you."

"You weren't Mom!"

Taryn jerked as if slapped. She didn't recognize the woman in front of her. This wasn't her sweet younger sister, who stayed up to watch scary movies with her, shopped with her, and baked sweets. This woman was selfish. She was . . . malicious.

Boyd turned his head to Payton and gazed at her as if she were his everything. "It was Payton's idea. Everything you've endured. She has the most brilliant mind I've ever encountered. There has never been anyone as well matched to me as her."

Payton smiled lovingly up at Boyd and touched his cheek before kissing him.

Taryn swallowed the bile that rose in her throat as her brain comprehended what Boyd had just shared. "What?"

Payton snapped her gaze back to Taryn, hatred burning in her eyes so brightly that Taryn was surprised she didn't fry to a crisp. "You wouldn't shut up about moving in with you. I told you over and over that I wanted to be on my own, but you wouldn't listen. I didn't need you. Dad and Ben didn't need you. But you had to control everyone. Why do you think Ben started doing drugs with Dad? Because you were constantly on his case."

"To do something with his life and not get caught up in the never-ending shit that was Dad's life," Taryn retorted, as she became enraged. "You call that controlling. I call it looking out for my brother. I wanted him to be happy, to have a life."

"And look what you did to him."

Taryn snorted as she raked her gaze over Payton. She thought of all the years she had been enslaved to Boyd for her sister's sake. And the entire time, Payton had been living it up, enjoying life. All while Taryn prayed that she got through each day without being killed and thinking of ways to free her and Payton. So many wasted years. "You want to put his death on me? That's rich. I'm not the one who has to carry that weight. You are. That's not on me. He followed Dad down the drug-addiction path." Then it hit Taryn. All of it. And she understood what loathing and disgust truly were. "Boyd said all of this was your fault. I always wondered how Dad and Ben could afford the cocaine. It came from you, didn't it?"

Payton smiled in response.

Taryn was caught between wanting to cry and

scream. "You got Ben and Dad started selling for Boyd. You knew they wouldn't be able to help themselves, and you made sure they didn't tell me. Then you got Boyd to come in and take all of us."

"About time you pieced it together," Boyd told her.

But that didn't make Taryn feel any better. She didn't take her eyes off Payton, nor did she think about Brick or the other armed men near her. "All you had to do was leave. Why did you have to pull all of us into this"—she looked around as her animosity grew— "this fucking hellhole!"

"Because it amused me," Payton replied with a smile.

Taryn swallowed, realizing then that Payton had been lying to everyone for years. The sweet sister act had been just that, an act. Taryn fought back tears as she thought about her father, who had been lost when her mother died. Of Ben, who had tried to be the dutiful son and brother but was so easily swayed. Taryn couldn't believe that she had been blind to it all. "You're the one who got Dad hooked on drugs after Mom died. You pushed him down that path."

"It was so easy," Payton said with a shrug. "Too easy. I actually thought it would be more difficult. There were times I thought you'd figure it out, but you were too caught up with Jace to notice. Even when I got Ben hooked on drugs, I thought you'd finally piece it together, but you didn't. Instead, you started poking into my life, wanting the two of us to move out together. I had Dad and Ben right where I wanted them. The only one in the way was you. I thought you'd move in with Jace, but you stayed and continued messing with my plans."

Taryn shook her head in amazement and confusion. "You ruined all our lives."

"You had a chance to get free, but I knew if the rest of us disappeared, you'd come looking. So, I told Boyd that you had to come, as well. He didn't want to include you at first, but then I told him you'd do anything for your family."

"I would have. I *did*," Taryn bit out, her hands fisting with her fury.

Payton laughed and rolled her eyes again. "Even now, you came back. Not that you would've gotten far had you tried to leave. I made sure you were followed closely. I know everything, big sis. Including the fact that you got married this morning."

Boyd's eyes widened as he smiled. "And we both know that Jace wouldn't allow you to return without a plan to get you back. Where is he?"

Taryn's stomach dropped to her feet like a rock. This was her worst fear. She couldn't lose Jace. She wouldn't. Not to her deranged sister and her boyfriend. "I don't know."

"But he's here," Payton said as she took a few steps closer to Taryn. "Isn't he?"

"You expect me to answer that after all you've done to me? To Dad? To Ben?"

Payton crossed her arms over her chest and gave Taryn a knowing look, complete with a sardonic smile. "I know you will."

"No," Taryn said with a shake of her head. "You purposefully ruined Dad's life. He could've found some peace after Mom's death, but you made sure that didn't happen. Then you put Ben on that same path simply to see if you could. Instead of going out on your own, you put the three of us into servitude, beholden to a maniac. He killed Dad and Ben, Payton. Did you know that?"

"Of course. I'm the one who told Boyd to do it. I

also made sure to put you and me in a dire situation so you'd think we were in danger. Then I told Boyd to take me away from you. I knew you'd do absolutely anything he wanted after that." Payton's cocky smile said it all. "Because you wanted to *save me*."

And she had. Taryn couldn't believe she hadn't seen the truth before now. Was Payton that good of a liar? Or was Taryn simply that blind? That was something she'd have to debate later. Right now, she was more concerned with getting out with her life. And given the way Payton looked at her, Taryn wasn't sure that would happen. Not to mention, she had no way of alerting Jace to the fact that things had changed. All she could hope for was that they witnessed what was going on.

Payton held out a hand to Boyd, who put a pistol in it. Her sister then turned and pointed the gun at Taryn's head.

Taryn stared into her sister's psychopathic eyes and lifted her chin. "You must hate me a great deal to want to kill me."

"You've given me no choice. I know Jace and his buddies. They'll be here soon for you. When they arrive, all they'll find is your body. But don't worry, I've got a trap set for them. They'll be framed for your murder. You'll be dead, Jace and his friends will be in jail, and Boyd and I will get away to continue building our empire."

Boyd gazed adoringly at Payton. "No one can come up with a plan like my beautiful girl."

Taryn smiled then. She struggled not to laugh as a calmness washed over her. Now she understood why Jace had told her to go over the plans again and again. She had forgotten them for a moment, but they filled her mind once more, and she couldn't help but grin.

Because if there was one thing she could depend on, it was Jace.

Payton's eyes narrowed into dangerous slits. "What's so funny?"

"The fact that you think you've thought of everything."

"I have," Payton stated.

Taryn shook her head. "Hate to break it to you, but you haven't."

Boyd's smile disappeared as he moved to stand beside Payton. He glared at Taryn. "Tell us what you mean."

She shrugged and wiggled her fingers, a sign to Jace and the others that it was time. Taryn then slapped Payton's hand away at the same time she leaned to the side. The gun went off, the sound deafening Taryn in one ear. Gunshots erupted from the guards next to Boyd as he grabbed Payton and tried to pull her to him.

Taryn held a hand to her ear and started turning away just as Payton pulled the trigger again. Taryn jerked in surprise, and a bellow of pain ripped from her when the bullet entered her shoulder.

Chapter 27

The moment Jace saw that Payton wasn't a prisoner, he notified the others that he was shifting positions. He rushed down the stairs to the bottom floor in an effort to get closer to Taryn. His heart hammered erratically in his chest because he knew that things were about to hit the fan.

They had imagined all sorts of scenarios, but the one option they hadn't taken into consideration was that Payton was working *with* Boyd. And while none of them could hear what was said between Taryn, Boyd, and Payton, Jace saw the surprise and wrath on Taryn's face through his scope, as well as Payton cuddling up to Boyd. That's all he needed to realize what was going on.

He reached the window and looked through the scope to find Payton with a gun trained on Taryn. He saw Taryn wiggle her fingers, but Jace couldn't get a clean shot at Payton from his current position. He pressed the button on his COMs and told the others, "Shoot Payton!"

Before he could finish the sentence, Payton's gun went off. Jace's heart stopped. "Noooooo!" he bellowed and began shooting the guards near Taryn.

When he saw Taryn go down to one knee, Jace lowered his gun and ran to the exit. He kicked it open and lifted the rifle to his shoulder once more. Men poured out from everywhere as gunfire erupted from all angles. He aimed at Payton, but before he could get off a shot, the unmistakable sound of a sniper rifle sounded, and the bullet hit Payton center mass. She went down instantly.

Jace had no idea who or where the shooter was or why they had shot Payton, but he was glad for it. He took out two more guards as he made his way to Taryn. When Jace had nearly reached her, he found Boyd in his scope, right as the bastard rushed into a building. Immediately behind Boyd was the tall, black-haired man who had stood beside Boyd. Except this time, he had a knife in hand.

Another loud crack sounded just as Jace turned to find a guard getting ready to fire at him. The guard's head snapped back with the force of the sniper round before he slumped to the ground. In Jace's ear, he heard the other members of the team asking who the sniper was. No one had spotted the shooter yet.

It felt like an eternity before Jace got to Taryn. He saw the blood as it soaked her shirt and ran down her arm. When she spotted him, tears filled her eyes. Jace grabbed her good arm and helped her to her feet, moving her next to the vehicle to help shield them from oncoming bullets.

"You're clear, Jace!" Brice shouted over the COMs. "Come toward us."

Jace caught Taryn's gaze. "We've got to make a run for it. Can you do it?"

"Yes," she said as she held her wounded arm against her body.

Jace checked to make sure all was good, then gave her a nod. They took off toward the warehouse. Jace fired two shots when a guard stepped in front of him. The same man was hit three more times, his body jerking with each strike of the bullets. Jace jumped over the guard's prone body on the way to the building.

The moment he had Taryn inside, he motioned for her to get behind a stack of crates to take cover from the bullets flying at them. Jace used a broken window near him to sight in targets and fire. Then, as quickly as it had started, the battle was finished. The sound of sirens filled the air when the gunfire ceased.

"Time to leave," Cooper said over the COMs.

Jace took one last look around to make sure no more of Boyd's men were moving. Many were dead on the ground, but a few had run off when they realized that they were losing. Unfortunately, Boyd was also gone. Jace spun and went to Taryn to check on her wound.

She sat with her back against the crates, holding her arm tightly against her side with her eyes closed. When he kneeled beside her, her lids lifted, and her beautiful green eyes met his. She smiled despite the pain that was evident in her shallow breathing.

"You did good," he told her.

She licked her lips and shook her head. "You're being kind."

Myles came up beside him then. He nodded at Taryn. "I'm Myles."

"He's a friend," Jace told her. "And a hell of a good medic."

It killed Jace to see Taryn wince when Myles examined her shoulder. Jace knew how lucky she was to be alive. If she hadn't pushed the gun Payton held at her away, if Taryn hadn't turned and tried to leave, things could be much, much worse.

"I don't think the bullet hit the bone. I can't be sure, though, until we get to a hospital," Myles told them.

Caleb walked up with Brice then. "We're not going to get that chance if we don't bug out of here now."

"Go," Jace told them. "Meet up with Cooper and Cash and get out of here."

There was a loud snort as Cooper and Cash walked into the room. "Like we'd do that."

"There's no need for everyone to go to jail," Taryn said. Her gaze landed on Jace. "Leave. All of you."

Jace shot her a smile. "I'm not going anywhere."

"Stubborn," she said with a laugh.

Brice slung his rifle over his shoulder. "We recently learned how hard Jace's head really is. Stubborn doesn't even begin to define him."

Jace got to his feet and looked at his friends. "What are y'all doing? Get out of here. There's still time."

"No," Cash said. "We're going to ride this out. Whatever happens."

Jace couldn't believe them. Then again, if he were in their shoes, he'd likely be saying the same thing. He knew how lucky he was to have such people in his life, but he couldn't let them sacrifice their lives like this. "Brice, you have a wife and a son. Go home to them. Caleb, Cooper, your wives are waiting for your return."

"Don't try that bullshit with me," Myles said.

Cash shot Jace a dry look. "I'm not going anywhere, so don't waste your breath."

"Please," Taryn said as she looked at the faces of the men who had helped her. "Jace is right. Go home to your families. And take Jace with you."

"What?" he asked as his head snapped to her.

She smiled up at him, then put her fingers over his lips to silence him. "I love you more than anything. You've gotten me out of a tough situation. Let me do the same for you."

"No." Jace couldn't believe she was even saying this.

Cash set his rifle on the floor beside him and jerked his chin to the approaching lights coming through the broken windows. "Looks like it's too late anyway. We're about to be surrounded."

"Keep pressure on her wound," Myles said as he quickly tossed aside his M4 and got to his feet to face the door.

Jace followed everyone else and set down his weapons. He had just put his hands on Taryn's wound when men busted through the door with guns drawn and lights shining in Jace's and the other's eyes.

"We're unarmed," Cooper said.

Jace held Taryn's gaze as he hollered, "And we have someone who needs medical attention."

"Hands in the air!" someone shouted.

With guns aimed at them, Jace had no choice but to do as commanded. His hands were covered with Taryn's blood. With the dark room and the lights blinding them, Jace could only make out the forms of the men swarming into the room. He heard more moving about the building. Suddenly, he was hauled to his feet and pulled away from Taryn.

He immediately elbowed the man who had grabbed

him and tried to get back to Taryn. She reached out her hand and yelled something he couldn't make out. The next thing Jace knew, he was being hauled back while his team yelled at the authorities.

"Take it easy," Cash whispered in his ear.

Jace relaxed when he realized it was Cash who had him. Once that happened, the tension in the room eased. They lowered their arms, and the men with guns took their fingers off the triggers.

"Damn. Y'all are intense."

Their heads turned at the sound of the new voice. With the flick of a switch, the room was suddenly bathed in light. Jace blinked as his eyes adjusted. He saw a tall, solidly built man walking toward them with a black windbreaker on. He had short, dark hair graying at his temples. The man's light brown gaze moved over each of them until he saw Taryn.

The man then shouted for a medic. Jace breathed a sigh of relief when they arrived. But that quickly dissolved when Taryn was helped to her feet and led from the room. Her gaze sought his, and when Jace tried to go to her again, the man stepped in front of him.

"You're Jace Wilder."

Jace clenched his hands and glanced at the door through which Taryn had just disappeared. "I am."

The man grinned. He said each of their names, his gaze landing on them one at a time.

Cooper crossed his arms over his chest. "And you are?"

"Bobby Flannigan. I'm part of the FBI office of Fort Worth. Seems you boys have a lot of friends in high places."

Caleb released a long breath. "Comes with the territory, as I'm sure you know."

Bobby nodded his head. "That I do." He glanced at his men. "Lower your weapons. Finish checking the buildings for more of Walters's men."

No one said anything until the armed men were gone, leaving only their group and Bobby. Jace wanted to ask so much, but he didn't want to step wrong in this situation. He didn't know who had called in the FBI. The fact that Flannigan had mentioned those in high places made Jace think a couple of people might have put calls in on their behalf.

Bobby sighed loudly and rocked back on his heels. He wore a grin that made him appear happy-go-lucky, but no one in the room was fooled by it. They all recognized that Bobby Flannigan wasn't a man they should cross.

"Well, we've certainly got ourselves quite the pickle," Bobby said into the silence.

Jace took a step forward. "This is my fault. No one else's. They came to help after everything was all over."

Bobby's gaze swung to him. "Is that right?"

"He's lying," Cooper said. "I was here."

Caleb nodded. "Me, too."

"And me," Cash said.

Brice flashed a grin. "Yep. I was here."

Bobby looked at Myles. "What about you?"

"Of course, I was here," Myles replied with a smile.

Jace wanted to kick all of them. He was trying to get them back to their families, but they were being stubborn. Just as he would be in their places.

The FBI agent scratched his eyebrow. "Do any of you know how long we've had Boyd Walters under surveillance?"

"This couldn't wait," Jace said.

"So I've been told." Bobby glanced at the ceiling. "Things could've gotten out of control here. I don't need to tell any of you that. Based on your military records, you all know exactly how bad things can get. Which is why I can't believe you took matters into your own hands."

Cash shrugged. "When the facts showed that Boyd had connections to branches of the government, the judicial system, and law enforcement, we were left with very few options. Taryn's life was at stake. We believed her sister was being kept under duress, as well."

"Taryn and her family were kidnapped in the middle of the night years ago," Jace said. "She watched her father and brother be murdered right before her eyes. You're damn right we were going to help."

"I appreciate the candor. Let me give you some in return." The agent stepped over a rifle on the floor and leaned against a crate. "If it were up to me, I'd have all of you in cuffs. Anyone thinking they can take the law into their own hands causes more problems than it solves. But I don't get a say in this. I've been ordered to let you go."

Myles frowned, confusion evident on his face. "What?"

"You heard me," Bobby stated. "Get your weapons and go home."

One by one, they gathered their guns and knives and walked out of the room until only Jace and Bobby remained. Jace bent to retrieve his rifle and slung the strap over his shoulder as he looked at the Fed. "Where is Taryn?"

"We're going to need a statement from her after she's been tended to by a medical professional."

"She's my wife. Where is she?"

Bobby blew out a breath and pushed away from the crate. "You're a smart man, Jace. Things have gone your way tonight. Don't push it."

"I'm not leaving without my wife," he stated emphatically.

Chapter 28

Ryan watched through the sniper scope as police, black SUVs, and helicopters swarmed Boyd's compound. He wasn't sure if his friends were all right or not. He had helped them out as much as he could, but it was time for him to go.

Choppers moved over the area with spotlights, looking for anyone trying to escape. He moved back onto his knees and lifted his rifle to put it away when one of the spotlights landed on him. Ryan rolled into the darkness, holding his weapon tightly against him. The helicopter blades drowned out all noise.

Then the spotlight found him again. Ryan lay on his back, looking up at the chopper. He had known this might happen. With a sigh, he carefully set aside his rifle and held up his hands. He didn't have long to wait before someone appeared.

"Keep your hands where I can see them!"

"I'm a cop!" Ryan shouted over the whirl of the helicopter. "My badge is in my pocket."

Suddenly, men were all around him. They flipped

him roughly onto his stomach and patted him down after his hands were cuffed. When they reached his back pocket, they pulled out his wallet. Ryan waited, wondering if they would let him go because he was a police officer. Or arrest him for being out of his jurisdiction with a sniper rifle atop a building.

Seconds ticked by. Just when he thought he was done for, the spotlight on him vanished, and the chopper flew away. Someone uncuffed him and helped him to his feet. When he turned around, Ryan found himself looking at a familiar face.

"Danny?" he asked in shock.

Danny motioned over his shoulder with his thumb. "I happen to know a division head for the Rangers up here. I had a feeling you might help."

"I . . . Why didn't you tell me you were coming?"

"It's not easy when you have friends like ours, and they get into situations like these. We have to toe the line of our positions, and yet we want to help."

Ryan swallowed, trying to take it all in. "How did you know it was Boyd?"

"It took some doing. I understood Taryn's position in not wanting our help, so I was careful. I ran the plates for the car she was driving. Turned out, they were registered to one of Boyd's legal businesses. I kept tabs on everyone, and the minute Taryn left town, I came up here."

"To the Rangers?" Ryan asked as he glanced at the men in cowboy hats standing behind Danny.

Danny chuckled. "Clayton isn't the only one with connections. How did you find out?"

Ryan glanced at the ground, wishing he could tell his friend the truth.

"I see," Danny said with a nod. "I know that look. You got information, but you can't say from who."

"I wish I could."

"You don't need to explain anything to me, of all people," Danny said with a grin.

Ryan glanced behind him to where the authorities were gathered. "What do you know about our friends and Taryn? I saw she was injured."

"She'll live. She's being taken to the hospital, and the Feds want a statement from her."

"And the others?"

Danny had a smile on his face. "Being let go to return home."

Ryan was flabbergasted. "Are you serious?"

"You're not being detained either," Danny pointed out.

Ryan chuckled and looked back at the buildings where the dead were being put into body bags. "They're one lucky group."

"I wish we would've spoken to each other about our plans. Things could've gone smoother."

"I can't believe no one was seriously injured or killed." Ryan ran a hand down his face. "Fuck. I can't believe we aren't being arrested."

Danny winced as he looked at Ryan. "Trust me, there are some noses bent out of joint right now. The best thing everyone can do is return to Clearview immediately."

"You don't have to tell me twice."

Abby let out a cry and rushed to Clayton when they received word that no one was being detained. Clayton squeezed his eyes shut, thankful that they had once more gotten out of a difficult situation with very little flack.

Taryn was injured, but it wasn't life-threatening. Payton was dead. As for Boyd, they were still waiting to hear about him. Clayton didn't think the worm could get away, but bastards like Boyd always managed to land on their feet, uncaring of who got hurt in the process.

"Everyone is coming home," Clayton told Abby. "Our family will be whole again."

She sniffed and nodded her head against him. "With a new member. I'm so excited that Jace and Taryn got married."

"We'll do something for them when they return, and Taryn feels up to it."

Abby leaned back and looked up at him, tears running down her face. "I honestly don't know how much more my heart can take. This might be the final straw."

He smiled and smoothed her hair away from her face. "Life is messy and cruel and merciless. We've got an amazing family, and people come into our lives when we can help them. I know you, Abby East, there's no way you'd refuse a friend in need, no matter how dangerous the situation."

"You know me too well," she said with a chuckle.

"It's one of the reasons I fell in love with you." He kissed her softly, then pulled her against him so he could wrap his arms around her. "Yet I also wonder how many more times we can rush into danger without someone getting seriously injured. Or worse, killed."

Abby sniffed again. "Let's hope that doesn't happen."

"Yeah. I'm keeping my fingers crossed that our children live very quiet lives."

But Clayton understood the odds. So did the others. Those odds meant nothing when someone you loved was in danger. There were still nights he woke in a panic when the nightmare of Abby being shot by the cattle rustlers returned. He had known that day that he would do absolutely anything for her, to keep her safe. Because of that, he would never say a word to Brice, Caleb, Cooper, Jace, Danny, Ryan—or his children—about not following their hearts.

Chapter 29

When she opened her eyes to the bright lights of the hospital, it took a moment for Taryn to remember where she was. Blue curtains were drawn around her, and she could hear others moving about, tending to patients on either side of her.

The pain in her shoulder had lessened so she could think clearer, but she could also tell that she had been given a heavy dose of painkillers. She was groggy, and though sleep pulled at her, she forced her eyes to remain open. The nightmare of the past years was over. So, why did she feel so paranoid? Was it because she had lived in fear for so long that she didn't know any other way to be?

No. She hadn't felt the panic and alarm as she did now when she had been with Jace. Taryn realized that a part of that was because she trusted Jace and knew that she was safe with him. But another part had known that when she was in Clearview, she was out of the fire, so to speak.

She shifted on the bed. Her limbs felt weighted

down. It was the morphine or whatever they had given her. Her gaze took in the feet and legs of the hospital staff moving about from where she could see them below the curtain. The moment someone came to check on her, she was going to ask for Jace.

Taryn swallowed, her mouth dry. The second she had been in FBI custody, she had been rushed to a hospital, and her wound seen to. Because of the location of the gunshot in her shoulder, they'd had to go in and get the bullet out, which meant that she had been under anesthesia. Taryn had no idea how long it had been since she last saw Jace, but she couldn't stop the rising tide of dread that grew with each breath she took.

Someone pushed the curtains open and a young, petite nurse with a blond pixie cut and a bright smile greeted her. "You're awake. I wasn't expecting that. How are you feeling?"

"Jace," Taryn said, barely able to get the word out. "I . . . need . . . him."

The nurse patted her hand. "I'm sure he'll be here shortly. You woke much earlier than normal. Take your time. We'll get Jace."

Taryn's eyes welled with tears as she tried to get the words past her lips, but they wouldn't form correctly. The nurse moved around her, checking her vitals, completely unaware that Taryn was drowning in fear.

"Rest, dear," the nurse said with a smile before she vanished through the curtains.

A tear fell down Taryn's face. It took great effort to lift her arm and wipe it away. So much for the nightmare being over. Then again, she hadn't known the full scope of what had been going on with Boyd until recently. She still couldn't comprehend what her sister had done.

That's when it hit Taryn that she had no more family. She was the last one. She couldn't even find it in her to be upset that Payton was dead. Her sister had made her choices, and she'd paid for them. After all, Payton had tried to kill Taryn. If she hadn't, Taryn wouldn't be lying in a hospital right now.

She closed her eyes for a heartbeat, and that's all it took for the pain meds to nearly pull her under once more. Something deep within her ran cold with dread, and some nameless fear surfaced. She clawed her way out of the darkness and opened her eyes. Somehow, she knew if she fell asleep, she wouldn't wake again. She didn't know how she knew it, only that she did.

"Jace," she whispered.

She knew him. He would be there with her if he could. Had he been arrested? Were they keeping him from her? She had no answers, and there was no one around to ask. Taryn was beginning to think that she wouldn't see anyone she recognized.

The hospital buzzed with activity. People moved around her constantly, but the curtains kept her separate from everyone. She was thankful for the small bit of kindness that allowed her to remain hidden. But at the same time, it prevented her from seeing anyone.

She tried to sit up. It was the wrong thing to do. Pain shot through her, and she wasn't able to stop herself from crying out. Instantly, the blond nurse was back.

"What are you doing?" she chastised Taryn. "You need to relax. Rest."

Taryn gripped the nurse's arm, holding her as tightly as she could, though Taryn wasn't sure it was barely more than a touch. "Jace. I need Jace. Emergency."

The nurse stared at her for a long minute. Then she nodded. "You're the one they brought in with the FBI?"

"Yes. Jace. Please, find him. It's important." Her speech was better, but still not normal.

The nurse glanced around her. Then she whispered, "I'll see what I can do."

Taryn released her and slumped back on the bed. Maybe the alarm she felt would dissipate now. Perhaps all she had to do was get someone to find Jace—if he was even in the hospital.

With that thought, her panic doubled. She wouldn't be able to wait for them to find Jace. She had to get out. Now.

"What the fuck do you mean I can't see her?" Jace demanded as he got up in Bobby's face.

The FBI agent kept calm. "Taryn's in recovery. When they say you can see her, they'll come get you."

"I need to see her now," Jace insisted.

Cooper walked over to him and put a hand on his arm. "We get it, but you need to take it easy. Everything is over."

Jace ran a hand down his face and squeezed his eyes shut for a moment. The sight of Taryn wounded, of her blood on his hands, had sent him spiraling into an abyss of fear that he hadn't been able to break free from—and wouldn't until he saw her again.

"Coop's right," Brice said. "She's going to be fine."

Jace opened his eyes and nodded at his friends. Then he looked at Bobby Flannigan and lifted his chin. Jace walked to the chairs in the waiting area and sank into one. He couldn't explain to anyone the driving need that hounded him to find Taryn.

To his surprise, Bobby came to sit beside him. The agent stretched out his legs and crossed his ankles as he folded his hands over his midsection. "You lost her once, and you didn't know what happened. Then you found her. She needed your help, and you were more than willing to lend it. Now that she's hurt, you're worried you'll lose her again. Does that about sum it up?"

"It does," Jace admitted without looking at Bobby.

"We have agents all over the hospital. Some under-cover. There's no safer place."

Jace slowly turned his head to Bobby. "Why are there agents here?"

"A precaution."

"For what?" Jace pushed, a knot forming in his stomach.

Bobby pressed his lips together, unable to meet Jace's gaze. "A precaution."

Fury exploded within Jace as it all came together. "You don't have Boyd."

"What?" Caleb asked, having overheard them.

Bobby glared at Jace before he looked at the others, who quickly converged on him. The agent hissed, "Keep your damn voices down."

"Tell us what we want to know," Cash stated.

The agent blew out a resigned breath. "No, we don't have Walters. He slipped away. The agent we had un-dercover was injured trying to apprehend him."

"And you're just telling us now?" Jace said as he got to his feet. "You've got two choices. You can take me to Taryn, or I'm going to rip apart anyone who stands between my wife and me."

Out of the corner of his eye, Jace saw Cooper, Myles, Cash, Brice, and Caleb join him.

"Fine," Bobby said as he threw up his hands. "I think you're all being ridiculous. Walters is getting as far from here as he can. He's not going to come here just to try to get to Taryn."

Myles snorted. "We'll be the judge of that."

Brice touched Jace's arm to get his attention. "Caleb, Myles, and I will go scout the entrances."

"I'll check this floor with Cash," Cooper said.

Bobby started to reach for his cell phone when Jace grabbed his hand and said, "I don't trust anyone in the FBI. You aren't talking to anyone, but you *are* coming with us."

They walked from the waiting room, splitting up to go in separate directions. Jace and Bobby made their way to the nurse's station.

Bobby showed his badge. "Show me to Taryn Hillman, please."

The nurse checked her computer. "She's still in recovery."

"This is FBI business," Jace said. "We need to see her immediately."

The nurse looked between the two of them before she nodded and rose from behind the counter. She walked around and motioned for them to follow her. The entire time they walked down the stark hall with its bright lights, all Jace could think about was all the different ways someone could get in—and out—without being noticed.

His heart thumped with dread, but he also held tightly to hope. He couldn't get Taryn back, only to lose her again. The bullet had missed any major organs or bone, leaving only a scar. Though in his opinion, that was enough after all she had suffered at Boyd's and Payton's hands.

But he didn't get to decide.

He should've listened to his instincts earlier when something had told him to remain with Taryn. It wasn't like he could go into the operating room with them, but that didn't matter. There was still danger out there, and he had just found out about it.

"Boyd won't get to her," Bobby said. "Not here."

Jace glanced at the FBI agent. "You'd better hope to hell he doesn't. I won't be responsible for what I do to you if anything happens to her."

"There are agents everywhere here."

"And he got away from your undercover agent," Jace pointed out, not bothering to hide the rage in his voice.

Bobby's lips twisted as he glanced at Jace. "Fair enough."

"Do you know how Boyd got away?"

"I wish I did. We found our undercover agent unconscious. He was brought here with Taryn, and I've not had a chance to check on or speak with him."

That only confirmed that Jace had to get to Taryn immediately. He quickened his steps. The nurse ahead of them glanced over her shoulder. He didn't care if she had heard their conversation or not. All that mattered was getting to Taryn. Jace would remain by her side, making sure she wasn't alone again until they found Boyd and put him behind bars.

"There," the nurse said as she pointed to the closed curtains.

Jace hurried over and opened them. Only to find an empty bed.

Chapter 30

Adrenaline pushed Taryn to keep moving despite the stabbing pain of her wound. And both had wiped out every drop of painkiller within her.

Getting out of her bed had been easy. Yanking the IV out of her arm had been a little more difficult. She pressed against the small wound the needle had left behind when she pulled it out so blood didn't drip on the floor and give her away.

She'd thought the hardest part would be slipping away from her bed, but that had been the easy part. Once she was in the hallway, looking for a place to hide, she realized that anyone could be after her. Taryn hoped that she ran into Jace. Maybe then he could tell her if she was being rational or if she had completely lost her mind.

Her heart beat a quick rhythm as she slid against the wall and walked in an effort to stay upright. A few nurses gave her questioning looks, but she smiled at them. That was all it took to keep them at bay.

"Can I help you?"

Taryn jerked to a stop as she looked at the older nurse who stepped before her. So much for thinking she was fooling everyone. Taryn licked her lips and smiled. "I'm fine. Just walking around."

"You're bleeding," the woman said and nodded to Taryn's hand, her short, graying hair in its neatly styled fashion bobbing.

Taryn glanced down at her forearm to see that blood had oozed through her fingers and even now dripped onto the floor. Her mind blanked as she tried to come up with a reason for the blood.

"I'll put a bandage on that," the nurse said with a chuckle. "You aren't the first patient to yank out an IV, and you won't be the last, honey."

Taryn couldn't believe her luck. She slumped against the wall as the nurse hurried away, only to return a moment later with everything needed to dress a minor wound. Even as the nurse tended to her, Taryn looked around. She seriously doubted her sanity at the moment, but there was no denying the persistent and constant urging from her instincts, telling her that she was in danger.

When the nurse finished, she looked up at Taryn with kind, brown eyes that crinkled at the corners. "Now, why don't you tell me what you're really doing out of bed?"

"Walking," Taryn replied.

The nurse clucked her tongue as she gave Taryn a stern look. "You've walked out of the recovery area, which tells me you've only recently come out of surgery."

"No. I'm walking like I was told to do."

"Why don't I help you?" the nurse said as she pulled up the neckline of Taryn's gown.

It hit Taryn then that the garment's back was open, showing off her bare backside to everyone. She hadn't thought about that when she had been running for her life.

"I need to find my husband," Taryn said.

The nurse nodded and moved around behind her to tie off the back of the gown. "All right. I can help with that. Why don't I take you back to your bed?"

"I need to find Jace."

"Okay," the nurse said as she came back around to Taryn's front. "I can see that you don't want to return to your bed. Come. Lean on me as we walk together. I'm sure your husband is in the waiting area."

Taryn accepted the nurse's arm to lean on as they began a slow walk down the hall. "Thank you."

"Hey, Mona," a doctor called out as he walked past.

Mona smiled at him. "How are you, Dr. Davis?"

"Couldn't be better," he replied with a grin.

A wash of emotion filled Taryn. She couldn't believe that she had found someone who could not only help her but would also keep whoever might be after her at bay.

"Honey, you look plum wore out," Mona said in a motherly tone. "Wait here. I'm going to get a wheel-chair for you."

Taryn nodded as tears filled her eyes and spilled over to fall down her cheeks. It had been so long since any-one had looked after her like her mother had. It felt good to be surrounded by that kind of protectiveness again.

"There, there. It's going to be just fine. You'll see. Things always have a way of working out like they should." Mona smiled and patted her hand before hur-rying away to get the chair.

When she returned, Taryn eagerly sank into it. Her shoulder throbbed, and she wasn't entirely sure how much longer her legs would've held her up. As Mona wheeled her to an elevator, talking nonstop about nothing in particular, Taryn's mind wondered. Her decision to leave recovery had been reckless and idiotic. She didn't know this hospital or anyone in it. Wanting to get out and actually doing it were two different things.

Her eyes grew heavy, and it became harder and harder to keep them open. Taryn let them close. Mona's words were like a song, lulling Taryn to sleep. She knew she should stay awake, but it was hard. Besides, she was safe with Mona. None of Boyd's men could get to her with the nurse beside her—someone who knew everyone at the hospital.

Jace whirled around to Bobby. Fury consumed him, but terror dwarfed it. He feared for Taryn's life. "Where is she?"

"I-I don't know," Bobby said as he stared stupidly at the empty bed.

Jace looked to the nurse. "Why wasn't someone with her?"

The nurse took a step back. "Sir, I need you to calm down."

"Calm down?" Jace asked in a cold tone. "A lunatic has held my wife prisoner for years. She was shot tonight and brought here. Now you have no idea where she is?"

"This is recovery," the nurse said in a high-pitched voice.

An Indian woman with thick, black hair pulled back in a ponytail walked up as she put her hands in the pockets of her white lab coat. "What's going on here?" she asked.

Jace glanced at her name sewn onto her coat. Dr. Anika Patel. "Doctor, my wife is missing."

"The gunshot victim?" Dr. Patel asked.

"Taryn. Her name is Taryn."

The doctor motioned for the nurse to leave, then looked at Jace. "I'm the one who performed the surgery. What do you mean she's missing?"

Jace stepped aside and swung out his arm, indicating the empty bed. "She's gone."

Dr. Patel looked from Jace to Bobby and then back to Jace. "She can't have gone far."

"Is there any reason for a nurse to take her?" Bobby asked.

"None," the doctor answered with a frown.

Jace ran his hand down his face, feeling frustrated and helpless at the same time. "She wouldn't have left that bed unless something was wrong. Those who shot her tonight, they're . . . a few got away."

The moment those words were out of his mouth, Dr. Patel turned and stopped one of the nurses. After a few quick words, the floor suddenly became a flurry of activity.

"I can call for backup," Bobby said.

Jace shook his head. "For all I know, one of your men is involved."

"You can't know that."

"And you can't say for certain they aren't," Jace spat.

Dr. Patel returned. "The floor is being searched. I have hospital security headed to every exit just in case. If they spot Taryn, they'll stop whoever is with her."

"I've got some friends checking those exits, as well,"

Jace warned her. Then he turned in a circle, trying to imagine which way he would go if he were Taryn. "Where is the nearest exit?"

Dr. Patel pointed to the left. "There's one on either side, but this one is the closest to her bed."

"Where does it lead?" Bobby asked.

"To rooms," the doctor answered.

Jace walked to the doors with her and Bobby following him. He pressed the button on the wall, and the large doors slowly slid open. "Any place for someone to hide?"

"Plenty," Dr. Patel replied. "Like I said, the floor is being searched."

Bobby blew out a breath as he glanced at Jace. "You better have the entire hospital searched."

"All floors?" the doctor asked in surprise.

Bobby nodded. "All of them."

She pulled out her cell phone and shot Bobby a disappointed look. "I think the FBI should've had someone guarding Taryn."

Jace didn't bother to agree. Bobby knew exactly what his thoughts were at the moment. With every second that passed without any sign of Taryn, Jace's gut clenched in dread. The last thing he planned to do was stand around and wait for someone else to find his wife.

"Wait," Dr. Patel said as she hurried after Jace.

He glanced at the doctor and Bobby, both of whom kept pace with him. "What?"

"We're coming with you," Bobby said. "Three sets of eyes are better than one. Then I can prove that I'm not in league with Boyd."

The doctor halted, her face going slack. "Boyd Walters?"

"The very one," Bobby said after he stopped and swiveled to look at her.

Jace turned and walked until he stood before Dr. Patel. "Why? Do you know him?"

"He's a generous donor to the hospital. His mother has worked here for years," Dr. Patel told them.

Jace fought for breath. It felt as if someone had punched him in the gut. "Who is this woman? Is she working tonight?"

"Mona. Her name is Mona," Dr. Patel said in bewilderment.

Bobby's brows lifted on his forehead. "Where does she usually work?"

The doctor's forehead creased as she suddenly looked panicked. "Here. In recovery."

"Shit," Jace murmured.

Bobby blew out a breath and took a step closer to Dr. Patel. "Do you know if Mona was working tonight?"

"I saw her earlier," she answered in a soft voice.

Jace looked around to make sure that no one was near. "We need to confirm if she's still on duty and in the building."

"This way," the doctor said and took them down another hall to a nurses' station.

Bobby stopped her before they got there and told her, "Go on your own. If Mona is near and sees either me or Jace, it might spook her."

Dr. Patel nodded, swallowing nervously. "I'll be right back."

They watched as she made her way to the station and chatted with a few of the nurses for a moment. Jace was able to make out when she asked for Mona. The other nurses confirmed that Mona was still there, but they didn't know where she was now. Dr. Patel smiled her thanks and made her way back to Jace.

"She was seen just a little while ago," she said.

Jace was about to reply when a tall black man in a lab coat looked their way after talking to a nurse. "Hang on. We might have company."

"What?" Dr. Patel asked with a frown.

The man eyed Jace and Bobby as he walked up. "Excuse me. Anika?"

Dr. Patel turned around. When she saw who it was, she smiled, her relief evident. "Oh, hi, Chad."

"Is everything all right?" he asked her in a low voice.

Dr. Patel glanced at Jace. "Yes. Everything is fine."

"Judy said you were looking for Mona."

"We are," she said.

Chad's nearly black eyes looked Bobby over before sliding to Jace. "Has she done something?"

The doctor let out a breath. "I can't do this. I can't lie to him."

"Lie to me?" Chad asked, his frown deepening. "What are these two forcing you to do?"

"We aren't forcing her to do anything," Jace said. "She's helping us search for my wife, who is missing."

That didn't appease Chad at all. "And that involves Mona how?"

"His wife was shot tonight," Dr. Patel said and blew out a breath. "It happened at Boyd Walters's warehouses."

Chad blinked and stood tall. He stared at Jace for a long moment. "Where was your wife shot?"

"Her right shoulder."

"I saw Mona about five minutes ago. She was with a young woman who had her right shoulder heavily bandaged," he said.

Dr. Patel swung her head to Jace, her eyes wide. "Five minutes isn't that long."

"It is when someone wants to harm another," Bobby replied. Then he looked at Chad. "Which way did they go?"

Chad motioned to the elevator. "I don't know if they went up or down."

"Down." Dr. Patel nodded as she glanced at Chad. "They went down. Part of the basement is under construction."

Jace pulled out his phone and texted Cooper as he and Bobby rushed to the elevator.

Chapter 31

The jarring movement of the wheelchair jolted Taryn awake. She cracked open her eyes and then immediately closed them once more. All she wanted to do was sleep. At least then, the pain wasn't so bad.

Right before she fell back asleep, Mona's words registered.

"I have no choice. A mother has to do what a mother has to do."

Taryn came instantly awake. Something in Mona's voice sent chills of foreboding racing down her spine. She looked around, only to discover that they weren't in a brightly lit hallway anymore. The lights were on, but not all of them. And the construction equipment, as well as the plastic sheeting hanging in rooms they passed, made Taryn's heart race.

"He was such a beautiful baby," Mona continued. "Always smiling, always happy. Everyone loved him. So many girls." She chuckled. "My Boyd was never without a woman. He loved them all, and they all loved him. But he never could settle on just one. He had a new woman on his arm every month or so."

Taryn wiggled her toes, happy to see that they moved better than they had a little while ago. Her hands were in her lap, but she didn't want to move them and bring Mona's attention to her.

"Perfect grades," Mona said. "A head for business. There wasn't anything my Boyd couldn't do. The more money he had, the more he made. He kept buying me things. I told him I didn't need them, but he wouldn't listen. Kept bringing over presents. Small things at first, but they got bigger. The car was the first one. Came home with a white Mercedes for me. A year later, he walked me into a brand-new house he'd had built for me. Completely paid off. No mother could've been prouder."

Taryn wondered if Mona knew where most of that money had come from. Even if she did, Taryn was sure Mona wouldn't care. When it came to Boyd, the woman was blinded by her love.

"All those things written about him in the papers infuriate me. He's a great businessman. Can't they see that?"

Taryn remained silent, hoping Mona thought she was still asleep. Suddenly, the woman turned the wheelchair and rolled Taryn into an empty room. For a brief moment, Taryn thought she should pretend to be asleep, but she decided at the last minute that she would rather face her killer.

"What do you say to all of that?" Mona asked as she halted the wheelchair and came to stand in front of Taryn. "I know who you are. I know what you've done."

"I don't think you know as much as you believe you do," Taryn replied.

Mona laughed and crossed her arms over her chest. Gone was the kind, motherly woman. "My son told me everything."

"So you know he's a drug dealer?"

"Dozens of others do the same thing." Mona shrugged. "Boyd began that way. He had a knack for doubling money in a blink. He used the money he made from the drugs to buy legitimate businesses to make even more."

Taryn shouldn't be surprised that Mona was so flippant about Boyd selling drugs, but she was. "I'm not talking marijuana. I'm talking cocaine, heroin. Hard drugs. The kind that kill people."

"If people are stupid enough to take those drugs, then that's their problem. Boyd saw a market and made himself millions. What's wrong with that?"

Taryn moved her fingers, flexing them. They felt pretty good. So did her toes. She wasn't sure about her arms and legs quite yet. "I'm not going to debate this with you. The simple fact is, there are laws against the distribution of drugs. Boyd broke those laws."

"So did you," Mona said with a pleased smile.

"I had no choice."

"Everyone has a choice. The same ones those who take the drugs have."

Taryn eyed the older woman, suddenly seeing the similarities between her and Boyd. Same eyes. Same sarcastic sneer. "I was taken against my will."

"Your sister was a beautiful woman. I knew the minute I saw Payton that she was the one for my son. He was utterly smitten with her. And she, him. They had a bright future. A true power couple. You ruined everything."

"Me?" Taryn asked with shock. "They killed my father and brother. Payton shot me!"

Mona raked her gaze over her. "You deserve to die. The fact that Payton is lying in the morgue and you're here makes me sick."

In that one sentence, Taryn knew that Mona intended to kill her. The dread she'd felt earlier had been real. If only she had realized her savior was actually her would-be killer, Taryn wouldn't be in this mess.

"I called Boyd. He's on his way," Mona said with a grin. "He wants to be the one to kill you for taking Payton from him."

Taryn's gut clenched. She had thought Boyd had been caught. If she didn't get to Jace before Boyd found her, whatever future she and her husband might have together was over. "How about taking Jace from me? Did either of you think about that? Did any of you think about *my* life?"

"You're nobody. You gave us some amusement seeing the lengths you would go to in order to keep Payton safe. There was one time we actually thought you'd figured it out, but Payton assured us you hadn't. Then you tried to bargain with Boyd for your freedom. Payton was the one who told him to accept your offer to prove how stupid you were."

"Stupid? For wanting to keep my sister safe from a sociopath?" Taryn snorted loudly. "Yeah. You keep thinking whatever you want."

Mona quirked an eyebrow. "You don't think I'm a threat to you."

It was a statement, not a question, so Taryn didn't bother to answer. The fact was, Mona didn't have a weapon. She had brought Taryn to some unused part of the hospital so Boyd could find them and kill her. That meant Taryn had some time to get free of Mona.

At that moment, Mona pulled a small pistol from the pocket of her shirt and aimed it at Taryn. "Bet you think I'm a threat now."

"Your son is the one who broke the law, not you. You kill me, and they will arrest you."

Mona laughed. "Why? Because the FBI is in the building? Or because your husband and his friends have connections? They don't have near the connections my son does. Do you have any idea how many times the authorities have arrested Boyd, only to let him go because the charges didn't stick? Too many to count."

A sarcastic remark was quick to the tip of Taryn's tongue, but she decided it would be better not to push Mona. At least, not yet. Taryn grabbed the arms of the wheelchair and tried to get to her feet.

"Nope," Mona said and waved the gun. "You're going to stay put."

"I was shot and had surgery."

Mona gave her a flat look. "Exactly. Why do you need to move at all?"

"You were in recovery, weren't you?" Taryn said, hoping to keep Mona talking until she could figure out how to get away from the woman.

Mona shrugged one shoulder. "I knew the moment I heard they'd brought a gunshot victim in that it was you. It was a sign from God. You were delivered to me to give Boyd a second chance at killing you."

"Wouldn't it be better if he left? Why chance things?"

"You know too much!"

Mona's outburst shocked Taryn. The nurse had been

mild-mannered at first and calm until just then. It was the first chink in Mona's armor that Taryn had seen. "You mean because I can give the Feds all kinds of information that will make charges stick?"

"That isn't going to happen."

"Your son is a criminal. He will pay for his crimes one way or another."

Mona threw back her head and issued a bark of laughter. "Why? Because he makes money? Because he is good at what he does?"

"Because he's a murderer and a drug dealer."

Mona rolled her eyes. "Everyone kills someone."

"I never have."

In response, Mona just stared at her.

Taryn's blood went cold at what Mona's silence stated.

"You should see your face," Mona said with a chuckle. "You have disrupted my son's life. You've taken away his love. And you will pay dearly for it."

"I've already paid by being kept prisoner and forced to sell drugs, watching first my father, and then my brother be killed." Taryn shook her head. "Oh, I've paid."

The sound of an elevator dinging reached them. Then footsteps. They were distant at first but quickly grew closer and closer. Taryn knew it was Boyd. Mona's smile was proof of that.

Taryn looked around, trying to find a way to get free or at least defend herself, but Mona had chosen the location wisely. Not only was it isolated from everyone and everything else, but nothing in the room could be used as a weapon—or for protection. And the only way in or out was the door they had entered through, the same one Boyd was about to appear in.

Jace. I love you.

Taryn wouldn't get to tell him that again, but he knew. He had waited for her all these years. That was proof of his love. The last few days with Jace ran through her head on fast forward—the kisses, the laughter, the conversations, the love. She had found the love of her life, but unfortunately, family and bad decisions had ruined the happiness she could've had. At least she'd had a little time with him. It hadn't been nearly enough, but some was better than nothing.

Boyd's frame filled the doorway. He no longer wore his sardonic smile. His face was grim and smudged with dirt. His clothes were in disarray. Fury laced his blue eyes. "Thank you, Momma."

"Anything for you, my sweet."

Boyd walked to Mona and took the gun from her before he turned to Taryn. "I wish I had time to make you truly suffer as I have suffered this night. It's going to be enough to watch you die."

"I've had to listen to your mother. I don't want to hear your whining, as well. Just shut up and pull the trigger," Taryn told him.

His nostrils flared. "You took my Payton from me."

"I didn't pull the trigger."

"You're still responsible. You're the one who brought Jace and the others to my compound."

Taryn rolled her eyes. "Payton even said you were expecting them. It isn't anyone's fault but your own for not being more prepared."

"She was killed by a sniper!" Boyd shouted, spittle flying from his mouth. He drew in a deep breath and cocked the pistol as he aimed it at her. "And you will die for it."

Taryn looked down the barrel, steeling herself. She

wanted to cry, to beg, to reach out for Jace, but she was alone with two lunatics. And it was entirely her fault because she'd left recovery. All she could hope was that Jace had helped to track down Boyd. She prayed that Cooper and the others would stop Jace from killing Boyd, though, because the last thing she wanted was to have Jace end up in jail over some lowlife like Boyd Walters.

"I'm going to enjoy this," Boyd said as his finger curled around the trigger.

Near the door, movement drew Taryn's attention as someone dove for Boyd, taking him to the ground and causing the gun to clatter and slide across the floor.

Taryn looked from the gun to Mona. Without a second thought, Taryn leapt from the chair.

Chapter 32

Jace was the first one out of the stairwell. They had taken the stairs in an attempt to keep from alerting Mona or anyone else to their arrival. Jace's hands felt empty without a weapon, but right now, all he wanted was to find Taryn—preferably unharmed.

He hated that he hadn't listened to his instincts earlier and gone to find Taryn himself. If he had, he might have prevented everything that was happening now. Jace knew it was foolish to let his mind wander down such paths. He needed to focus on the facts at hand and come up with ways to defuse the potential situation.

If he got to Taryn in time.

Jace inwardly kicked himself. He couldn't think like that. So many things could happen. He needed to be prepared for any eventuality. But if Taryn had gotten hurt in any way, Jace would hunt Boyd down and exact his revenge—no matter how long it took.

He glanced behind him, meeting Bobby's gaze. Despite his and Bobby's attempts to keep Dr. Patel and

Chad away, both physicians were with them. Jace put his finger to his lips to warn them not to make a sound. The pair nodded silently.

Jace looked both ways down the short corridor before turning left and heading to the main hall and the elevator. He heard voices and strained to hear Taryn's. When he did, he had to stop himself from rushing to her.

As they reached the main foyer, Jace slowed when he heard something. He motioned for the doctors to stay back as he and Bobby took up their positions. Bobby was the first around the corner, his weapon drawn. Jace followed right after—and found himself staring into familiar eyes.

"Jace," Ryan said in a shocked whisper. "What the fuck?"

"We could ask the same thing," Bobby replied.

Before Jace could reply, Danny leaned to the side and jerked his thumb over his shoulder to where they could still hear talking.

Jace touched Bobby's shoulder to get him to lower his gun. Then he whispered, "We need to move fast."

"Boyd's here," Ryan mouthed.

Jace's gaze moved down the semi-lit hallway, trying to determine which room they might be in. He motioned for his friends and Bobby to move stealthily. Then he looked back and held up his palm to tell the doctors to stay put. Thankfully, Dr. Patel and Chad listened, though they leaned around the corner to watch them.

At the sound of Boyd's bellow, Jace's heart skipped a beat. Then he saw the blur of a shadow diving into the room. Without a word to the others, Jace ran.

In her efforts to get the gun, Taryn had forgotten the wound on her right shoulder and instinctively reached with that arm. She landed heavily on the injury and cried out from the pain that washed over her. Still, she didn't take her eyes off the gun. She landed inches from it. So close, but yet so far.

Behind her, she heard a struggle. She wanted to look at whoever had come into the room and to see where Mona was, but Taryn didn't dare. She feared if she took her eyes off the weapon, it would disappear.

Something slammed into her left ribs, knocking the breath from her lungs. She gripped that side, only realizing when she was hit again that Mona was kicking her. Something warm and wet dripped from her wounded shoulder. Taryn ignored it and tried to push herself to the gun with her feet and her good arm.

She moved slightly, but it wasn't enough. And she couldn't take another kick from Mona. Pain blinded her, but she knew if she didn't get the gun, she was dead. She had no choice but to push through the agony that radiated through her body. Out of the corner of her eye, Taryn saw Mona swing back her leg to kick once more. Taryn shifted onto her side and swept her right leg forward, knocking Mona on her ass, hard. Taryn used that to her advantage and pulled herself forward with both hands. She got close enough to put her fingers on the gun, but before she could get the weapon in hand, Mona's foot connected with her head. A moment later, a loud crash sounded as the wheelchair toppled over, and Boyd and whoever fought him crashed onto her legs.

Taryn couldn't hold back the yell of pain. Tears stung her eyes as she looked at the gun, once more only a few inches from her. But with the men rolling around on her legs, she couldn't move.

She heard a snap, and the men stopped moving.

Taryn glanced over her shoulder to see Boyd's head hanging at an odd angle as he sat on the floor. Her gaze lifted, and Taryn found herself staring into Brick's brown eyes. She wasn't sure she registered the truth of what was going on through her haze of pain.

Mona let out a half-scream, half-bellow at the sight of her dead son. Taryn swung her head around and stretched out her wounded arm for the gun, but Mona's fingers wrapped around the grip and lifted it, firing three shots into Brick's chest.

Taryn watched, horrified, as Brick's body jerked with each impact. With tears streaming down her face, Mona turned the weapon on Taryn. Taryn steeled herself, knowing this was likely the end. When the gun went off, she jerked, expecting to feel more pain, but there was nothing. A heartbeat of silence passed, then multiple rounds were fired—all into Mona. The woman's feet slipped out from under her as she slid to the floor, the gun falling from her fingers as her lifeless eyes stared at Taryn.

Relief slammed into Taryn, but it was quickly drowned out by the surging pain radiating throughout her body. All Taryn wanted to do was close her eyes and sink into the waiting darkness.

"Baby? Baby, I need you to look at me. Come on, Taryn, turn those beautiful green eyes my way."

She pulled herself from the brink as she registered Jace's voice. She met his gaze and saw happiness fill his face as a tear fell from his eye. Her own tears came then as it dawned on her that, somehow, she had come out of this alive.

Suddenly, people swarmed the room. A woman barked orders from somewhere behind Jace. Dimly, Taryn heard someone tell her to ready herself. She was about to ask what for when they moved her. Taryn cried out, dark spots dotting her vision. Somehow, she managed to stay conscious. Jace didn't let go of her hand even when they put her on a gurney and wheeled her out of the room.

As they left, Taryn saw Ryan and Danny near Brick as hospital staff worked to save him. But by the looks on their faces, it wasn't good.

"It's over," Jace murmured next to her face.

She looked at him and saw the lights over his head moving faster and faster. He smiled and said something, but she couldn't make it out as she lost consciousness.

Jace had washed Taryn's blood from his hands and arms again, but it was still on his clothing. He paced the area, waiting to hear from Dr. Patel for a second time. FBI agents were stationed all over the hospital now. Not that it mattered since Boyd and Mona were both dead. But the remaining men in Boyd's organization might think to attack.

"Hey."

Jace turned to find Cooper standing with a cup of coffee extended in his direction. Jace accepted it. "Thanks."

"She's going to be fine."

Jace took a drink, not caring that it didn't have nearly enough sugar in it. He was drained emotionally, mentally, and physically. All he wanted was to hold his wife in his arms. He forced himself to sit in one of the chairs. "Did you find out anything from Ryan or Danny?"

"Did I," Cooper said with his brows raised. He sank into a chair diagonal to Jace's. "Turns out, Brick is Ryan's cousin. He was also the undercover agent."

"Well, shit."

Cooper nodded. "I'm pretty sure I said that exact same thing. By the way, you can thank Ryan for Payton. He was the sniper."

Jace leaned forward and braced his forearms on his knees. "Son of a bitch."

"He saved Taryn, and I'm certain he saved our asses, as well."

"I'm in agreement. How is Brick?"

Cooper's smile faded as his lips twisted ruefully. "I haven't heard. By the time Myles and I got to the basement, they had already taken Brick into surgery. I don't know where Ryan is. Danny was there and filled us in on everything. If y'all hadn't gotten there when you did . . ."

"I know." Jace dropped his chin to his chest. "I'll never forget hearing those gunshots. When I turned the corner and saw Boyd's mother aiming the gun at Taryn, everything went into slow motion." Jace raised his head to look at Cooper. "I didn't have a weapon, but I was going to do whatever was needed to stop Mona. Ryan was right behind me and got off the first shot before Mona could pull the trigger. Danny and Bobby joined in, ending any attempt Mona had at killing Taryn."

Cooper blew out a breath. "It's been a hell of a day."

Jace was about to reply when Dr. Patel filled the doorway. She was still in her scrubs, a cap covering her hair, and a face mask around her neck. He jumped up and rushed to her. It was only when she smiled that he allowed himself to breathe.

"I've repaired the damage to Taryn's shoulder," the doctor said. "Her ribs are bruised from the kicking, but there is no other damage. We also gave her some blood to help with the amount she lost. She's in recovery now if you want to see her."

Jace hurried past her. Then he looked over his shoulder and said, "Thanks, doc!"

His heart pounded with excitement as he found Taryn. He exchanged a smile with the nurse currently checking Taryn's vitals. Then his gaze landed on his wife. She was still unconscious, but just looking at her made him happy.

He didn't want to think about how many people had tried to kill her or the trauma she had endured, but they would have to face it. He had some experience with these kinds of things, so he could help. Taryn was one of the strongest people he knew. She would get through it, and he would be there to help her through both the good days and the bad.

Her hand twitched on the bed. Jace walked around to the side and slipped his fingers around hers. Her lids fluttered open, and her beautiful green eyes met his.

"Hello, darlin'. 'Bout time you joined us," he said with a smile.

Her lips curved in response. "Jace."

"I'm here. I'll always be here."

"Love you," she whispered as her eyes closed once more.

Jace leaned over and kissed her forehead. And though she couldn't hear him because she had drifted back to sleep, he said, "And I love you."

Chapter 33

It was good to be home. Taryn had tried to tell Jace that she was all right, but he doted on her. And truth be told, she loved it.

"Here's your tea," Jace said as he set the mug on the table beside her.

Her right arm was heavily bandaged. It would be weeks before she could move it properly. She had already set up physical therapy appointments for when the time came. She smiled and reached for the giant mug with her left hand. "Thank you."

"How's the pain?"

Right before Taryn took a sip, she said, "Manageable."

"I know we just got home, but . . ."

She quirked a brow when Jace trailed off. "But people want to come over," she said with a grin.

"I can tell them no."

"As long as I can sit right here and drink my tea, they're welcome."

Jace leaned over her and kissed her forehead. "That's good because they're all outside. Cooper just texted me."

Taryn laughed and shook her head. "Go let them in."

"Come in, y'all!" Jace yelled.

A heartbeat later, the door opened. Within minutes, Taryn was surrounded. She saw balloons wishing her well, flowers, and gift bags, all set around her. She looked at the people who were a part of Jace's life—and now hers—and started crying.

"Baby?" Jace asked as he rushed to her. "Are you in pain?"

She shook her head, hating that her emotions had run so high since the incident at the hospital. Taryn wiped at her tears and smiled at everyone. "Some might feel sorry for me because I've lost my family. They would be wrong. Because as I look at everyone in this house, I realize that I have a family."

"A rather large one," Sharon, Jace's mother, said as she walked up. "Honey, I'm so happy you're back and married to Jace."

More tears fell from Taryn's eyes as she hugged Sharon.

"I've waited a long time to have a daughter-in-law," Jace's father, Alan, said as he approached and hugged Taryn. Then he turned to Jace. "We'll have a talk later about you leaving for such a mission without telling your mom and me."

Jace sat beside Taryn and took her left hand. "When it comes to Taryn, I'll do whatever it takes to keep her safe."

They shared a smile as conversation started among the others. Then Ryan approached.

"I should've told you," he said then looked at Jace. "I should've told you both."

Taryn shook her head. "You were protecting your cousin."

Ryan removed his cowboy hat and ran a hand through his hair. "Yeah. We haven't spoken in years. It was a shock to find him in Clearview."

"We tried to get information about Brick before we left the hospital, but no one would tell us anything. And I couldn't get in touch with you," Jace said.

Ryan turned his hat around in his hands. "Between talking to doctors and the FBI, I turned off my phone. Brick is alive, but he has a long recovery ahead of him. One of the bullets missed his heart by millimeters." The chief shook his head. "One entered his lung, and the other got lodged in a rib. That doesn't even include the one he took to the back that Boyd managed to fire off when Brick attacked."

"Boyd must have known that Brick was undercover," Jace replied.

Ryan shrugged. "Brick said he followed Boyd into the building, and Boyd was there with a gun. They fought, and Brick knocked the weapon away, but Boyd had another."

Taryn sipped her tea. "How did Brick know that Boyd was in the hospital?"

"He knew Boyd's mother worked there. Once he realized that both of you had been taken there, he knew it was only a matter of time before Boyd or someone came for you," Ryan explained. "Brick was on his way to recovery to watch over you when he saw you slip away. He tried to get to you when Mona found you. After that, it was just a matter of him following you and waiting for Boyd to get there."

"I owe him so much," she said.

Jace tightened his fingers around her hand. "We both do."

Ryan's gaze dropped to the floor. "He was just doing

his job, but if I see him, I'll let him know what y'all said."

Taryn frowned. "What do you mean *if* you see him?"

"We've not had the best relationship." Ryan cleared his throat and put his hat back on his head. "There's a lot of bad history between us."

Taryn caught his gaze. "You nearly lost him. The past shouldn't mean as much as we make it out to. Forget it, and the old hurts. Embrace the fact that you have your cousin back in your life."

"If I'm able, I want to talk him into coming and living with me." Ryan's lips tilted into a smile. "He always did love horses, and I've got plenty for him to be around. It would give him a place to heal and would let us connect again."

Jace shot Ryan a wide smile. "I think that sounds like a wonderful idea. You should probably tell him soon."

"Yeah," Ryan said with an absentminded nod. "I should."

And with that, the police chief jumped up and rushed out of the house.

"What was that all about?" Danny asked as he walked over.

Jace shook his head with a grin. "I think Ryan is making another trip back to Fort Worth."

"To see his cousin? Good," Danny said. He looked at them. "Can I sit?"

Jace motioned to a chair. "Of course."

Once seated, Danny sighed. "I wanted to say that while I still don't agree with what all of you did, I'm glad it turned out as well as it did."

"I hear you're part of the reason," Jace said.

Taryn jerked her head to Jace. "What?"

Jace glanced at her before he looked back at Danny.

"Seems Danny called some friends and was in Fort Worth at the same time we were. He was the one who vouched for Ryan when the Rangers found him."

"I had no idea," Taryn said to Danny. "Thank you."

Danny bowed his head. "I'm glad I could help."

"I'm sorry I didn't trust you and Ryan," Taryn said.

Danny raised his hand to stop her. "There's no need for you to apologize. You had your reasons, and I respect that. I just wanted to say congratulations on the nuptials."

"Thank you," Jace said as he gave her a quick kiss.

Taryn smiled at Danny. "Yes, thank you."

"Looks like the only single one left is Ryan," Danny pointed out.

"Don't forget Cash and Brick." Taryn then frowned. "Or is Brick married?"

Danny and Jace exchanged a look before Jace shrugged. "None of us know much about Brick. Is that even his real name?"

"He's been undercover for years," Danny said. "I'm sure there is a lot about him no one knows. I did find out that he worked intelligence in the military before moving to the FBI."

Jace's brows shot up on his forehead. "Interesting."

Danny got to his feet and tipped his hat to Taryn. "Welcome home. I'm sure we'll be seeing much more of each other."

The moment Danny left, Clayton, Abby, and their three kids came to talk. Taryn loved getting to meet the children. Eventually, everyone made their way over to her and Jace to share a few words.

When they finally got a few minutes to themselves, Taryn chuckled and looked at Jace. "Is everything with Boyd really over?"

"I think so, but he had a large organization. We'll need to be careful for a while. Bobby will keep tabs on things."

"You trust him?"

"I do. He's only telling a select few agents, who will continue monitoring both Fort Worth and Clearview. If anything happens, he'll know which ones to talk to," Jace said.

Taryn set aside her mug. "I hope that we won't always have to keep looking over our shoulders."

"We won't," he vowed.

She looked around at the houseful of people and smiled.

"I haven't had a chance to say I'm sorry about Payton."

At the mention of her sister, Taryn's grin faded. She swung her gaze to Jace. "All the signs were there. I just didn't see them."

"You can't blame yourself."

"Maybe if I hadn't been so wrapped up in you, I would have."

Jace shook his head. "Remember what you just told Ryan? You can't hold onto the past."

"I know." She blew out a breath. "When I think about Payton and what she did, I'm just . . ." She shook her head, unable to find words.

Jace brought her hand to his mouth and kissed it. "It's going to take time to deal with everything that happened with her."

Taryn looked down at their joined hands. She hadn't taken the wedding ring off since the hospital. "And what happened at the hospital with Boyd and Mona."

"If I could take that from you, I would."

Her eyes lifted as she smiled at Jace. "I know, but I can handle it. Like you said, it's just going to take time."

"If anyone can do it, it's you. Look at everything you've gotten through these past years."

She drew in a deep breath and slowly released it. "Did you suspect Payton?"

"Not at all. They knew just what to say and do to ensure that you believed everything they told you. None of us had reason to believe that Payton would turn out to be the one who masterminded everything."

"She was my sister," Taryn said as tears stung her eyes. "All I wanted was for her to be happy and have a life. I tried to take care of my family."

Jace touched his finger to her chin to get her attention. "Baby, you did. The simple truth is that Payton was just a bad apple. You couldn't have thought she would turn your father and brother onto drugs or have all of you kidnapped and made all but slaves to Boyd."

"She had my father and brother killed," Taryn said, her tears giving way to anger. She shook her head as her ire grew. "She took me away from you, robbed us of years we could've been happy."

Jace shot her a sexy grin. "But we triumphed. We're here, together. She tried her damnedest to keep us apart, but it didn't work."

"No, it didn't." Taryn's smile was wide as she realized she had many things to rejoice about—the main one being that she was with Jace.

"Are you ready?"

She cocked her head to the side. "For what?"

"For the future."

"Oh, yeah," she said with a nod. "I dreamed about it every night while I was away."

He shot her a wink. "No need to dream anymore. It's right here, darlin'."

Epilogue

Four months later

Jace had been waiting for this day for some time. He wasn't sure how everyone—including himself—had managed to keep it all a secret. But they had.

"I'm just about ready," Taryn called from the bedroom. "Just putting on my boots."

He smiled, thinking how absolutely glorious life with her had been. Their journey to each other might have taken a bit of a detour, but it had all worked out in the end. Although there had been some close calls.

Taryn walked from their bedroom in a pair of jeans, boots, and a green plaid shirt. Her long hair was loose as she walked to him where he stood next to the island, and kissed him as they wound their arms around each other. "I can't believe this day is finally here. No more physical therapy."

"That's right. Now it's time to celebrate with some good food."

"And a horseback ride." She pulled back and quirked

a brow at him. "You said I'd get to ride. My physical therapist said it was fine."

Jace gave a nod. "You're going to get to ride."

"Then what are we waiting for? We need to get to your parents', visit, and have lunch so we can saddle up the horses and ride to the river."

He smiled at her enthusiasm. It was on the tip of his tongue to spill the secret, but he managed to keep it to himself as they locked up the house and hurried to his truck. The entire drive to his parents', she sang along with the radio and looked out the window. Jace looked at their linked hands and sighed in happiness.

When they reached his parents' house, his mom and dad greeted them at the door. Jace kept hold of Taryn's hand as they made their way to the kitchen. His mother had the double back doors open to let the cool fall air in. Jace spotted all their friends outside. He tugged Taryn away from his mom long enough to bring her out to the backyard where everyone waited.

"Oh, my God," Taryn said when she saw everybody.

Jace stood beside her, watching her greet everyone until she finally saw her surprise. Everyone went silent as Taryn's mouth fell open at the sight of the silver buckskin mare held near a fence by Caleb. Jace had jumped through many hoops to do this for her, even had Caleb and Cooper travel to Wyoming to acquire the animal.

"She's all yours, sweetheart," Jace told Taryn.

Her eyes teared up as she covered her mouth with her hands, looking from Jace to the horse with its black mane, tail, muzzle, and ears. Two of her legs were also black. Silver buckskins were rare in the horse world, but the mare was as unique as his wife—making them perfect for each other.

Taryn threw her arms around him. "Jace. What did you do?"

"Bought my wife a present."

"Thank you." She gave him a kiss then hurried to the horse.

As Taryn stroked her hand down the mare's back, she looked over her shoulder at Jace and mouthed, "*I love you*." He blew her a kiss and grabbed a beer as his parents gave her a black saddle and matching tack.

"You look content," Cooper said as he walked up.

Jace nodded, unable to take his eyes from Taryn. "More than you can imagine."

"I think we've all earned some peace."

"I'll drink to that." They clinked their beer bottles. Jace looked around at the friends and family that made up their circle. "We've all survived a lot. We're lucky to be here."

Cooper nodded as he drank. "And to find women who will put up with our shit."

"Not all of us," Jace said as he nodded at Ryan.

"Oh, his time will come."

Jace chuckled. "That just might be one for the ages. But, I'll admit, I'd love to see it. Ryan's a good man. He deserves to find a good woman like we have."

"Are you thinking what I am?" Cooper asked mischievously.

Jace's mouth widened in a smile. "Damn straight. We need to start setting him up."

"I'll go tell Caleb and Brice."

Jace waited until Cooper had walked away before he went to his wife. Taryn and the mare were getting to know one another. Already, Jace could see it would be a strong bond.

"She's the most beautiful thing I've ever seen," Taryn said when he reached her.

"Caleb has had her for the last month, making sure she was trained properly. You can ride her now."

Taryn's green eyes lit up. Then she frowned as she looked at everyone. "Later."

"Whenever you want. We can go now."

She shook her head. "Our family is all together. That's not easy for such a large group. We're going to take advantage of it. We'll go for a ride later, just the two of us. Be sure to pack a blanket."

"Oh, woman," he said as he drew her against him. "You read my mind."

Don't miss the next book by *New York Times*
bestseller Donna Grant

HOME FOR A COWBOY CHRISTMAS

Coming in October 2021
from St. Martin's Paperbacks